POKÉMON®

ULTIMATE

HANDBOOK

ISBN-13: 978-0-545-07886-3
ISBN-10: 0-545-07886-5

© 2008 Pokémon. © 1995-2008 Nintendo/Creatures Inc./GAME FREAK inc.
™ and ® are trademarks of Nintendo. All rights reserved.

Published by Scholastic Inc.
SCHOLASTIC and associated logos are trademarks and/or registered trademarks of Scholastic Inc.

12 11 10 9 8 7 6 5 4 3 2 1          8 9 10 11 12/0

Book design: Henry Ng, Cheung Tai, and Kay Petronio
Printed in the U.S.A.
First printing, September 2008

# POKÉMON

## ULTIMATE
## HANDBOOK

by Cris Silvestri

**SCHOLASTIC INC.**

New York   Toronto   London   Auckland   Sydney
Mexico City   New Delhi   Hong Kong   Buenos Aires

# WELCOME TO THE COMPLETE WORLD OF POKÉMON!

Pokémon Trainers know that the key to success with Pokémon is staying informed. Certain things, like a Pokémon's type, species, weight, and more can make the difference in raising, battling, and evolving Pokémon.

In this book, you'll have the once in a lifetime complete National Pokédex, which contains everything you need to know about each and every Pokémon. From Abomasnow to Zubat, you'll find out how each Pokémon evolves, which moves are most common to them, and even which region they hail from. And it's all in alphabetical order for easy reference.

Get ready, Trainers: with this handy guide, you'll be able to master almost any Pokémon challenge!

# HOW TO READ THE ULTIMATE HANDBOOK

*NAME:* A Pokémon's name—the first step in knowing your Pokémon.

*SPECIES:* All Pokémon belong to a specific Species. These are interesting classes that highlight what makes some Pokémon so unique. Did you know Pikachu was a Mouse Species Pokémon?

*PRONOUNCED:* How can you train a Pokémon if you can't pronounce its name correctly? Learn how to pronounce each name with this handy entry.

*POSSIBLE MOVES:* There are a ton of moves that Pokémon could be taught, but there are only a few that might be naturally instilled into your Pokémon. This is that list.

*TYPE:* Some Pokémon have one type, some are dual types—but every Pokémon has a type, and there are 17 in total. Types allow you to anticipate what a Pokémon's strengths and weaknesses will be in battle.

*HEIGHT:* Who's the tallest? The shortest?

*WEIGHT:* Who's the heaviest? The lightest?

*REGION:* There are four main Regions to the Pokémon world—Kanto, Johto, Hoenn, and Sinnoh, and each Region has Pokémon particular to it.

*DESCRIPTION:* Cool facts about your Pokémon—some of which you may never have known if it were not for this guide! Read up and become a true Pokémon expert!

*EVOLUTION:* Some Pokémon evolve into other Pokémon—others don't evolve at all. Learning the evolutions for each Pokémon will help you become a well-informed Trainer.

ARE YOU READY?

*YOUR POKÉMON JOURNEY BEGINS WHEN YOU TURN THE PAGE!*

# ABOMASNOW
## FROST TREE POKÉMON

Known as the Ice Monster, Abomasnow can create blizzards across wide areas in the mountains.

| | |
|---|---|
| **Pronounced:** uh-BOM-a-snow | |
| **Possible Moves:** Ice Punch, Powder Snow, Leer, Razor Leaf, Icy Wind, GrassWhistle, Swagger, Mist, Ice Shard, Ingrain, Wood Hammer, Blizzard, Sheer Cold | |
| **Type:** Grass-Ice | |
| **Height:** 7'03"  **Weight:** 298.7 lbs. | |
| **Region:** Sinnoh | |

SNOVER

ABOMASNOW

# ABRA
## PSYCHIC POKÉMON

This Pokémon has the ability to teleport itself at any time.

| | |
|---|---|
| **Pronounced:** AH-bra | |
| **Possible Moves:** Teleport | |
| **Type:** Psychic | |
| **Height:** 2'11"  **Weight:** 43.0 lbs. | |
| **Region:** All Regions | |

ABRA

KADABRA

ALAKAZAM

# ABSOL
## DISASTER POKÉMON

When you see Absol, it means that disaster is imminent—so don't stay put! Absol only appears to those it wants to warn.

**Pronounced:**
AB-sol

**Possible Moves:** Scratch, Leer, Taunt, Quick Attack, Razor Wind, Pursuit, Swords Dance, Bite, Double Team, Slash, Future Sight, Sucker Punch, Detect, Night Slash, Me First, Psycho Cut, Perish Song

**Type:** Dark

**Height:** 3'11"

**Weight:** 103.6 lbs.

**Region:** Hoenn

## DOES NOT EVOLVE

# AERODACTYL
## FOSSIL POKÉMON

Aerodactyl's teeth are as sharp as blades, and it has flown the skies since the time of dinosaurs.

| | |
|---|---|
| **Pronounced:** AIR-row-DACK-tull | |
| **Possible Moves:** Ice Fang, Fire Fang, Thunder Fang, Wing Attack, Supersonic, Bite, Scary Face, Roar, Agility, AncientPower, Crunch, Take Down, Iron Head, Hyper Beam, Rock Slide, Giga Impact | |
| **Type:** Rock-Flying | |
| **Height:** 5'11"    **Weight:** 130.1 lbs. | |
| **Region:** Kanto | |

DOES NOT EVOLVE

# AGGRON
## IRON ARMOR POKÉMON

Aggron digs tunnels by burrowing through bedrock with its steel horns. It digs the tunnels while seeking iron for food.

| | |
|---|---|
| **Pronounced:** AGG-ron | |
| **Possible Moves:** Tackle, Harden, Mud-Slap, Headbutt, Metal Claw, Iron Defense, Roar, Take Down, Iron Head, Protect, Metal Sound, Iron Tail, Double-Edge, Metal Burst | |
| **Type:** Steel-Rock | |
| **Height:** 6'11"    **Weight:** 793.7 lbs. | |
| **Region:** Hoenn | |

ARON

LAIRON

AGGRON

# AIPOM
## LONG TAIL POKÉMON

Aipom uses its tail to grab things that are out of his reach, since its tail is more effective than its hands.

| | |
|---|---|
| **Pronounced:** AY-pom | |
| **Possible Moves:** Scratch, Tail Whip, Sand-Attack, Astonish, Baton Pass, Tickle, Fury Swipes, Swift, Screech, Agility, Double Hit, Fling, Nasty Plot, Last Resort | |
| **Type:** Normal | |
| **Height:** 2'07" | **Weight:** 25.4 lbs. |
| **Region:** Johto and Sinnoh | |

AMBIPOM

AIPOM

# ALAKAZAM
## PSYCHIC POKÉMON

With an IQ of over 5,000, Alakazam is a force to be reckoned with. It can recall everything it has ever done—including moves in battle.

| | |
|---|---|
| **Pronounced:** AH-la-kuh-ZAM | |
| **Possible Moves:** Teleport, Kinesis, Confusion, Disable, Miracle Eye, Psybeam, Reflect, Recover, Psycho Cut, Calm Mind, Psychic, Future Sight, Trick | |
| **Type:** Psychic | |
| **Height:** 4'11" | **Weight:** 105.8 lbs. |
| **Region:** Kanto and Sinnoh | |

ABRA

KADABRA

ALAKAZAM

# ALTARIA
## HUMMING POKÉMON

Altaria looks like a fluffy cloud, and likes to hum in a soprano voice.

**Pronounced:** all-TEAR-ee-uh

**Possible Moves:** Pluck, Peck, Growl, Astonish, Sing, Fury Attack, Safeguard, Mist, Take Down, Natural Gift, DragonBreath, Dragon Dance, Refresh, Dragon Pulse, Perish Song, Sky Attack

**Type:** Dragon-Flying

**Height:** 3'07"    **Weight:** 45.4 lbs.

**Region:** Hoenn

SWABLU

ALTARIA

# AMBIPOM
## LONG TAIL POKÉMON

Sometimes, two tails are better than one! Ambipom has been known to form big groups by linking its tails with other Ambipom.

**Pronounced:** AM-bih-pom

**Possible Moves:** Scratch, Tail Whip, Sand-Attack, Astonish, Baton Pass, Tickle, Fury Swipes, Swift, Screech, Agility, Double Hit, Fling, Nasty Plot, Last Resort

**Type:** Normal

**Height:** 3'11"    **Weight:** 44.8 lbs.

**Region:** Sinnoh

AIPOM

AMBIPOM

# AMPHAROS
## LIGHT POKÉMON

The tail on Ampharos shines so bright, people once used it to send signals.

| | |
|---|---|
| **Pronounced:** AMF-fah-ros | |
| **Possible Moves:** Fire Punch, Tackle, Growl, ThunderShock, Thunder Wave, Cotton Spore, Charge, ThunderPunch, Discharge, Signal Beam, Light Screen, Power Gem, Thunder | |
| **Type:** Electric | |
| **Height:** 4'07" | |
| **Weight:** 135.6 lbs. | |
| **Region:** Johto | |

MAREEP

FLAAFFY

AMPHAROS

# ANORITH
## OLD SHRIMP POKÉMON

Anorith uses its massive claws to hunt its prey. It lives in the sea and was reanimated from a fossil, just like Lileep.

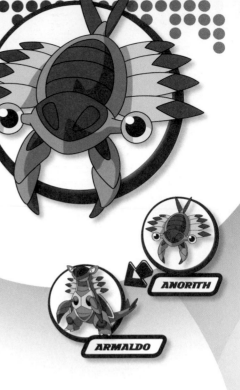

| | |
|---|---|
| **Pronounced:** AN-no-rith | |
| **Possible Moves:** Scratch, Harden, Mud Sport, Water Gun, Metal Claw, Protect, AncientPower, Fury Cutter, Slash, Rock Blast, Crush Claw, X-Scissor | |
| **Type:** Rock-Bug | |
| **Height:** 2'04"   **Weight:** 27.6 lbs. | |
| **Region:** Hoenn | |

ANORITH

ARMALDO

# ARBOK
## COBRA POKÉMON

Arbok uses the pattern on its belly to intimidate foes, but then constricts them while they are frozen with fear.

| |
|---|
| **Pronounced:** ARE-bock |
| **Possible Moves:** Ice Fang, Thunder Fang, Fire Fang, Wrap, Leer, Poison Sting, Bite, Glare, Screech, Acid, Crunch, Stockpile, Swallow, Spit Up, Mud Bomb, Gastro Acid, Haze, Gunk Shot |
| **Type:** Poison |
| **Height:** 11'06"   **Weight:** 143.3 lbs. |
| **Region:** Kanto |

EKANS

ARBOK

# ARCANINE
## LEGENDARY POKÉMON

Arcanine is a very proud and regal Pokémon, which makes it a favorite among humans.

| | |
|---|---|
| **Pronounced:** ar-KAY-nine | |
| **Possible Moves:** Thunder Fang, Bite, Roar, Fire Fang, Odor Sleuth, ExtremeSpeed | |
| **Type:** Fire | |
| **Height:** 6'03" | **Weight:** 341.7 lbs. |
| **Region:** Kanto | |

GROWLITHE

ARCANINE

# ARIADOS
## LONG LEG POKÉMON

Ariados can attach a silken thread to a foe, then follow the thread to its lair and attack it and any acquaintances that happen to be hanging around!

| | |
|---|---|
| **Pronounced:** AIR-ree-uh-dose | |
| **Possible Moves:** Bug Bite, Poison Sting, String Shot, Scary Face, Constrict, Leech Life, Night Shade, Shadow Sneak, Fury Swipes, Sucker Punch, Spider Web, Agility, Pin Missile, Psychic, Poison Jab | |
| **Type:** Bug-Poison | |
| **Height:** 3'07" | **Weight:** 73.9 lbs. |
| **Region:** Johto | |

SPINARAK

ARIADOS

# ARMALDO
## PLATE POKÉMON

Armaldo evolved into its sturdy armor after going ashore to track down foes and food sources.

| Pronounced: ar-MAL-do |
|---|
| **Possible Moves:** Scratch, Harden, Mud Sport, Water Gun, Metal Claw, Protect, AncientPower, Fury Cutter, Slash, Rock Blast, Crush Claw, X-Scissor |
| Type: Rock-Bug |
| Height: 4'11"    Weight: 150.4 lbs. |
| Region: Hoenn |

ANORITH

ARMALDO

# ARON
## IRON ARMOR POKÉMON

Hunger may drive Aron to eat railroad tracks and cars. It lives deep in mountains.

| Pronounced: AIR-ron |
|---|
| **Possible Moves:** Tackle, Harden, Mud-Slap, Headbutt, Metal Claw, Iron Defense, Roar, Take Down, Iron Head, Protect, Metal Sound, Iron Tail, Double-Edge, Metal Burst |
| Type: Steel-Rock |
| Height: 1'04"    Weight: 132.3 lbs. |
| Region: Hoenn |

ARON

LAIRON

AGGRON

# ARTICUNO
## FREEZE POKÉMON
### Legendary Pokémon

By freezing moisture in the air, Articuno can create blizzards.

**Pronounced:** ART-tick-COO-no

**Possible Moves:** Gust, Powder Snow, Mist, Ice Shard, Mind Reader, AncientPower, Agility, Ice Beam, Reflect, Roost, Tailwind, Blizzard, Sheer Cold, Hail

**Type:** Ice-Flying

**Height:** 5'07"

**Weight:** 122.1 lbs.

**Region:** Kanto

DOES NOT EVOLVE

# AZELF
## STONE POKÉMON
### *Legendary Pokémon*

*Also known as The Being of Willpower, this Pokémon keeps the world in balance. It is said that Uxie, Mesprit, and Azelf all came from the same egg.*

**Pronounced:**
AZ-elf

**Possible Moves:** Rest, Imprison, Detect, Confusion, Uproar, Future Sight, Nasty Plot, Extrasensory, Last Resort, Natural Gift, Explosion

**Type:** Psychic

**Height:** 1'00"

**Weight:** 0.7 lbs.

**Region:** Sinnoh

## DOES NOT EVOLVE

Azumarill has natural camouflage—the patterns on its body can fool even those standing right next to it.

| | |
|---|---|
| **Pronounced:** ah-ZU-mare-rill | |
| **Possible Moves:** Tackle, Defense Curl, Tail Whip, Water Gun, Rollout, BubbleBeam, Aqua Ring, Double-Edge, Rain Dance, Aqua Tail, Hydro Pump | |
| **Type:** Water | |
| **Height:** 2'07" | **Weight:** 62.8 lbs. |
| **Region:** Hoenn, Johto, and Sinnoh | |

AZURILL

MARILL

AZUMARILL

# AZURILL
## POLKA DOT POKÉMON

Azurill is a water-dwelling Pokémon that loves to bounce on its springy tail, which is filled with nutrients.

| | |
|---|---|
| **Pronounced:** uh-ZOO-rill | |
| **Possible Moves:** Splash, Charm, Tail Whip, Bubble, Slam, Water Gun | |
| **Type:** Normal | |
| **Height:** 0'08" | **Weight:** 4.4 lbs. |
| **Region:** Hoenn and Sinnoh | |

AZURILL

MARILL

AZUMARILL

# BAGON
## ROCK HEAD POKÉMON

Bagon leaps off cliffs every day in the hopes that one day it will be able to fly.

**Pronounced:**
BAY-gon

**Possible Moves:** Rage, Bite, Leer, Headbutt, Focus Energy, Ember, DragonBreath, Zen Headbutt, Scary Face, Crunch, Dragon Claw, Double-Edge

**Type:** Dragon

**Height:** 2'00"

**Weight:** 92.8 lbs.

**Region:** Hoenn

BAGON

SHELGON

SALAMENCE

# BALTOY
## CLAY DOLL POKÉMON

Considered a very rare Pokémon, Baltoy was discovered in ancient ruins.

| | |
|---|---|
| **Pronounced:** BALL-toy | |
| **Possible Moves:** Confusion, Harden, Rapid Spin, Mud-Slap, Psybeam, Rock Tomb, Selfdestruct, AncientPower, Power Trick, Sandstorm, Cosmic Power, Earth Power, Heal Block, Explosion | |
| **Type:** Ground-Psychic | |
| **Height:** 1'08" | **Weight:** 47.4 lbs. |
| **Region:** Hoenn | |

**CLAYDOL**

**BALTOY**

# BANETTE
## MARIONETTE POKÉMON

Banette became a Pokémon after being abandoned by its owner. It spends most of its time seeking out that owner.

| | |
|---|---|
| **Pronounced:** bane-NETT | |
| **Possible Moves:** Knock Off, Screech, Night Shade, Curse, Spite, Shadow Sneak, Will-O-Wisp, Faint Attack, Shadow Ball, Sucker Punch, Embargo, Snatch, Grudge, Trick | |
| **Type:** Ghost | |
| **Height:** 3'07" | **Weight:** 27.6 lbs. |
| **Region:** Hoenn | |

**SHUPPET**

**BANETTE**

# BARBOACH
## WHISKERS POKÉMON

Barboach is able to use its sensitive whiskers to detect prey. It covers its body in slimy fluid so it's harder for predators to grasp.

**Pronounced:** bar-BOACH

**Possible Moves:** Mud-Slap, Mud Sport, Water Sport, Water Gun, Mud Bomb, Amnesia, Water Pulse, Magnitude, Rest, Snore, Aqua Tail, Earthquake, Future Sight, Fissure

**Type:** Water-Ground

**Height:** 1'04"   **Weight:** 4.2 lbs.

**Region:** Hoenn and Sinnoh

BARBOACH

WHISCASH

# BASTIODON
## SHIELD POKÉMON

Bastiodon protect their young by forming a wall with other Bastiodon. It is a calm Pokémon that feeds on berries and grass.

**Pronounced:** BAS-tee-oh-donn

**Possible Moves:** Tackle, Protect, Taunt, Metal Sound, Take Down, Iron Defense, Swagger, AncientPower, Block, Endure, Metal Burst, Iron Head

**Type:** Rock-Steel

**Height:** 4'03"   **Weight:** 329.6 lbs.

**Region:** Sinnoh

SHIELDON

BASTIODON

# BAYLEEF
## LEAF POKÉMON

Need a pick-me-up? Hang out around Bayleef! The spicy aroma from the rings around its neck can improve the mood of people nearby.

**Pronounced:** BAY-leaf

**Possible Moves:** Tackle, Growl, Razor Leaf, PoisonPowder, Synthesis, Reflect, Magical Leaf, Natural Gift, Sweet Scent, Light Screen, Body Slam, Safeguard, Aromatherapy, SolarBeam

**Type:** Grass

**Height:** 3'11"    **Weight:** 34.8 lbs.

**Region:** Johto

MEGANIUM

BAYLEEF

CHIKORITA

# BEAUTIFLY
## BUTTERFLY POKÉMON

Beautifly uses its long, narrow mouth to drain fluid from prey.

**Pronounced:** BUƐ-tee-fly

**Possible Moves:** Absorb, Gust, Stun Spore, Morning Sun, Mega Drain, Whirlwind, Attract, Silver Wind, Giga Drain, Bug Buzz

**Type:** Bug-Flying

**Height:** 3'03"    **Weight:** 62.6 lbs.

**Region:** Hoenn and Sinnoh

WURMPLE

SILCOON

BEAUTIFLY

# BEEDRILL
## POISON BEE POKÉMON

Beedrill loves to stick and move—flying around at high speeds and stinging enemies, then flying away.

**Pronounced:** BEE-dril

**Possible Moves:** Fury Attack, Focus Energy, Twineedle, Rage, Pursuit, Toxic Spikes, Pin Missile, Agility, Assurance, Poison Jab, Endeavor

**Type:** Bug-Poison

**Height:** 3'03"    **Weight:** 65.0 lbs.

**Region:** Kanto

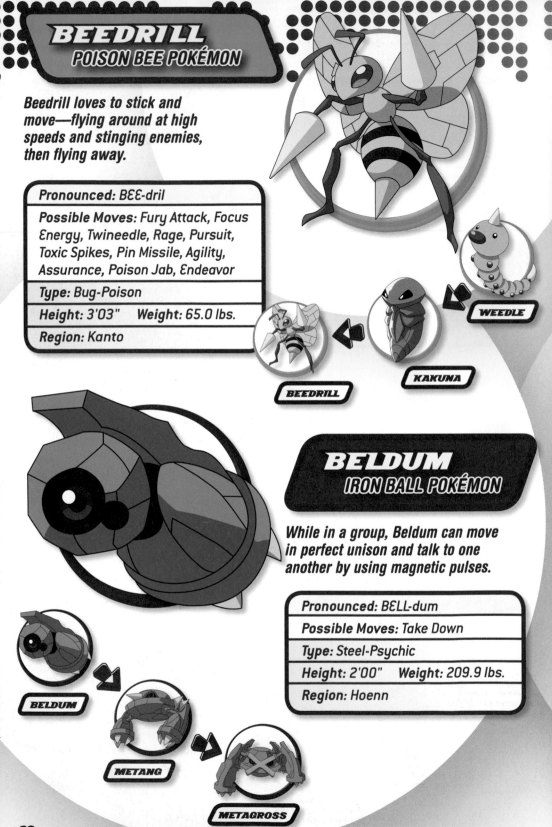

WEEDLE

KAKUNA

BEEDRILL

# BELDUM
## IRON BALL POKÉMON

While in a group, Beldum can move in perfect unison and talk to one another by using magnetic pulses.

**Pronounced:** BELL-dum

**Possible Moves:** Take Down

**Type:** Steel-Psychic

**Height:** 2'00"    **Weight:** 209.9 lbs.

**Region:** Hoenn

BELDUM

METANG

METAGROSS

# BELLOSSOM
## FLOWER POKÉMON

Bellossom will dance in the open sunlight after the rainy season ends.

| | |
|---|---|
| **Pronounced:** bell-LAHS-um | |
| **Possible Moves:** Mega Drain, Sweet Scent, Stun Spore, Sunny Day, Magical Leaf, Leaf Storm | |
| **Type:** Grass | |
| **Height:** 1'04" | **Weight:** 12.8 lbs. |
| **Region:** Johto | |

ODDISH

BELLOSSOM

GLOOM

# BELLSPROUT
## FLOWER POKÉMON

Bellsprout uses its vines to capture prey and likes to live in hot environments.

| | |
|---|---|
| **Pronounced:** BELL-sprout | |
| **Possible Moves:** Vine Whip, Growth, Wrap, Sleep Powder, PoisonPowder, Stun Spore, Acid, Knock Off, Sweet Scent, Gastro Acid, Razor Leaf, Slam, Wring Out | |
| **Type:** Grass-Poison | |
| **Height:** 2'04" | **Weight:** 8.8 lbs. |
| **Region:** Kanto | |

BELLSPROUT

WEEPINBELL

VICTREEBEL

# BIBAREL
## BEAVER POKÉMON

Bibarel can swim fast in water, but moves slowly on land. Bibarel is known as a hard-working Pokémon.

| | |
|---|---|
| **Pronounced:** BEE-bear-ull | |
| **Possible Moves:** Tackle, Growl, Defense Curl, Rollout, Water Gun, Headbutt, Hyper Fang, Yawn, Amnesia, Take Down, Super Fang, Superpower | |
| **Type:** Normal-Water | |
| **Height:** 3'03"    **Weight:** 69.4 lbs. | |
| **Region:** Sinnoh | |

BIDOOF

BIBAREL

# BIDOOF
## PLUMP MOUSE POKÉMON

Bidoof is known to chew on rocks and logs to dull the edge of its sharp teeth. But be careful—this Pokémon is more agile than it appears.

| | |
|---|---|
| **Pronounced:** BEE-doof | |
| **Possible Moves:** Tackle, Growl, Defense Curl, Rollout, Headbutt, Hyper Fang, Yawn, Amnesia, Take Down, Super Fang, Superpower | |
| **Type:** Normal | |
| **Height:** 1'08"    **Weight:** 44.1 lbs. | |
| **Region:** Sinnoh | |

BIDOOF

BIBAREL

# BLASTOISE
## SHELLFISH POKÉMON

Beware of the jets from this Pokémon's shell—they can punch through thick steel.

Pronounced:
BLAS-toyce

Possible Moves: Flash Cannon, Tackle, Tail Whip, Bubble, Withdraw, Water Gun, Bite, Rapid Spin, Protect, Water Pulse, Aqua Tail, Skull Bash, Rain Dance, Hydro Pump

Type: Water

Height: 5'03"

Weight: 188.5 lbs.

Region: Kanto

SQUIRTLE

WARTORTLE

BLASTOISE

# BLAZIKEN
## BLAZE POKÉMON

Blaziken's knuckles are covered in flames that it uses to beat its foes.

**Pronounced:**
BLAZE-uh-ken

**Possible Moves:** Fire Punch, Scratch, Growl, Focus Energy, Ember, Double Kick, Peck, Sand-Attack, Bulk Up, Quick Attack, Blaze Kick, Slash, Brave Bird, Sky Uppercut, Flare Blitz

**Type:** Fire-Fighting

**Height:** 6'03"

**Weight:** 114.6 lbs.

**Region:** Hoenn

TORCHIC

COMBUSKEN

BLAZIKEN

# BLISSEY
## HAPPINESS POKÉMON

This Pokémon can sense feelings of sadness, and also nurses sick Pokémon back to health.

| |
|---|
| **Pronounced:** BLISS-sey |
| **Possible Moves:** Pound, Growl, Tail Whip, Refresh, Softboiled, DoubleSlap, Minimize, Sing, Fling, Defense Curl, Light Screen, Egg Bomb, Healing Wish, Double-Edge |
| **Type:** Normal |
| **Height:** 4'11"    **Weight:** 103.2 lbs. |
| **Region:** Johto and Sinnoh |

HAPPINY

CHANSEY

BLISSEY

# BONSLY
## BONSAI POKÉMON

Don't worry, Bonsly isn't sad! This Pokémon adjusts its fluid levels by eliminating the excess water from its body through tears.

| |
|---|
| **Pronounced:** BON-sly |
| **Possible Moves:** Fake Tears, Copycat, Flail, Low Kick, Rock Throw, Mimic, Block, Faint Attack, Rock Tomb, Rock Slide, Slam, Sucker Punch, Double-Edge |
| **Type:** Rock |
| **Height:** 1'08"    **Weight:** 33.1 lbs. |
| **Region:** Sinnoh |

BONSLY

SUDOWOODO

25

# BRELOOM
## MUSHROOM POKÉMON

Though Breloom appears to have short arms, they will stretch when Breloom throws punches at its foes.

**Pronounced:** BRELL-loom

**Possible Moves:** Absorb, Tackle, Stun Spore, Leech Seed, Mega Drain, Headbutt, Mach Punch, Counter, Force Palm, Sky Uppercut, Mind Reader, Seed Bomb, DynamicPunch

**Type:** Grass-Fighting

**Height:** 3'11"    **Weight:** 86.4 lbs.

**Region:** Hoenn

SHROOMISH

BRELOOM

# BRONZONG
## BRONZE BELL POKÉMON

This Pokémon was known in ancient times as the bringer of plentiful harvests, because it produced rain clouds.

BRONZOR

BRONZONG

**Pronounced:** brawn-ZONG

**Possible Moves:** Sunny Day, Rain Dance, Tackle, Confusion, Hypnosis, Imprison, Confuse Ray, Extrasensory, Iron Defense, Safeguard, Block, Gyro Ball, Future Sight, Faint Attack, Payback, Heal Block

**Type:** Steel-Psychic

**Height:** 4'03"    **Weight:** 412.3 lbs.

**Region:** Sinnoh

# BRONZOR
## BRONZE POKÉMON

Shaped like an ancient artifact, no one really knows what Bronzor is made out of.

**Pronounced:**
BRAWN-zor

**Possible Moves:** Tackle, Confusion, Hypnosis, Imprison, Confuse Ray, Extrasensory, Iron Defense, Safeguard, Gyro Ball, Future Sight, Faint Attack, Payback, Heal Block

**Type:** Steel-Psychic

**Height:** 1'08"

**Weight:** 133.4 lbs.

**Region:** Sinnoh

**BRONZOR**

**BRONZONG**

# BUDEW
## BUD POKÉMON

The pollen that is released from Budew's bud can cause runny noses and sneezing.

| | |
|---|---|
| **Pronounced:** Buh-DOO | |
| **Possible Moves:** Headbutt, Leer, Focus Energy, Pursuit, Take Down, Scary Face, Assurance, AncientPower, Endeavor, Zen Headbutt, Screech, Head Smash | |
| **Type:** Grass-Poison | |
| **Height:** 0'08" | **Weight:** 2.6 lbs. |
| **Region:** Sinnoh | |

ROSERADE

ROSELIA

BUDEW

# BUIZEL
## SEA WEASEL POKÉMON

The sac around Buziel's neck acts like an innertube, which allows it to float with its head above water. It moves by spinning its tail like a propeller.

| | |
|---|---|
| **Pronounced:** BWEE-zull | |
| **Possible Moves:** Growl, Water Sport, Quick Attack, Water Gun, Pursuit, Swift, Aqua Jet, Agility, Whirlpool, Razor Wind | |
| **Type:** Water | |
| **Height:** 2'04" | **Weight:** 65.0 lbs. |
| **Region:** Sinnoh | |

BUIZEL

FLOATZEL

# BULBASAUR
## SEED POKÉMON

*Shortly after being born, this Pokémon can obtain nourishment from the seed on its back.*

**Pronounced:** BUL-buh-sore

**Possible Moves:** *Tackle, Growl, Leech Seed, Vine Whip, PoisonPowder, Sleep Powder, Take Down, Razor Leaf, Sweet Scent, Growth, Double-Edge, Worry Seed, Synthesis, Seed Bomb*

**Type:** *Grass-Poison*

**Height:** *2'04"*    **Weight:** *15.2 lbs.*

**Region:** *Kanto*

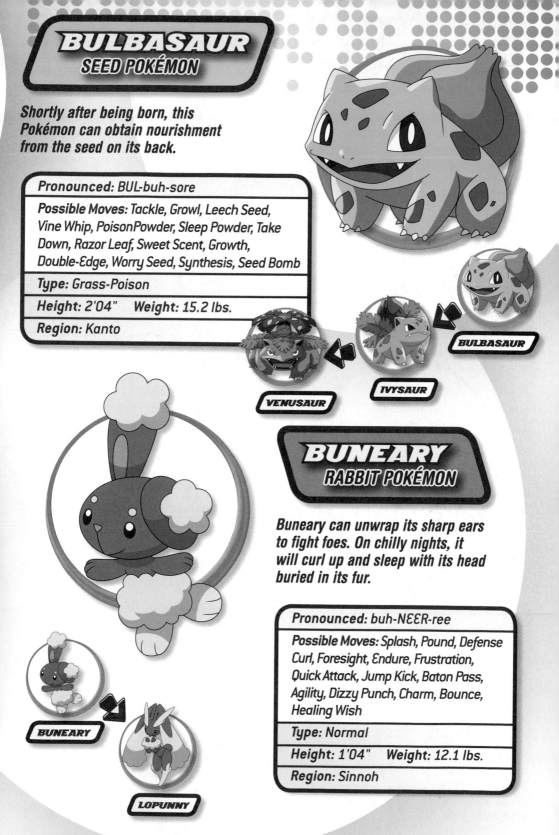

VENUSAUR

IVYSAUR

BULBASAUR

# BUNEARY
## RABBIT POKÉMON

*Buneary can unwrap its sharp ears to fight foes. On chilly nights, it will curl up and sleep with its head buried in its fur.*

**Pronounced:** buh-NEER-ree

**Possible Moves:** *Splash, Pound, Defense Curl, Foresight, Endure, Frustration, Quick Attack, Jump Kick, Baton Pass, Agility, Dizzy Punch, Charm, Bounce, Healing Wish*

**Type:** *Normal*

**Height:** *1'04"*    **Weight:** *12.1 lbs.*

**Region:** *Sinnoh*

BUNEARY

LOPUNNY

# BURMY GRASS CLOAK
## BAGWORM POKÉMON

Burmy can camouflage itself by burying itself in leaves and twigs. If it's uncovered in battle, it can quickly cover itself back up.

| | |
|---|---|
| **Pronounced:** BURR-mee | |
| **Possible Moves:** Protect, Tackle, Hidden Power | |
| **Type:** Bug | |
| **Height:** 0'08"  **Weight:** 7.5 lbs. | |
| **Region:** Sinnoh | |

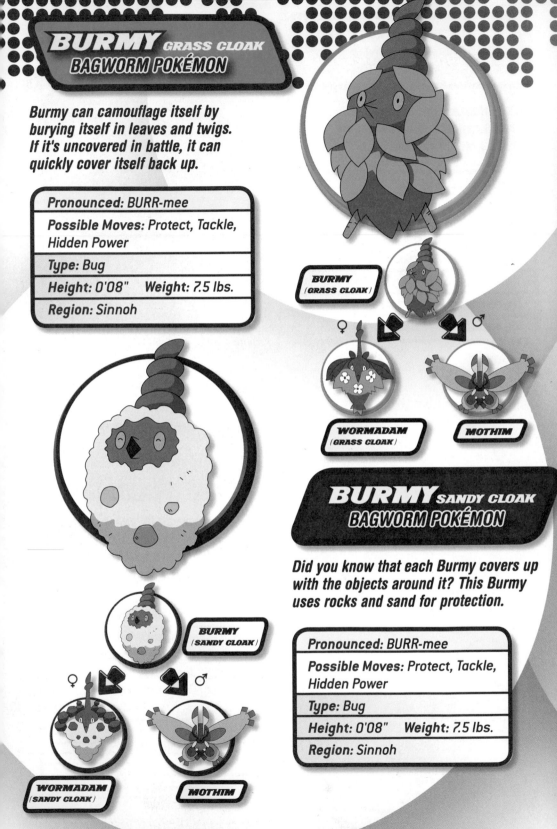

BURMY
(GRASS CLOAK)

♀

♂

WORMADAM
(GRASS CLOAK)

MOTHIM

# BURMY SANDY CLOAK
## BAGWORM POKÉMON

Did you know that each Burmy covers up with the objects around it? This Burmy uses rocks and sand for protection.

| | |
|---|---|
| **Pronounced:** BURR-mee | |
| **Possible Moves:** Protect, Tackle, Hidden Power | |
| **Type:** Bug | |
| **Height:** 0'08"  **Weight:** 7.5 lbs. | |
| **Region:** Sinnoh | |

BURMY
(SANDY CLOAK)

♀

♂

WORMADAM
(SANDY CLOAK)

MOTHIM

*If you're looking for Burmy with a Trash Cloak, try poking around inside a few buildings. You might get lucky!*

| | |
|---|---|
| **Pronounced:** BURR-mee | |
| **Possible Moves:** Protect, Tackle, Hidden Power | |
| **Type:** Bug | |
| **Height:** 0'08" | **Weight:** 7.5 lbs. |
| **Region:** Sinnoh | |

**BURMY** (TRASH CLOAK)

♀ **WORMADAM** (TRASH CLOAK)

♂ **MOTHIM**

# BUTTERFREE
## BUTTERFLY POKÉMON

*Butterfree can smell honey from great distances, and will often find its way to meadows with even minute traces of honey or pollen.*

CATERPIE

METAPOD

BUTTERFREE

| | |
|---|---|
| **Pronounced:** BUT-er-free | |
| **Possible Moves:** Confusion, PoisonPowder, Stun Spore, Sleep Powder, Gust, Supersonic, Whirlwind, Psybeam, Silver Wind, Tailwind, Safeguard, Captivate, Bug Buzz | |
| **Type:** Bug-Flying | |
| **Height:** 3'07" | **Weight:** 70.5 lbs. |
| **Region:** Kanto | |

31

# CACNEA
## CACTUS POKÉMON

Because of its balloon shape, Cacnea can survive up to thirty days in the desert by living off the water stored in its body.

| |
|---|
| Pronounced: CACK-nee-uh |
| Possible Moves: Poison Sting, Leer, Absorb, Growth, Leech Seed, Sand-Attack, Pin Missile, Ingrain, Faint Attack, Spikes, Sucker Punch, Payback, Needle Arm, Cotton Spore, Sandstorm, Destiny Bond |
| Type: Grass |
| Height: 1'04"   Weight: 113.1 lbs. |
| Region: Hoenn |

CACNEA

CACTURNE

# CACTURNE
## SCARECROW POKÉMON

Cacturne is a nocturnal Pokémon, and waits patiently for prey that are tired from traipsing around in the desert all day.

CACNEA

CACTURNE

| |
|---|
| Pronounced: CACK-turn |
| Possible Moves: Revenge, Poison Sting, Leer, Absorb, Growth, Leech Seed, Sand-Attack, Pin Missile, Ingrain, Faint Attack, Spikes, Sucker Punch, Payback, Needle Arm, Cotton Spore, Sandstorm, Destiny Bond |
| Type: Grass-Dark |
| Height: 4'03"   Weight: 170.6 lbs. |
| Region: Hoenn |

# CAMERUPT
## ERUPTION POKÉMON

*If too much magma builds up in Camerupt's body, the volcanoes on its back will shudder, then erupt violently.*

| | |
|---|---|
| **Pronounced:** CAM-err-rupt | |
| **Possible Moves:** Growl, Tackle, Magnitude, Ember, Focus Energy, Take Down, Amnesia, Lava Plume, Rock Slide, Earth Power, Earthquake, Eruption, Fissure | |
| **Type:** Fire-Ground | |
| **Height:** 6'03"    **Weight:** 485.0 lbs. | |
| **Region:** Hoenn | |

**NUMEL**

**CAMERUPT**

# CARNIVINE
## BUG CATCHER POKÉMON

*Carnivine attracts its prey by emitting a sweet-smelling scent. Once caught, it takes Carnivine a whole day to digest its prey.*

DOES NOT EVOLVE

| | |
|---|---|
| **Pronounced:** CAR-nuh-vine | |
| **Possible Moves:** Bind, Growth, Bite, Vine Whip, Sweet Scent, Ingrain, Faint Attack, Stockpile, Spit Up, Swallow, Crunch, Wring Out, Power Whip | |
| **Type:** Grass | |
| **Height:** 4'07"    **Weight:** 59.5 lbs. | |
| **Region:** Sinnoh | |

# CARVANHA
## SAVAGE POKÉMON

Carvanha's sharp fangs have been known to destroy boat hulls, and they swarm any foe that invades their territory.

| | |
|---|---|
| **Pronounced:** car-VAH-na | |
| **Possible Moves:** Leer, Bite, Rage, Focus Energy, Scary Face, Ice Fang, Screech, Swagger, Assurance, Crunch, Aqua Jet, Agility, Take Down | |
| **Type:** Water-Dark | |
| **Height:** 2'07"   **Weight:** 45.9 lbs. | |
| **Region:** Hoenn | |

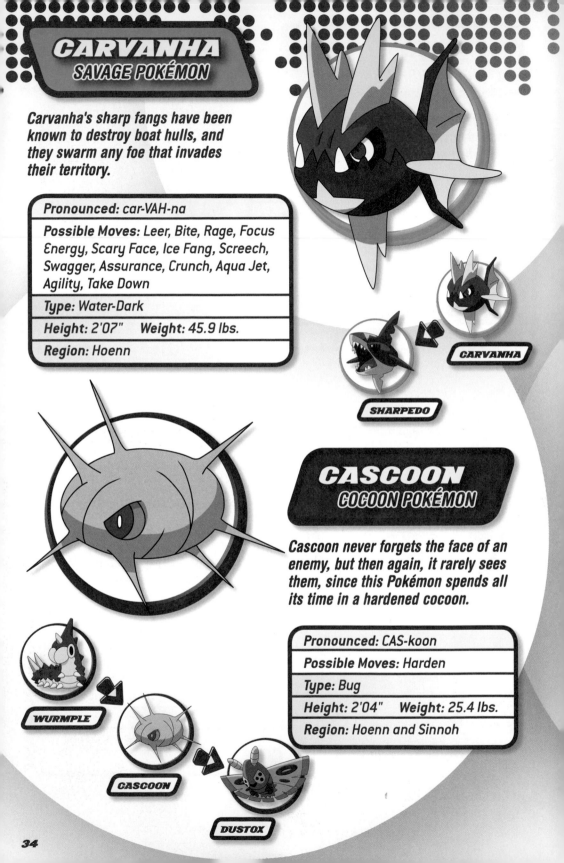

CARVANHA

SHARPEDO

# CASCOON
## COCOON POKÉMON

Cascoon never forgets the face of an enemy, but then again, it rarely sees them, since this Pokémon spends all its time in a hardened cocoon.

| | |
|---|---|
| **Pronounced:** CAS-koon | |
| **Possible Moves:** Harden | |
| **Type:** Bug | |
| **Height:** 2'04"   **Weight:** 25.4 lbs. | |
| **Region:** Hoenn and Sinnoh | |

WURMPLE

CASCOON

DUSTOX

# CASTFORM
## WEATHER POKÉMON

Castform has the ability to change its appearance to match changes of weather.

| | |
|---|---|
| **Pronounced:** CAST-form | |
| **Possible Moves:** Tackle, Water Gun, Ember, Powder Snow, Rain Dance, Sunny Day, Hail, Weather Ball | |
| **Type:** Normal | |
| **Height:** 1'00" | **Weight:** 1.8 lbs. |
| **Region:** Hoenn | |

DOES NOT EVOLVE

# CATERPIE
## WORM POKÉMON

How does Caterpie grow? By repeatedly shedding its skin. How does it survive? By releasing a horrible stench from its antennae.

| | |
|---|---|
| **Pronounced:** CAT-er-pee | |
| **Possible Moves:** Tackle, String Shot | |
| **Type:** Bug | |
| **Height:** 1'00" | **Weight:** 6.4 lbs. |
| **Region:** Kanto | |

CATERPIE

METAPOD

BUTTERFREE

# CELEBI
## TIME TRAVEL POKÉMON
### Legendary Pokémon

Celebi is rumored to appear only in peaceful times.

**Pronounced:**
SEL-ih-bee

**Possible Moves:** Leech Seed, Confusion, Recover, Heal Bell, Safeguard, Magical Leaf, AncientPower, Baton Pass, Natural Gift, Heal Block, Future Sight, Healing Wish, Leaf Storm, Perish Song

**Type:** Grass-Psychic

**Height:** 2'00"

**Weight:** 11.0 lbs.

**Region:** Johto

**DOES NOT EVOLVE**

# CHANSEY
## EGG POKÉMON

This is a very compassionate Pokémon, delivering happiness and sharing its egg with injured people and Pokémon.

**Pronounced:**
CHAN-see

**Possible Moves:** Pound, Growl, Tail Whip, Refresh, Softboiled, DoubleSlap, Minimize, Sing, Fling, Defense Curl, Light Screen, Egg Bomb, Healing Wish, Double-Edge

**Type:** Normal

**Height:** 3'07"

**Weight:** 76.3 lbs.

**Region:** Kanto and Sinnoh

HAPPINY

CHANSEY

BLISSEY

# CHARIZARD
## FLAME POKÉMON

You don't want to mess with Charizard after it has experienced a tense battle—the fire emanating from it burns hotter when it is stressed.

**Pronounced:**
CHAR-i-zard

**Possible Moves:** Dragon Claw, Shadow Claw, Air Slash, Scratch, Growl, Ember, SmokeScreen, Dragon Rage, Scary Face, Fire Fang, Slash, Wing Attack, Flamethrower, Fire Spin, Heat Wave, Flare Blitz

**Type:** Fire-Flying

**Height:** 5'07"

**Weight:** 199.5 lbs.

**Region:** Kanto

CHARMANDER

CHARMELEON

CHARIZARD

# CHARMANDER
## LIZARD POKÉMON

*If Charmander is healthy, the fire on its tail burns intensely.*

**Pronounced:**
CHAR-man-der

**Possible Moves:** Scratch, Growl, Ember, SmokeScreen, Dragon Rage, Scary Face, Fire Fang, Slash, Flamethrower, Fire Spin

**Type:** Fire

**Height:** 2'00

**Weight:** 18.7 lbs

**Region:** Kanto

CHARMANDER

CHARMELEON

CHARIZARD

# CHARMELEON
## FLAME POKÉMON

It's easy to spot a Charmeleon's lair in Kanto's rocky mountains: Each one shines with the power of intense starlight due to this Pokémon's fiery tail.

**Pronounced:**
char-MEAL-ee-ehn

**Possible Moves:** Scratch, Growl, Ember, SmokeScreen, Dragon Rage, Scary Face, Fire Fang, Slash, Flamethrower, Fire Spin

**Type:** Fire

**Height:** 3'07"

**Weight:** 41.9 lbs.

**Region:** Kanto

CHARMANDER

CHARMELEON

CHARIZARD

# CHATOT
## MUSIC NOTE POKÉMON

Chatot can learn human words. But even if it can't speak, Chatot can click its tail feathers to make a rhythmic sound.

| |
|---|
| **Pronounced:** CHAH-tot |
| **Possible Moves:** Peck, Growl, Mirror Move, Sing, Fury Attack, Chatter, Taunt, Mimic, Roost, Uproar, FeatherDance, Hyper Voice |
| **Type:** Normal-Flying |
| **Height:** 1'08"    **Weight:** 4.2 lbs. |
| **Region:** Sinnoh |

DOES NOT EVOLVE

# CHERRIM
## CHERRY BLOSSOM POKÉMON

While the sun is out, Cherrim will bloom to full strength, but will return to a bud when sunlight fades.

| |
|---|
| **Pronounced:** chuh-RIM |
| **Possible Moves:** Tackle, Growth, Leech Seed, Helping Hand, Magical Leaf, Sunny Day, Petal Dance, Worry Seed, Take Down, SolarBeam, Lucky Chant |
| **Type:** Grass |
| **Height:** 1'08"    **Weight:** 20.5 lbs. |
| **Region:** Sinnoh |

CHERUBI

CHERRIM

# CHERUBI
## CHERRY POKÉMON

The small ball attached to Cherubi holds the nutrition that Cherubi needs to evolve. While out in the sun, it will change its color to red.

| | |
|---|---|
| **Pronounced:** chuh-ROO-bee | |
| **Possible Moves:** Tackle, Growth, Leech Seed, Helping Hand, Magical Leaf, Sunny Day, Worry Seed, Take Down, SolarBeam, Lucky Chant | |
| **Type:** Grass | |
| **Height:** 1'04" | **Weight:** 7.3 lbs. |
| **Region:** Sinnoh | |

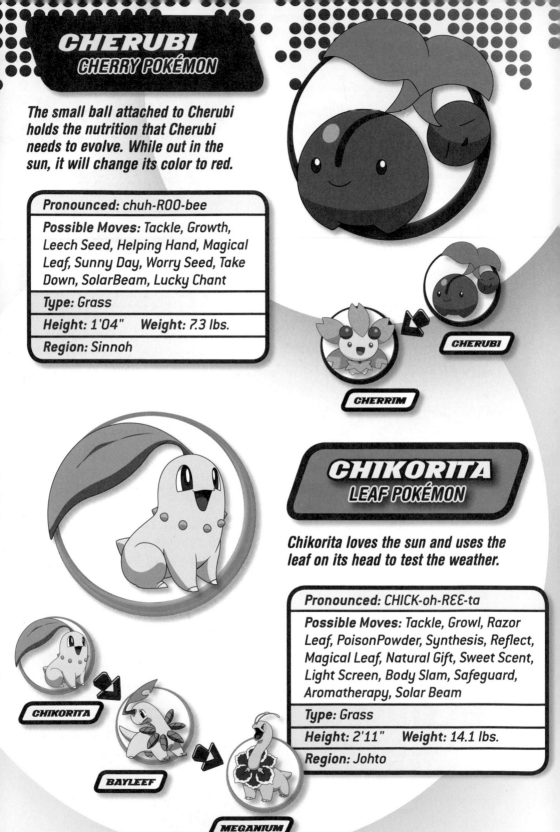

CHERRIM

CHERUBI

# CHIKORITA
## LEAF POKÉMON

Chikorita loves the sun and uses the leaf on its head to test the weather.

| | |
|---|---|
| **Pronounced:** CHICK-oh-REE-ta | |
| **Possible Moves:** Tackle, Growl, Razor Leaf, PoisonPowder, Synthesis, Reflect, Magical Leaf, Natural Gift, Sweet Scent, Light Screen, Body Slam, Safeguard, Aromatherapy, Solar Beam | |
| **Type:** Grass | |
| **Height:** 2'11" | **Weight:** 14.1 lbs. |
| **Region:** Johto | |

CHIKORITA

BAYLEEF

MEGANIUM

# CHIMCHAR
## CHIMP POKÉMON

Even the rain can't put out Chimchar's fiery tail, which is fueled by the gases in its stomach.

**Pronounced:**
CHIM-char

**Possible Moves:** Scratch, Leer, Ember, Taunt, Fury Swipes, Flame Wheel, Nasty Plot, Torment, Facade, Fire Spin, Slack Off, Flamethrower

**Type:** Fire

**Height:** 1'08"

**Weight:** 13.7 lbs.

**Region:** Sinnoh

CHIMCHAR

MONFERNO

INFERNAPE

# CHIMECHO
## WIND CHIME POKÉMON

Chimecho can use seven different cries to knock out its prey.

**Pronounced:** chime-ECK-ko

**Possible Moves:** Wrap, Growl, Astonish, Confusion, Uproar, Take Down, Yawn, Psywave, Double-Edge, Heal Bell, Safeguard, Extrasensory, Healing Wish

**Type:** Psychic

**Height:** 2'00"    **Weight:** 2.2 lbs.

**Region:** Hoenn and Sinnoh

CHINGLING

CHIMECHO

# CHINCHOU
## ANGLER POKÉMON

Chinchou's electric attacks are possible thanks to the energy it charges between its two antennae.

**Pronounced:** CHIN-chow

**Possible Moves:** Bubble, Supersonic, Thunder Wave, Flail, Water Gun, Confuse Ray, Spark, Take Down, BubbleBeam, Signal Beam, Discharge, Aqua Ring, Hydro Pump, Charge

**Type:** Water-Electric

**Height:** 1'08"    **Weight:** 26.5 lbs.

**Region:** Johto

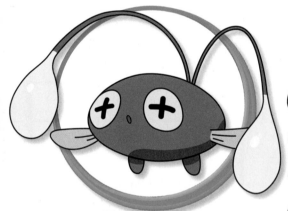

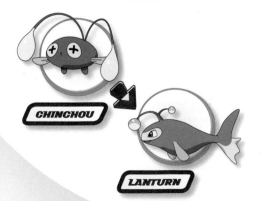

CHINCHOU

LANTURN

# CHINGLING
## BELL POKÉMON

Chingling defeats its foes by using a cry that comes from an orb in the back of its throat. But when not in battle, it makes a ringing sound as it moves and hops around.

| | |
|---|---|
| **Pronounced:** CHING-ling | |
| **Possible Moves:** Wrap, Growl, Astonish, Confusion, Uproar, Last Resort | |
| **Type:** Psychic | |
| **Height:** 0'08"   **Weight:** 1.3 lbs. | |
| **Region:** Sinnoh | |

CHINGLING

CHIMECHO

# CLAMPERL
## BIVALVE POKÉMON

Clamperl will only produce one pearl in its lifetime, which is said to enhance psychic power.

| | |
|---|---|
| **Pronounced:** CLAM-perl | |
| **Possible Moves:** Clamp, Water Gun, Whirlpool, Iron Defense | |
| **Type:** Water | |
| **Height:** 1'04"   **Weight:** 115.7 lbs. | |
| **Region:** Hoenn | |

CLAMPERL

HUNTAIL

GOREBYSS

# CLAYDOL
## CLAY DOLL POKÉMON

Claydol was formed when a mysterious ray of light shone down upon an ancient clay figurine.

| | |
|---|---|
| **Pronounced:** CLAY-doll | |
| **Possible Moves:** Teleport, Confusion, Harden, Rapid Spin, Mud-Slap, Psybeam, Rock Tomb, Selfdestruct, AncientPower, Power Trick, Hyper Beam, Sandstorm, Cosmic Power, Earth Power, Heal Block, Explosion | |
| **Type:** Ground-Psychic | |
| **Height:** 4'11" | **Weight:** 238.1 lbs. |
| **Region:** Hoenn | |

BALTOY

CLAYDOL

# CLEFABLE
## FAIRY POKÉMON

This Pokémon is very shy. It lives mostly near deserted lakebeds. Clefable can hear you coming, too—its hearing can detect a pin drop from over half a mile away.

| | |
|---|---|
| **Pronounced:** cluh-FAY-bull | |
| **Possible Moves:** Sing, DoubleSlap, Minimize, Metronome | |
| **Type:** Normal | |
| **Height:** 4'03" | **Weight:** 88.2 lbs. |
| **Region:** Kanto and Sinnoh | |

CLEFFA

CLEFAIRY

CLEFABLE

# CLEFAIRY
## FAIRY POKÉMON

This is one of the most difficult Pokémon to find—it flies mostly at night, collecting moonlight on its wings.

**Pronounced:** cluh-FAIR-ee

**Possible Moves:** Pound, Growl, Encore, Sing, DoubleSlap, Defense Curl, Follow Me, Minimize, Wake-Up Slap, Cosmic Power, Lucky Chant, Metronome, Gravity, Moonlight, Light Screen, Meteor Mash, Healing Wish

**Type:** Normal

**Height:** 2'00"    **Weight:** 16.5 lbs.

**Region:** Kanto and Sinnoh

CLEFFA

CLEFAIRY

CLEFABLE

# CLEFFA
## STAR SHAPE POKÉMON

Cleffa is usually found when swarms of shooting stars descend, but they're gone by sunrise.

**Pronounced:** CLEFF-uh

**Possible Moves:** Pound, Charm, Encore, Sing, Sweet Kiss, Copycat, Magical Leaf

**Type:** Normal

**Height:** 1'00"    **Weight:** 6.6 lbs.

**Region:** Johto and Sinnoh

CLEFFA

CLEFAIRY

CLEFABLE

# CLOYSTER
## BIVALVE POKÉMON

Cloyster fights by shooting spikes from its body and then closing its shell for protection.

| |
|---|
| **Pronounced:** CLOY-stir |
| **Possible Moves:** Toxic Spikes, Withdraw, Supersonic, Aurora Beam, Protect, Spikes, Spike Cannon |
| **Type:** Water-Ice |
| **Height:** 4'11"    **Weight:** 292.1 lbs. |
| **Region:** Kanto |

SHELLDER

CLOYSTER

# COMBEE
## TINY BEE POKÉMON

Combee collects honey for the rest of the colony and delivers it to Vespiquen.

| |
|---|
| **Pronounced:** COHM-bee |
| **Possible Moves:** Sweet Scent, Gust |
| **Type:** Bug-Flying |
| **Height:** 1'00"    **Weight:** 12.1 lbs. |
| **Region:** Sinnoh |

COMBEE

VESPIQUEN

# COMBUSKEN
## YOUNG FOWL POKÉMON

Using cries to intimidate its foes, Combusken can kick ten times per second.

Pronounced:
com-BUS-ken

**Possible Moves:** Scratch, Growl, Focus Energy, Ember, Double Kick, Peck, Sand-Attack, Bulk Up, Quick Attack, Slash, Mirror Move, Sky Uppercut, Flare Blitz

**Type:** Fire-Fighting

**Height:** 2'11"

**Weight:** 43.0 lbs.

**Region:** Hoenn

TORCHIC

COMBUSKEN

BLAZIKEN

# CORPHISH
## RUFFIAN POKÉMON

Corphish will use its pincers to grab hold of its prey. Its sturdy nature enables it to adapt to almost any environment.

| | |
|---|---|
| **Pronounced:** COR-fish | |
| **Possible Moves:** Bubble, Harden, ViceGrip, Leer, BubbleBeam, Protect, Knock Off, Taunt, Night Slash, Crabhammer, Swords Dance, Crunch, Guillotine | |
| **Type:** Water | |
| **Height:** 2'00"  **Weight:** 25.4 lbs. | |
| **Region:** Hoenn | |

CORPHISH

CRAWDAUNT

DOES NOT EVOLVE

# CORSOLA
## CORAL POKÉMON

Corosla must live in clean seas (usually in the south) because they can't live in polluted waters.

| | |
|---|---|
| **Pronounced:** COR-soh-la | |
| **Possible Moves:** Tackle, Harden, Bubble, Recover, Refresh, Rock Blast, BubbleBeam, Lucky Chant, AncientPower, Aqua Ring, Spike Cannon, Power Gem, Mirror Coat, Earth Power | |
| **Type:** Water-Rock | |
| **Height:** 2'00"  **Weight:** 11.0 lbs. | |
| **Region:** Johto | |

# CRADILY
## BARNACLE POKÉMON

Cradily captures its prey by digging up the beaches of warm seas during low tide.

| | |
|---|---|
| **Pronounced:** cray-DILLY | |
| **Possible Moves:** Astonish, Constrict, Acid, Ingrain, Confuse Ray, Amnesia, AncientPower, Gastro Acid, Energy Ball, Stockpile, Spit Up, Swallow, Wring Out | |
| **Type:** Rock-Grass | |
| **Height:** 4'11"    **Weight:** 133.2 lbs. | |
| **Region:** Hoenn | |

LILEEP

CRADILY

# CRANIDOS
## HEADBUTT POKÉMON

Cranidos uses its ironclad head to ram into its foes and take them down.

| | |
|---|---|
| **Pronounced:** CRANE-ee-dose | |
| **Possible Moves:** Headbutt, Leer, Focus Energy, Pursuit, Take Down, Scary Face, Assurance, AncientPower, Zen Headbutt, Screech, Head Smash | |
| **Type:** Rock | |
| **Height:** 2'11"    **Weight:** 69.4 lbs. | |
| **Region:** Sinnoh | |

CRANIDOS

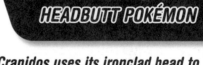

RAMPARDOS

# CRAWDAUNT
## ROGUE POKÉMON

Crawdaunt is highly territorial. It will use its pincers to toss away any intruders that venture near.

CORPHISH

CRAWDAUNT

**Pronounced:** CRAW-daunt

**Possible Moves:** Bubble, Harden, ViceGrip, Leer, BubbleBeam, Protect, Knock Off, Swift, Taunt, Night Slash, Crabhammer, Swords Dance, Crunch, Guillotine

**Type:** Water-Dark

**Height:** 3'07"   **Weight:** 72.3 lbs.

**Region:** Hoenn

DOES NOT EVOLVE

# CRESSELIA
## CRESCENT MOON POKÉMON
### Legendary Pokémon

The crescent moon shape of Cresselia's wings will sometimes emit shiny particles, making it look like a veil.

**Pronounced:** cres-SEL-ee-uh

**Possible Moves:** Confusion, Double Team, Safeguard, Mist, Aurora Beam, Future Sight, Slash, Moonlight, Psycho Cut, Psycho Shift, Lunar Dance, Psychic

**Type:** Psychic

**Height:** 4'11"   **Weight:** 188.7 lbs.

**Region:** Sinnoh

# CROAGUNK
## POISON POKÉMON

The sacs on Croagunk's cheeks hold a toxic poison. It surprises its foes by jabbing them with its toxic fingers.

**Pronounced:**
CROW-gunk

**Possible Moves:** Astonish, Mud-Slap, Poison Sting, Taunt, Pursuit, Faint Attack, Revenge, Swagger, Mud Bomb, Sucker Punch, Nasty Plot, Poison Jab, Sludge Bomb, Flatter

**Type:** Poison-Fighting

**Height:** 2'04"

**Weight:** 50.7 lbs.

**Region:** Sinnoh

GROAGUNK

TOXICROAK

# CROBAT
## BAT POKÉMON

How does Crobat fly so fast and so quietly? Its lower legs evolved into an extra pair of wings!

**Pronounced:** CROW-bat

**Possible Moves:** Cross Poison, Screech, Leech Life, Supersonic, Astonish, Bite, Wing Attack, Confuse Ray, Air Cutter, Mean Look, Poison Fang, Haze, Air Slash

**Type:** Poison-Flying

**Height:** 5'11"    **Weight:** 165.3 lbs.

**Region:** Johto, Hoenn, and Sinnoh

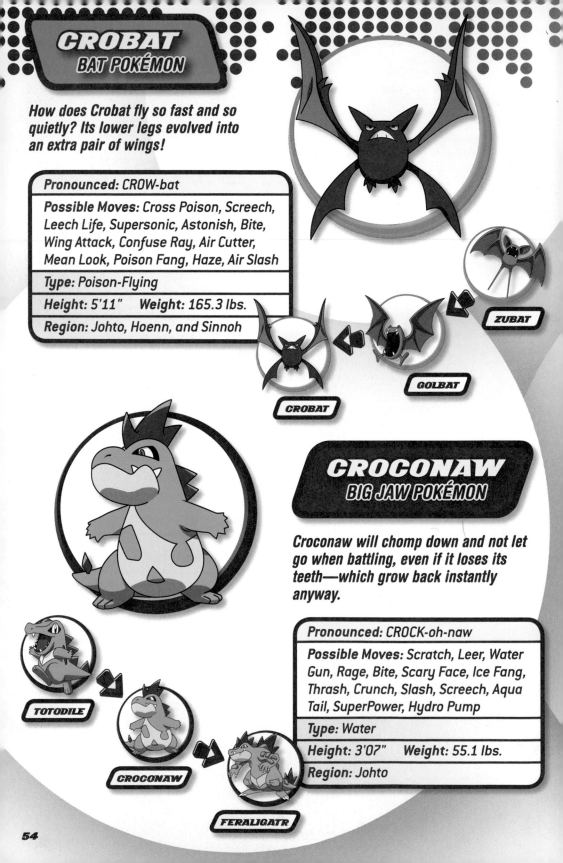

ZUBAT

GOLBAT

CROBAT

# CROCONAW
## BIG JAW POKÉMON

Croconaw will chomp down and not let go when battling, even if it loses its teeth—which grow back instantly anyway.

**Pronounced:** CROCK-oh-naw

**Possible Moves:** Scratch, Leer, Water Gun, Rage, Bite, Scary Face, Ice Fang, Thrash, Crunch, Slash, Screech, Aqua Tail, SuperPower, Hydro Pump

**Type:** Water

**Height:** 3'07"    **Weight:** 55.1 lbs.

**Region:** Johto

TOTODILE

CROCONAW

FERALIGATR

# CUBONE
## LONELY POKÉMON

The skull it wears rattles loudly when it cries.

| | |
|---|---|
| **Pronounced:** CUE-bone | |
| **Possible Moves:** Growl, Tail Whip, Bone Club, Headbutt, Leer, Focus Energy, Bonemerang, Rage, False Swipe, Thrash, Fling, Bone Rush, Endeavor, Double-Edge | |
| **Type:** Ground | |
| **Height:** 1'04" | **Weight:** 14.3 lbs. |
| **Region:** Kanto | |

**CUBONE**

**MAROWAK**

# CYNDAQUIL
## FIRE MOUSE POKÉMON

The flames on Cyndaquil's back will burn more brightly if it is startled.

| | |
|---|---|
| **Pronounced:** SIN-da-kwill | |
| **Possible Moves:** Tackle, Leer, SmokeScreen, Ember, Quick Attack, Flame Wheel, Defense Curl, Swift, Lava Plume, Flamethrower, Rollout, Double-Edge, Eruption | |
| **Type:** Fire | |
| **Height:** 1'08" | **Weight:** 17.4 lbs. |
| **Region:** Johto | |

**CYNDAQUIL**

**QUILAVA**

**TYPHLOSION**

# DELCATTY
## PRIM POKÉMON

Female Trainers love Delcatty for its beautiful fur—and because it never makes a nest.

| | |
|---|---|
| Pronounced: dell-CAT-tee | |
| Possible Moves: Fake Out, Attract, Sing, DoubleSlap | |
| Type: Normal | |
| Height: 3'07" | Weight: 71.9 lbs. |
| Region: Hoenn | |

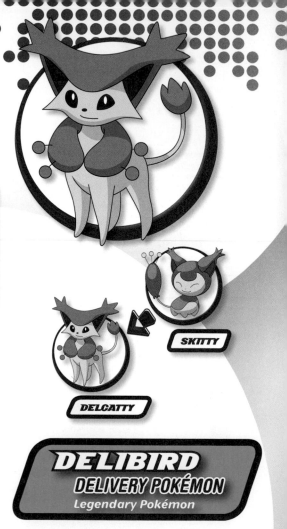

SKITTY

DELCATTY

DOES NOT EVOLVE

# DELIBIRD
## DELIVERY POKÉMON
### Legendary Pokémon

If people get lost in the mountains, Delibird will share its food, which it carries in its tail.

| | |
|---|---|
| Pronounced: DELL-ee-bird | |
| Possible Moves: Present | |
| Type: Ice-Flying | |
| Height: 2'11" | Weight: 35.3 lbs. |
| Region: Johto | |

# DEOXYS
## DNA POKÉMON
*Legendary Pokémon*

**Deoxys was formed when a meteor that carried an alien virus underwent a DNA mutation after falling to Earth.**

**Pronounced:**
dee-OCKS-iss

**Possible Moves:** Leer, Wrap, Night Shade, Teleport, Knock Off, Pursuit, Psychic, Snatch, Psycho Shift, Zen Headbutt, Cosmic Power, Recover, Psycho Boost, Hyper Beam

**Type:** Psychic

**Height:** 5'07"

**Weight:** 134.0 lbs.

**Region:** Hoenn

## DOES NOT EVOLVE

# DEWGONG
## SEA LION POKÉMON

Because its coat is pure white, it can blend in snow to protect it from being seen by predators.

**Pronounced:**
DOO-gong

**Possible Moves:** Headbutt, Growl, Signal Beam, Icy Wind, Encore, Ice Shard, Rest, Aqua Ring, Aurora Beam, Aqua Jet, Brine, Sheer Cold, Take Down, Dive, Aqua Tail, Ice Beam, Safeguard

**Type:** Water-Ice

**Height:** 5'07"

**Weight:** 264.6 lbs.

**Region:** Kanto

SEEL

DEWGONG

# DIALGA
## TIME POKÉMON
### Legendary Pokémon

This Legendary Pokémon has the ability to distort time—as a matter of fact, it is said that time began when Dialga was born.

**Pronounced:**
dee-AL-guh

**Possible Moves:**
DragonBreath, Scary Face, Metal Claw, AncientPower, Dragon Claw, Roar of Time, Heal Block, Earth Power, Slash, Flash Cannon, Aura Sphere

**Type:** Steel-Dragon

**Height:** 17'09"

**Weight:** 1505.8 lbs.

**Region:** Sinnoh

*DOES NOT EVOLVE*

# DIGLETT
## MOLE POKÉMON

*Diglett avoids the sunlight and lives underground. It is so used to the dark recesses that bright sunlight repels it.*

**DIGLETT**

**DUGTRIO**

| |
|---|
| **Pronounced:** DIG-lit |
| **Possible Moves:** Scratch, Sand-Attack, Growl, Astonish, Magnitude, Mud-Slap, Dig, Sucker Punch, Earth Power, Mud Bomb, Slash, Earthquake, Fissure |
| **Type:** Ground |
| **Height:** 0'08"     **Weight:** 1.8 lbs. |
| **Region:** Kanto |

DOES NOT EVOLVE

# DITTO
## TRANSFORM POKÉMON

*Ditto has the ability to transform into anything it sees by reconstituting and restructuring its cellular composition.*

| |
|---|
| **Pronounced:** DID-oh |
| **Possible Moves:** Transform |
| **Type:** Normal |
| **Height:** 1'00"     **Weight:** 8.8 lbs. |
| **Region:** Kanto |

# DODRIO
## TRIPLE BIRD POKÉMON

Dodrio evolves from Doduo after one of Doduo's heads splits in two. This Pokémon is able to run at almost forty mph!

| | |
|---|---|
| **Pronounced:** doe-DREE-oh | |
| **Possible Moves:** Pluck, Peck, Growl, Quick Attack, Rage, Fury Attack, Pursuit, Uproar, Acupressure, Tri Power, Agility, Drill Peck, Endeavor | |
| **Type:** Normal-Flying | |
| **Height:** 5'11"    **Weight:** 187.8 lbs. | |
| **Region:** Kanto | |

DODUO

DODRIO

DODUO

DODRIO

# DODUO
## TWIN BIRD POKÉMON

Using a telepathic power, the two heads of Doduo can communicate emotions to each other.

| | |
|---|---|
| **Pronounced:** DOE-doo-oh | |
| **Possible Moves:** Peck, Growl, Quick Attack, Rage, Fury Attack, Pursuit, Uproar, Acupressure, Double Hit, Agility, Drill Peck, Endeavor | |
| **Type:** Normal-Flying | |
| **Height:** 4'07"    **Weight:** 86.4 lbs. | |
| **Region:** Kanto | |

DODRIO

# DONPHAN
## ARMOR BIRD POKÉMON

Donphan attacks by curling up
into a ball and rolling into foes,
and can bowl over a house in
one hit.

Pronounced: DON-fan

Possible Moves: Fire Fang, Thunder Fang,
Horn Attack, Growl, Defense Curl, Flail,
Rapid Spin, Knock Off, Rollout, Magnitude,
Slam, Fury Attack, Assurance, Scary Face,
Earthquake, Giga Impact

Type: Ground

Height: 3'07"    Weight: 264.6 lbs.

Region: Johto

PHANPY

DONPHAN

# DRAGONAIR
## DRAGON POKÉMON

Living in seas and lakes, Dragonair
can change weather patterns if its
body is affected by auras.

Pronounced: drag-uh-NAIR

Possible Moves: Wrap, Leer, Thunder
Wave, Twister, Dragon Rage, Slam, Agility,
Aqua Tail, Dragon Rush, Safeguard,
Dragon Dance, Outrage, Hyper Beam

Type: Dragon

Height: 31'01"    Weight: 36.4 lbs.

Region: Kanto

DRATINI

DRAGONAIR

DRAGONITE

# DRAGONITE
## DRAGON POKÉMON

Dragonite is known for helping guide shipwrecked crews to land.

**Pronounced:**
drag-uh-NITε

**Possible Moves:** Fire Punch, ThunderPunch, Roost, Wrap, Leer, Thunder Wave, Twister, Dragon Rage, Slam, Agility, Aqua Tail, Dragon Rush, Safeguard, Dragon Dance, Wing Attack, Outrage, Hyper Beam

**Type:** Dragon-Flying

**Height:** 7'03"

**Weight:** 463.0 lbs.

**Region:** Kanto

DRATINI

DRAGONAIR

DRAGONITE

# DRAPION
## OGRE SCORP POKÉMON

Drapion is able to turn its head 180 degrees to see its surroundings. It will use its mighty clawed arms to hold onto its prey.

Pronounced:
DRAP-pee-on

Possible Moves: Thunder Fang, Ice Fang, Fire Fang, Bite, Poison Sting, Leer, Pin Missile, Acupressure, Knock Off, Scary Face, Toxic Spikes, Poison Fang, Crunch, Cross Poison

Type: Poison-Dark

Height: 4'03"

Weight: 135.6 lbs.

Region: Sinnoh

SKORUPI

DRAPION

# DRATINI
## DRAGON POKÉMON

Dratini is so rare that people are only aware of its existence because of the shed skin it leaves behind.

Pronounced: druh-TEE-nee

Possible Moves: Wrap, Leer, Thunder Wave, Twister, Dragon Rage, Slam, Agility, Aqua Tail, Dragon Rush, Safeguard, Dragon Dance, Outrage, Hyper Beam

Type: Dragon

Height: 5'11"    Weight: 7.3 lbs.

Region: Kanto

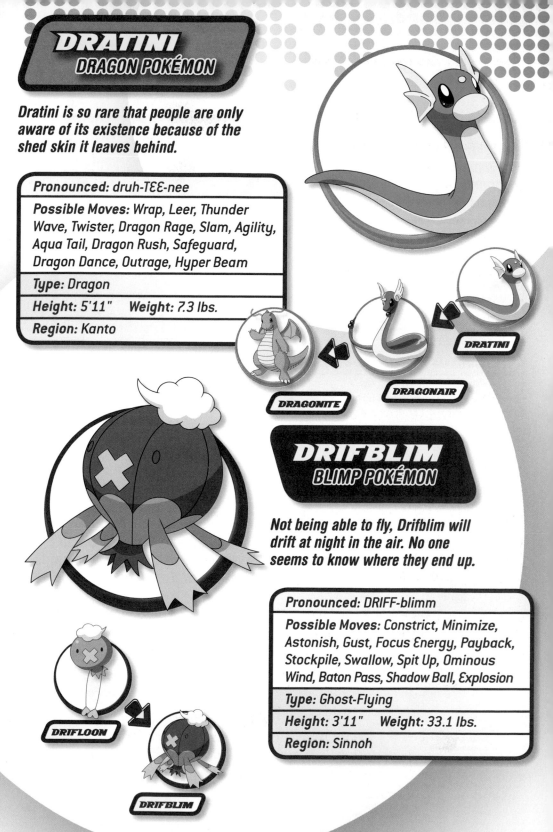

DRATINI

DRAGONAIR

DRAGONITE

# DRIFBLIM
## BLIMP POKÉMON

*Not being able to fly, Drifblim will drift at night in the air. No one seems to know where they end up.*

Pronounced: DRIFF-blimm

Possible Moves: Constrict, Minimize, Astonish, Gust, Focus Energy, Payback, Stockpile, Swallow, Spit Up, Ominous Wind, Baton Pass, Shadow Ball, Explosion

Type: Ghost-Flying

Height: 3'11"    Weight: 33.1 lbs.

Region: Sinnoh

DRIFLOON

DRIFBLIM

# DRIFLOON
## BALLOON POKÉMON

Difloon tries to pull on the hands of children to steal them away, but this lightweight Pokémon doesn't have the power to lift them from the ground. Usually, it's Drifloon that ends up getting pulled around!

| | |
|---|---|
| **Pronounced:** DRIFF-loon | |
| **Possible Moves:** Constrict, Minimize, Astonish, Gust, Focus Energy, Payback, Stockpile, Swallow, Spit Up, Ominous Wind, Baton Pass, Shadow Ball, Explosion | |
| **Type:** Ghost-Flying | |
| **Height:** 1'04"  **Weight:** 2.6 lbs. | |
| **Region:** Sinnoh | |

DRIFLOON

DRIFBLIM

# DROWZEE
## HYPNOSIS POKÉMON

Drowzee loves fun dreams! It can tell where the dreams are by using its nose to sniff around.

| | |
|---|---|
| **Pronounced:** DROW-zee | |
| **Possible Moves:** Pound, Hypnosis, Disable, Confusion, Headbutt, Poison Gas, Meditate, Psybeam, Psych Up, Swagger, Psychic, Nasty Plot, Zen Headbutt, Future Sight | |
| **Type:** Psychic | |
| **Height:** 3'03"  **Weight:** 71.4 lbs. | |
| **Region:** Kanto | |

DROWZEE

HYPNO

# DUGTRIO
## MOLE POKÉMON

Using its three heads, Dugtrio is able to dig through soil at depths that sometimes reach sixty miles.

**Pronounced:** dug-TREE-oh

**Possible Moves:** Night Slash, Tri Power, Scratch, Sand-Attack, Growl, Astonish, Magnitude, Mud-Slap, Dig, Sucker Punch, Sand Tomb, Earth Power, Mud Bomb, Slash, Earthquake, Fissure

**Type:** Ground

**Height:** 2'04"    **Weight:** 73.4 lbs.

**Region:** Kanto

DIGLETT

DUGTRIO

# DUNSPARCE
## LAND SNAKE POKÉMON

Dunsparce is able to fly for short bursts, but uses its tail to make maze-like nests in the ground.

DOES NOT EVOLVE

**Pronounced:** DUN-sparce

**Possible Moves:** Rage, Defense Curl, Yawn, Glare, Rollout, Spite, Pursuit, Screech, Roost, Take Down, AncientPower, Dig, Endeavor, Flail

**Type:** Normal

**Height:** 4'11"    **Weight:** 30.9 lbs.

**Region:** Johto

# DUSCLOPS
## BECKON POKÉMON

Dusclops' body is hollow, but don't look too closely—it is believed that if you gaze into its body you can be lost in the void.

**Pronounced:** DUS-klops

**Possible Moves:** Fire Punch, Ice Punch, ThunderPunch, Gravity, Bind, Leer, Night Shade, Disable, Disable, Foresight, Astonish, Confuse Ray, Shadow Sneak, Pursuit, Curse, Will-O-Wisp, Shadow Punch, Mean Look, Payback, Future Sight

**Type:** Ghost

**Height:** 5'03"    **Weight:** 67.5 lbs.

**Region:** Hoenn

DUSKULL

DUSCLOPS

DUSKNOIR

# DUSKNOIR
## GRIPPER POKÉMON

Dusknoir receives messages from the antennae on its head. Sometimes, it is commanded to take people to the spirit world.

**Pronounced:** DUSK-nwar

**Possible Moves:** Fire Punch, Ice Punch, ThunderPunch, Gravity, Bind, Leer, Night Shade, Disable, Foresight, Astonish, Confuse Ray, Shadow Sneak, Pursuit, Curse, Will-O-Wisp, Shadow Punch, Mean Look, Payback, Future Sight

**Type:** Ghost

**Height:** 7'03"    **Weight:** 235.0 lbs.

**Region:** Sinnoh

DUSKULL

DUSCLOPS

DUSKNOIR

# DUSKULL
## REQUIEM POKÉMON

Duskull is a nocturnal Pokémon that spends most of its time seeking out enemies and prey.

| |
|---|
| **Pronounced:** DUS-kull |
| **Possible Moves:** Leer, Night Shade, Disable, Foresight, Astonish, Confuse Ray, Shadow Sneak, Pursuit, Curse, Will-O-Wisp, Mean Look, Payback, Future Sight |
| **Type:** Ghost |
| **Height:** 2'07"     **Weight:** 33.1 lbs. |
| **Region:** Hoenn |

DUSKULL

DUSCLOPS

DUSKNOIR

# DUSTOX
## POISONMOTH POKÉMON

This nocturnal Pokémon loves to scavenge leafy goodness from tree-lined boulevards, and is attracted to streetlights.

| |
|---|
| **Pronounced:** DUS-tocks |
| **Possible Moves:** Confusion, Gust, Protect, Moonlight, Psybeam, Whirlwind, Light Screen, Silver Wind, Toxic, Bug Buzz |
| **Type:** Bug-Poison |
| **Height:** 3'11"     **Weight:** 69.7 lbs. |
| **Region:** Hoenn and Sinnoh |

WURMPLE

CASCOON

DUSTOX

# EEVEE
## EVOLUTION POKÉMON

**Pronounced:**
EE-vee

**Possible Moves:** Tackle, Tail Whip, Helping Hand, Sand-Attack, Growl, Quick Attack, Bite, Baton Pass, Take Down, Last Resort, Trump Card

**Type:** Normal

**Height:** 1'00

**Weight:** 14.3 lbs.

**Region:** Kanto

Eevee is able to take on many different evolutionary forms and adapts to almost any environment.

VAPOREON

JOLTEON

GLACEON

FLAREON

EEVEE

ESPEON

LEAFEON

UMBREON

# EKANS
## SNAKE POKÉMON

Ekans is sneaky, gaining the advantage in battle by taking its enemies by surprise.

| | |
|---|---|
| **Pronounced:** ECK-ehns | |
| **Possible Moves:** Wrap, Leer, Poison Sting, Bite, Glare, Screech, Acid, Stockpile, Swallow, Spit Up, Mud Bomb, Gastro Acid, Haze, Gunk Shot | |
| **Type:** Poison | |
| **Height:** 6'07" | **Weight:** 15.2 lbs. |
| **Region:** Kanto | |

ARBOK

EKANS

# ELECTABUZZ
## ELECTRIC POKÉMON

Because it eats so much electricity from power plants, Electabuzz can cause blackouts.

| | |
|---|---|
| **Pronounced:** ee-LECK-tuh-buzz | |
| **Possible Moves:** Quick Attack, Leer, ThunderShock, Low Kick, Swift, Shock Wave, Light Screen, ThunderPunch, Discharge, Thunderbolt, Screech, Thunder | |
| **Type:** Electric | |
| **Height:** 3'07" | **Weight:** 66.1 lbs. |
| **Region:** Kanto | |

ELEKID

ELECTABUZZ

ELECTIVIRE

# ELECTIVIRE
## THUNDERBOLT POKÉMON

*This Pokémon uses the tips of its two tails to let loose with twenty thousand volts of power.*

**Pronounced:**
e-LECT-uh-vire

**Possible Moves:** Fire Punch, Quick Attack, Leer, ThunderShock, Low Kick, Swift, Shock Wave, Light Screen, ThunderPunch, Discharge, Thunderbolt, Screech, Thunder, Giga Impact

**Type:** Electric

**Height:** 5'11"

**Weight:** 305.6 lbs.

**Region:** Sinnoh

ELEKID

ELECTABUZZ

ELECTIVIRE

# ELECTRIKE
## LIGHTNING POKÉMON

This Pokémon gains reaction speed by stimulating its muscles via electricity stored in its fur.

**Pronounced:**
ee-LEK-trike

**Possible Moves:** Tackle, Thunder Wave, Leer, Howl, Quick Attack, Spark, Odor Sleuth, Bite, Thunder Fang, Roar, Discharge, Charge, Thunder

**Type:** Electric

**Height:** 2'00"

**Weight:** 33.5 lbs.

**Region:** Hoenn

ELECTRIKE

MANECTRIC

# ELECTRODE
## BALL POKÉMON

When Electrode is bloated to bursting with electricity, it can drift on the wind.

| | |
|---|---|
| **Pronounced:** ee-LECK-trode | |
| **Possible Moves:** Charge, Tackle, Sonic Boom, Spark, Rollout, Screech, Light Screen, Charge Beam, Selfdestruct, Swift, Magnet Rise, Gyro Ball, Explosion, Mirror Coat | |
| **Type:** Electric | |
| **Height:** 3'11" | **Weight:** 146.8 lbs. |
| **Region:** Kanto | |

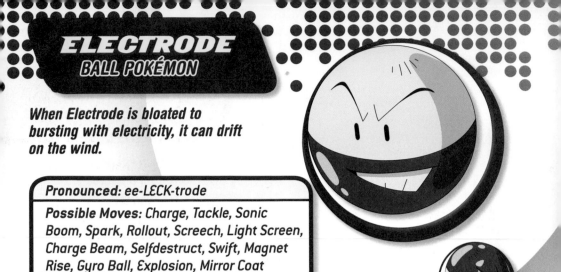

VOLTORB

ELECTRODE

# ELEKID
## ELECTRIC POKÉMON

Elekid spins its arms to create electricity, but it cannot store the electricity it creates.

| | |
|---|---|
| **Pronounced:** el-EH-kid | |
| **Possible Moves:** Quick Attack, Leer, ThunderShock, Low Kick, Swift, Shock Wave, Light Screen, ThunderPunch, Discharge, Thunderbolt, Screech, Thunder | |
| **Type:** Electric | |
| **Height:** 2'00" | **Weight:** 51.8 lbs. |
| **Region:** Johto | |

ELEKID

ELECTABUZZ

ELECTIVIRE

# EMPOLEON
## EMPEROR POKÉMON

You can tell the leader in a pack of Empoleon by the size of its horns—the leader has the biggest ones, of course! It can swim at speeds that rival jet boats.

**Pronounced:**
im-PO-lee-on

**Possible Moves:** Tackle, Growl, Bubble, Swords Dance, Peck, Metal Claw, Swagger, BubbleBeam, Fury Attack, Brine, Aqua Jet, Whirlpool, Mist, Drill Peck, Hydro Pump

**Type:** Water-Steel

**Height:** 5'07"

**Weight:** 186.3 lbs.

**Region:** Sinnoh

PIPLUP

PRINPLUP

EMPOLEON

# ENTEI
## VOLCANO POKÉMON
### Legendary Pokémon

*Somewhere around the globe, a volcano will erupt when Entei roars.*

**Pronounced:**
EN-tay

**Possible Moves:** Bite, Leer, Ember, Roar, Fire Spin, Stomp, Flamethrower, Swagger, Fire Fang, Lava Plume, Extrasensory, Fire Blast, Calm Mind

**Type:** Fire

**Height:** 6'11"

**Weight:** 436.5 lbs.

**Region:** Johto

## DOES NOT EVOLVE

# ESPEON
## SUN POKÉMON

When Espeon uses psychic power, the orb on its head will glow. Its fur has the look and feel of velvet.

| | |
|---|---|
| **Pronounced:** ESS-pee-on | |
| **Possible Moves:** Tackle, Tail Whip, Helping Hand, Sand-Attack, Confusion, Quick Attack, Swift, Psybeam, Future Sight, Last Resort, Psych Up, Psychic, Morning Sun | |
| **Type:** Psychic | |
| **Height:** 2'11" | **Weight:** 58.4 lbs. |
| **Region:** Johto | |

EEVEE

ESPEON

# EXEGGCUTE
## EGG POKÉMON

Exeggcute communicates with the other five in its group by using telepathy, and can gather quickly if separated.

| | |
|---|---|
| **Pronounced:** EGGS-egg-cute | |
| **Possible Moves:** Barrage, Uproar, Hypnosis, Reflect, Leech Seed, Bullet Seed, Stun Spore, PoisonPowder, Sleep Powder, Confusion, Worry Seed, Natural Gift, SolarBeam, Psychic | |
| **Type:** Grass-Psychic | |
| **Height:** 1'04" | **Weight:** 5.5 lbs. |
| **Region:** Kanto | |

EXEGGCUTE

EXEGGUTOR

# EXEGGUTOR
## COCONUT POKÉMON

Known also as The Walking Jungle, it can spawn an Exeggcute if its head becomes too big and falls off.

| | |
|---|---|
| **Pronounced:** EGGS-egg-you-tor | |
| **Possible Moves:** Seed Bomb, Barrage, Hypnosis, Confusion, Stomp, Egg Bomb, Wood Hammer, Leaf Storm | |
| **Type:** Grass-Psychic | |
| **Height:** 6'07"   **Weight:** 264.6 lbs. | |
| **Region:** Kanto | |

EXEGGCUTE

EXEGGUTOR

# EXPLOUD
## LOUD NOISE POKÉMON

This noisy Pokémon emits sound from every port on its body, and when it howls it can be heard from miles away.

| | |
|---|---|
| **Pronounced:** ecks-PLOWD | |
| **Possible Moves:** Ice Fang, Fire Fang, Thunder Fang, Pound, Uproar, Astonish, Howl, Bite, Supersonic, Stomp, Screech, Crunch, Roar, Rest, Sleep Talk, Hyper Voice, Hyper Beam | |
| **Type:** Normal | |
| **Height:** 4'11"   **Weight:** 185.2 lbs. | |
| **Region:** Hoenn | |

WHISMUR

LOUDRED

EXPLOUD

# FARFETCH'D
## WILD DUCK POKÉMON

Farfetch'd can't live without the stalk it constantly holds, which is why it will defend it to the death.

| | |
|---|---|
| **Pronounced:** FAR-fetcht | |
| **Possible Moves:** Poison Jab, Peck, Sand-Attack, Leer, Fury Cutter, Fury Attack, Knock Off, Aerial Ace, Slash, Air Cutter, Swords Dance, Agility, Night Slash, Air Slash, False Swipe | |
| **Type:** Normal-Flying | |
| **Height:** 2'07" | **Weight:** 33.1 lbs. |
| **Region:** Kanto | |

*DOES NOT EVOLVE*

# FEAROW
## BEAK POKÉMON

Its powerful wings let it fly all day, but its needle-sharp beak is what you have to watch out for.

| | |
|---|---|
| **Pronounced:** FEER-oh | |
| **Possible Moves:** Pluck, Peck, Growl, Leer, Fury Attack, Pursuit, Aerial Ace, Mirror Move, Agility, Assurance, Roost, Drill Peck | |
| **Type:** Normal-Flying | |
| **Height:** 3'11" | **Weight:** 83.8 lbs. |
| **Region:** Kanto | |

SPEAROW

FEAROW

# FEEBAS
## FISH POKÉMON

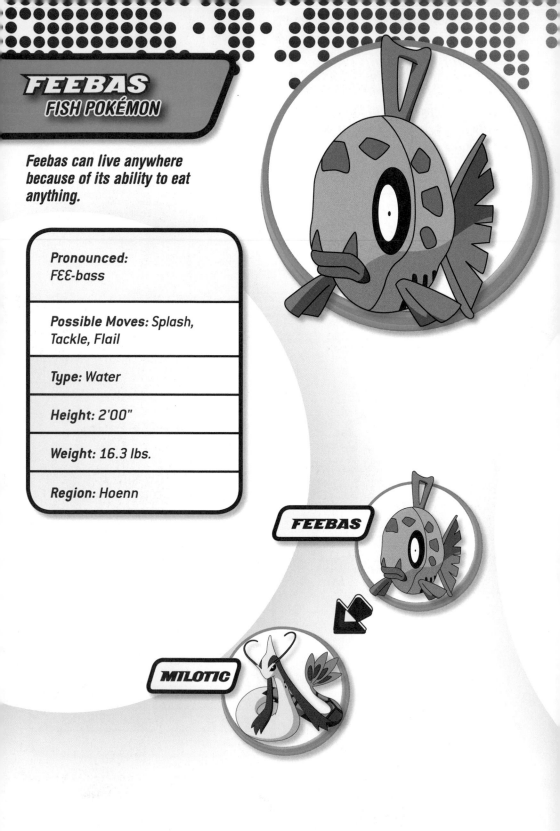

Feebas can live anywhere because of its ability to eat anything.

**Pronounced:**
FEE-bass

**Possible Moves:** Splash, Tackle, Flail

**Type:** Water

**Height:** 2'00"

**Weight:** 16.3 lbs.

**Region:** Hoenn

FEEBAS

MILOTIC

# FERALIGATR
## BIG JAW POKÉMON

It's easy to be fooled by Feraligatr's slow gait, but be warned that it becomes lightning fast when battling.

**Pronounced:** fer-AL-ee-gay-tur

**Possible Moves:** Scratch, Leer, Water Gun, Rage, Bite, Scary Face, Ice Fang, Thrash, Agility, Crunch, Slash, Screech, Aqua Tail, SuperPower, Hydro Pump

**Type:** Water

**Height:** 7'07"    **Weight:** 195.8 lbs.

**Region:** Johto and Sinnoh

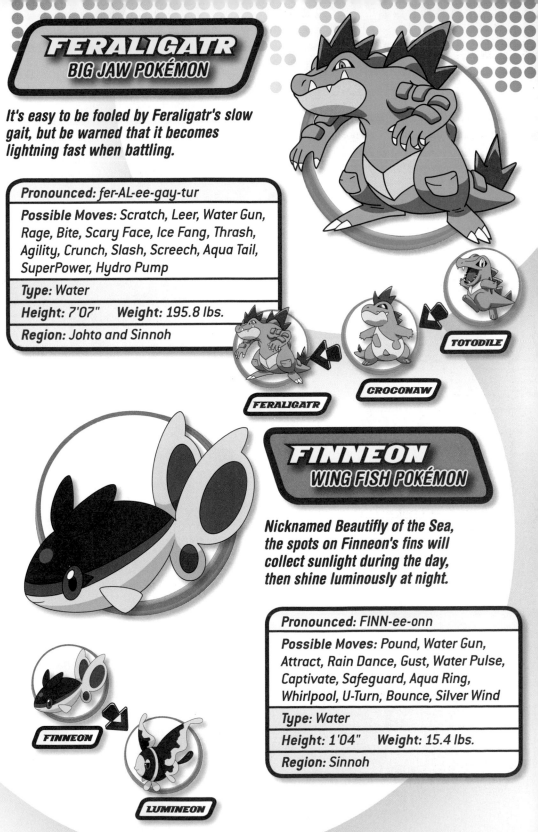

TOTODILE

CROCONAW

FERALIGATR

# FINNEON
## WING FISH POKÉMON

Nicknamed Beautifly of the Sea, the spots on Finneon's fins will collect sunlight during the day, then shine luminously at night.

**Pronounced:** FINN-ee-onn

**Possible Moves:** Pound, Water Gun, Attract, Rain Dance, Gust, Water Pulse, Captivate, Safeguard, Aqua Ring, Whirlpool, U-Turn, Bounce, Silver Wind

**Type:** Water

**Height:** 1'04"    **Weight:** 15.4 lbs.

**Region:** Sinnoh

FINNEON

LUMINEON

# FLAAFFY
## WOOL POKÉMON

Flaafy's tail will light up when its coat is completely charged with electricity—and it will shoot electrified hairs from its body!

**Pronounced:** FLAF-fee

**Possible Moves:** Tackle, Growl, ThunderShock, Thunder Wave, Cotton Spore, Charge, Discharge, Signal Beam, Light Screen, Power Gem, Thunder

**Type:** Electric

**Height:** 2'07"    **Weight:** 29.3 lbs.

**Region:** Johto

MAREEP

FLAAFFY

AMPHAROS

# FLAREON
## FLAME POKÉMON

Before a battle, it can raise its body temperature to 1650 degrees Fahrenheit via a flame sac in its body.

**Pronounced:** FLARE-ae-on

**Possible Moves:** Tackle, Tail Whip, Helping Hand, Sand-Attack, Ember, Quick Attack, Bite, Fire Spin, Fire Fang, Last Resort, Smog, Scary Face, Fire Blast

**Type:** Fire

**Height:** 2'11"    **Weight:** 55.1 lbs.

**Region:** Kanto

EEVEE

FLAREON

# FLOATZEL
## SEA WEASEL POKÉMON

Using its floatation tube around its neck, Floatzel can stay afloat easily, and has even assisted in the rescue of drowning people.

Pronounced: FLOAT-zull

**Possible Moves:** Ice Fang, SonicBoom, Growl, Water Sport, Quick Attack, Water Gun, Pursuit, Swift, Aqua Jet, Crunch, Agility, Whirlpool, Razor Wind

Type: Water

Height: 3'07"    Weight: 73.9 lbs.

Region: Sinnoh

BUIZEL

FLOATZEL

# FLYGON
## MYSTIC POKÉMON

Known as The Desert Spirit, Flygon can create sandstorms with the rapid flapping of its wings.

Pronounced: FLY-gon

**Possible Moves:** SonicBoom, Sand-Attack, Faint Attack, Sand Tomb, Supersonic, DragonBreath, Screech, Dragon Claw, Sandstorm, Hyper Beam

Type: Ground-Dragon

Height: 6'07"    Weight: 180.8 lbs.

Region: Hoenn

TRAPINCH

VIBRAVA

FLYGON

# FORRETRESS
## BAGWORM POKÉMON

The only internal workings of this Pokémon that are visible past its steel shell are its eyes.

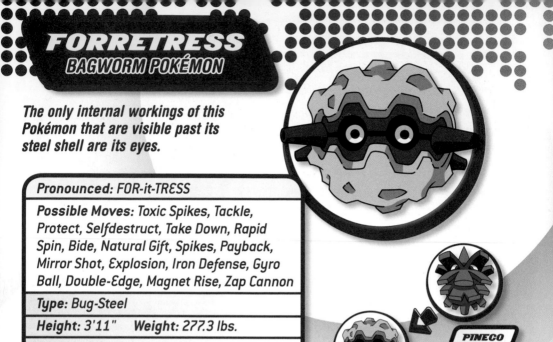

**Pronounced:** FOR-it-TRESS

**Possible Moves:** Toxic Spikes, Tackle, Protect, Selfdestruct, Take Down, Rapid Spin, Bide, Natural Gift, Spikes, Payback, Mirror Shot, Explosion, Iron Defense, Gyro Ball, Double-Edge, Magnet Rise, Zap Cannon

**Type:** Bug-Steel

**Height:** 3'11"    **Weight:** 277.3 lbs.

**Region:** Johto

PINECO

FORRETRESS

SNORUNT

GLALIE

FROSLASS

# FROSLASS
## SNOW COUNTRY POKÉMON

Froslass may seem to have a solid body, but it is actually hollow. It likes to freeze its foes.

**Pronounced:** FROS-lass

**Possible Moves:** Powder Snow, Leer, Double Team, Astonish, Icy Wind, Confuse Ray, Ominous Wind, Wake-Up Slap, Captive, Ice Shard, Hail, Blizzard, Destiny Bond

**Type:** Ice-Ghost

**Height:** 4'03"    **Weight:** 58.6 lbs.

**Region:** Sinnoh

# FURRET
## LONG BODY POKÉMON

Furret uses speed to outmaneuver foes, and lulls its offspring to sleep by curling up around them.

| | |
|---|---|
| **Pronounced:** FUR-ret | |
| **Possible Moves:** Scratch, Foresight, Defense Curl, Quick Attack, Fury Swipes, Helping Hand, Follow Me, Slam, Rest, Sucker Punch, Amnesia, Baton Pass, Me First, Hyper Voice | |
| **Type:** Normal | |
| **Height:** 5'11" | **Weight:** 71.6 lbs. |
| **Region:** Johto | |

**SENTRET**

**FURRET**

# GABITE
## CAVE POKÉMON

Rumor has it that using the scales from Gabite can heal even the most incurable diseases.

| | |
|---|---|
| **Pronounced:** guh-BITE | |
| **Possible Moves:** Tackle, Sand-Attack, Dragon Rage, Sandstorm, Take Down, Sand Tomb, Slash, Dragon Claw, Dig, Dragon Rush | |
| **Type:** Dragon-Ground | |
| **Height:** 4'07" | **Weight:** 123.5 lbs. |
| **Region:** Sinnoh | |

**GIBLE**

**GABITE**

**GARCHOMP**

# GALLADE
## BLADE POKÉMON

Gallade fights by extending the swords on its elbows, but it is very courteous when not battling.

**Pronounced:**
GAL-ade

**Possible Moves:** Leaf Blade, Night Slash, Leer, Confusion, Double Team, Teleport, Fury Cutter, Slash, Swords Dance, Psycho Cut, Helping Hand, Feint, False Swipe, Protect, Close Combat

**Type:** Psychic-Fighting

**Height:** 5'03"

**Weight:** 114.6 lbs.

**Region:** Sinnoh

RALTS

KIRLIA

GALLADE

# GARCHOMP
## MACH POKÉMON

By spreading its wings and folding up its body, Garchomp can fly as fast as a jet plane.

| | |
|---|---|
| **Pronounced:** gar-CHOMP | |
| **Possible Moves:** Fire Fang, Tackle, Sand-Attack, Dragon Rage, Sandstorm, Take Down, Sand Tomb, Slash, Dragon Claw, Dig, Crunch, Dragon Rush | |
| **Type:** Dragon-Ground | |
| **Height:** 6'03" | **Weight:** 209.4 lbs. |
| **Region:** Sinnoh | |

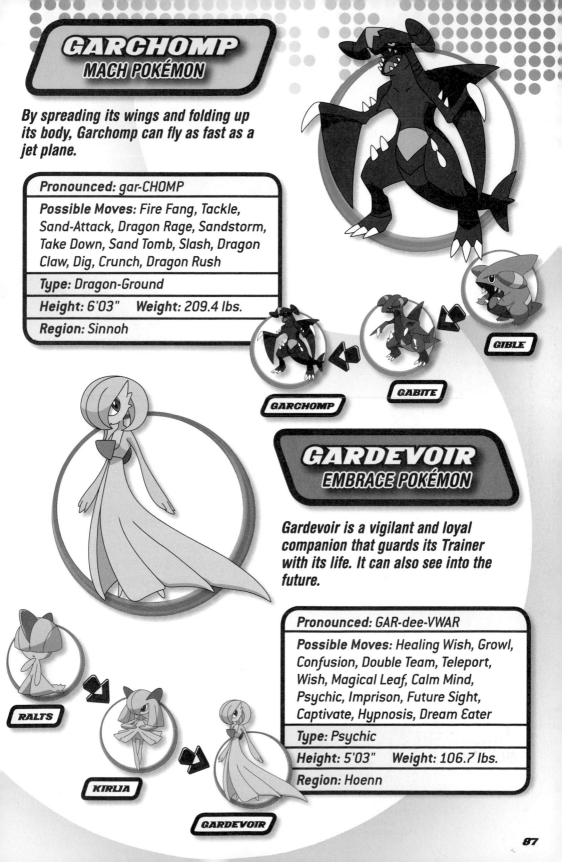

GARCHOMP

GABITE

GIBLE

# GARDEVOIR
## EMBRACE POKÉMON

Gardevoir is a vigilant and loyal companion that guards its Trainer with its life. It can also see into the future.

| | |
|---|---|
| **Pronounced:** GAR-dee-VWAR | |
| **Possible Moves:** Healing Wish, Growl, Confusion, Double Team, Teleport, Wish, Magical Leaf, Calm Mind, Psychic, Imprison, Future Sight, Captivate, Hypnosis, Dream Eater | |
| **Type:** Psychic | |
| **Height:** 5'03" | **Weight:** 106.7 lbs. |
| **Region:** Hoenn | |

RALTS

KIRLIA

GARDEVOIR

# GASTLY
## GAS POKÉMON

Although Gastly is ninety-five percent gas and can beat even a large foe, the gas is easily blown away by strong winds.

| | |
|---|---|
| **Pronounced:** GAST-lee | |
| **Possible Moves:** Hypnosis, Lick, Spite, Mean Look, Curse, Night Shade, Confuse Ray, Sucker Punch, Payback, Shadow Ball, Dream Eater, Dark Pulse, Destiny Bond, Nightmare | |
| **Type:** Ghost-Poison | |
| **Height:** 4'03"    **Weight:** 0.2 lbs. | |
| **Region:** Johto, Kanto, and Sinnoh | |

GENGAR

HAUNTER

GASTLY

# GASTRODON (EAST)
## SEA SLUG POKÉMON

Gastrodon has different colors depending upon where it's found. If you find your Gastrodon in the East Sea, it will be blue and green. If you found it in the west, it will be pink and brown.

| | |
|---|---|
| **Pronounced:** GAS-tro-donn | |
| **Possible Moves:** Mud-Slap, Mud Sport, Harden, Water Pulse, Mud Bomb, Hidden Power, Rain Dance, Body Slam, Muddy Water, Recover | |
| **Type:** Water-Ground | |
| **Height:** 2'11"    **Weight:** 65.9 lbs. | |
| **Region:** Sinnoh | |

SHELLOS (EAST SEA)

GASTRODON (EAST SEA)

# GASTRODON (WEST)
## SEA SLUG POKÉMON

Living in shallow waters, Gastrodon can grow back any body part that is ripped off.

Pronounced: GAS-tro-donn

**Possible Moves:** Mud-Slap, Mud Sport, Harden, Water Pulse, Mud Bomb, Hidden Power, Rain Dance, Body Slam, Muddy Water, Recover

**Type:** Water-Ground

**Height:** 2'11"    **Weight:** 65.9 lbs.

**Region:** Sinnoh

SHELLOS
(WEST SEA)

GASTRODON
(WEST SEA)

# GENGAR
## SHADOW POKÉMON

You can tell where Gengar is hiding when the temperature drops by ten degrees Fahrenheit.

Pronounced: GANG-are

**Possible Moves:** Hypnosis, Lick, Spite, Mean Look, Curse, Night Shade, Confuse Ray, Sucker Punch, Shadow Punch, Payback, Shadow Ball, Dream Eater, Dark Pulse, Destiny Bond, Nightmare

**Type:** Ghost-Poison

**Height:** 4'11"    **Weight:** 89.3 lbs.

**Region:** Kanto, Johto, and Sinnoh

GASTLY

HAUNTER

GENGAR

# GEODUDE
## ROCK POKÉMON

Geodude watches climbers while masquerading as half-buried rocks. They slam into each other to show how strong they are.

**Pronounced:** JEE-oh-dood

**Possible Moves:** Tackle, Defense Curl, Mud Sport, Rock Polish, Rock Throw, Magnitude, Selfdestruct, Rollout, Rock Blast, Earthquake, Explosion, Double-Edge, Stone Edge

**Type:** Rock-Ground

**Height:** 1'04"  **Weight:** 44.1 lbs.

**Region:** All Regions

GOLEM

GRAVELER

GEODUDE

# GIBLE
## LAND SHARK POKÉMON

Nesting in small holes in caves, Gible will pounce on any prey that comes too close.

**Pronounced:** GIBB-bull

**Possible Moves:** Tackle, Sand-Attack, Dragon Rage, Sandstorm, Take Down, Sand Tomb, Slash, Dragon Claw, Dig, Dragon Rush

**Type:** Dragon-Ground

**Height:** 2'04"  **Weight:** 45.2 lbs.

**Region:** Sinnoh

GIBLE

GABITE

GARCHOMP

# GIRAFARIG
## LONG NECK POKÉMON

Girafarig's tail can keep away foes that are trying to attack from behind. The tail has a small brain, and never sleeps.

**Pronounced:** jir-RAF-uh-rig

**Possible Moves:** Power Swap, Guard Swap, Astonish, Tackle, Growl, Confusion, Odor Sleuth, Stomp, Agility, Psybeam, Baton Pass, Assurance, Double Hit, Psychic, Zen Headbutt, Crunch

**Type:** Normal-Psychic

**Height:** 4'11"   **Weight:** 91.5 lbs.

**Region:** Johto, Hoenn, and Sinnoh

DOES NOT EVOLVE

# GIRATINA
## RENEGADE POKÉMON
### Legendary Pokémon

Giratina is rumored to live in a world on the reverse side of ours, and can be found near ancient cemeteries.

DOES NOT EVOLVE

**Pronounced:** gear-uh-TEE-na

**Possible Moves:** DragonBreath, Scary Face, Ominous Wind, AncientPower, Dragon Claw, Shadow Force, Heal Block, Earth Power, Slash, Shadow Claw, Aura Sphere

**Type:** Ghost-Dragon

**Height:** 14'09"   **Weight:** 1653.5 lbs.

**Region:** Sinnoh

# GLACEON
## FRESH SNOW POKÉMON

As a defensive measure, Glaceon freezes its fur so that its hairs are razor sharp needles.

| | |
|---|---|
| **Pronounced:** GLACE-ee-on | |
| **Possible Moves:** Tackle, Tail Whip, Helping Hand, Sand-Attack, Icy Wind, Quick Attack, Bite, Ice Shard, Ice Fang, Last Resort, Mirror Coat, Hail, Blizzard | |
| **Type:** Ice | |
| **Height:** 2'07"    **Weight:** 57.1 lbs. | |
| **Region:** Sinnoh | |

EEVEE

GLACEON

# GLALIE
## FACE POKÉMON

Glalie can freeze the moisture in the air to encase its body in an armor of ice.

| | |
|---|---|
| **Pronounced:** GLAY-lee | |
| **Possible Moves:** Powder Snow, Leer, Double Team, Bite, Icy Wind, Headbutt, Protect, Ice Fang, Crunch, Ice Beam, Hail, Blizzard, Sheer Cold | |
| **Type:** Ice | |
| **Height:** 4'11"    **Weight:** 565.5 lbs. | |
| **Region:** Hoenn | |

SNORUNT

GLALIE

FROSLASS

# GLAMEOW
## CATTY POKÉMON

*Even though Glameow can be very fickle, don't underestimate it. It can put a foe into hypnosis with its stare.*

| | |
|---|---|
| **Pronounced:** GLAM-meow | |
| **Possible Moves:** Fake Out, Scratch, Growl, Hypnosis, Faint Attack, Fury Swipes, Charm, Assist, Captivate, Slash, Sucker Punch, Attract | |
| **Type:** Normal | |
| **Height:** 1'08"   **Weight:** 8.6 lbs. | |
| **Region:** Sinnoh | |

GLAMEOW

PURUGLY

# GLIGAR
## FLYSCORPION POKÉMON

*Gligar will aim for a foe's face while descending from the sky.*

| | |
|---|---|
| **Pronounced:** GLY-gar | |
| **Possible Moves:** Poison Sting, Sand-Attack, Harden, Knock Off, Quick Attack, Fury Cutter, Faint Attack, Screech, Slash, Swords Dance, U-Turn, X-Scissor, Guillotine | |
| **Type:** Ground-Flying | |
| **Height:** 3'07"   **Weight:** 142.9 lbs. | |
| **Region:** Johto | |

GLIGAR

GLISCOR

# GLISCOR
## FANGSCORPION POKÉMON

While hanging upside down from branches, Gliscor patiently waits for prey upon which it will swoop at a moment's notice.

**Pronounced:**
GLY-skor

**Possible Moves:** Thunder Fang, Ice Fang, Fire Fang, Poison Jab, Sand-Attack, Harden, Knock Off, Quick Attack, Fury Cutter, Faint Attack, Screech, Night Slash, Swords Dance, U-Turn, X-Scissor, Guillotine

**Type:** Ground-Flying

**Height:** 6'07"

**Weight:** 93.7 lbs.

**Region:** Sinnoh

GLIGAR

GLISCOR

# GLOOM
## WEED POKÉMON

The drool of honey from Gloom's mouth is so noxious, you can smell it from a mile away.

**Pronounced:** GLOOM

**Possible Moves:** Absorb, Sweet Scent, Acid, PoisonPowder, Stun Spore, Sleep Powder, Mega Drain, Lucky Chant, Natural Gift, Moonlight, Giga Drain, Petal Dance

**Type:** Grass-Poison

**Height:** 2'07"   **Weight:** 19.0 lbs.

**Region:** Kanto

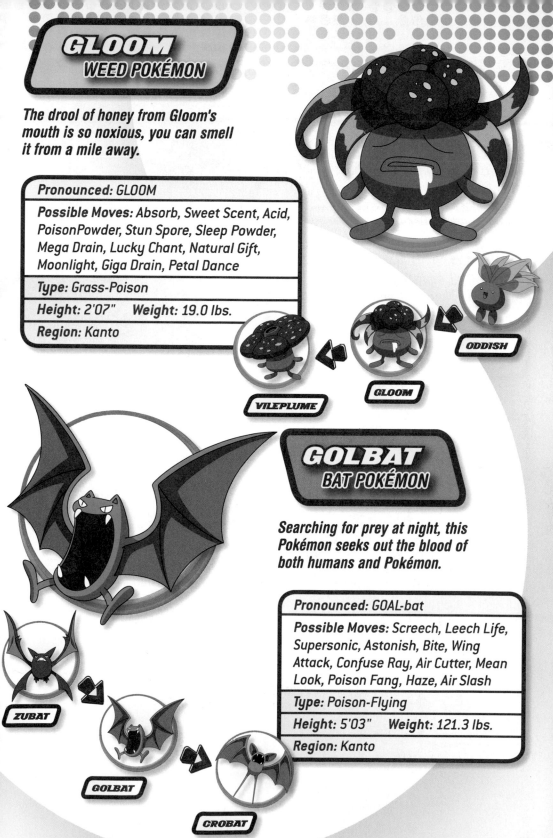

ODDISH

GLOOM

VILEPLUME

# GOLBAT
## BAT POKÉMON

Searching for prey at night, this Pokémon seeks out the blood of both humans and Pokémon.

**Pronounced:** GOAL-bat

**Possible Moves:** Screech, Leech Life, Supersonic, Astonish, Bite, Wing Attack, Confuse Ray, Air Cutter, Mean Look, Poison Fang, Haze, Air Slash

**Type:** Poison-Flying

**Height:** 5'03"   **Weight:** 121.3 lbs.

**Region:** Kanto

ZUBAT

GOLBAT

CROBAT

# GOLDEEN
## GOLDFISH POKÉMON

*Although imbued with the majesty of a queen, and a champion swimmer that reaches five knots, Goldeen relies on the sharp horn on its head for protection.*

| |
|---|
| **Pronounced:** GOAL-deen |
| **Possible Moves:** Peck, Tail Whip, Water Sport, Supersonic, Horn Attack, Water Pulse, Flail, Aqua Ring, Fury Attack, Waterfall, Horn Drill, Agility, Megahorn |
| **Type:** Water |
| **Height:** 2'00"    **Weight:** 33.1 lbs. |
| **Region:** All Regions |

GOLDEEN

SEAKING

# GOLDUCK
## DUCK POKÉMON

*Known as the fastest swimmer, this Pokémon lives in lakes. It is faster than any recorded human swimmer.*

| |
|---|
| **Pronounced:** GOAL-duck |
| **Possible Moves:** Water Sport, Scratch, Tail Whip, Water Gun, Disable, Confusion, Water Pulse, Fury Swipes, Screech, Psych Up, Zen Headbutt, Amnesia, Hydro Pump |
| **Type:** Water |
| **Height:** 5'07"    **Weight:** 168.9 lbs. |
| **Region:** All Regions |

PSYDUCK

GOLDUCK

# GOLEM
## ROCK POKÉMON

Not even big blasts of dynamite can harm this rocky-looking Pokémon, which sheds its skin only once a year.

**Pronounced:** GOAL-um

**Possible Moves:** Tackle, Defense Curl, Mud Sport, Rock Polish, Rock Throw, Magnitude, Selfdestruct, Rollout, Rock Blast, Eartquake, Explosion, Double-Edge, Stone Edge

**Type:** Rock-Ground

**Height:** 4'07"    **Weight:** 661.4 lbs.

**Region:** All Regions

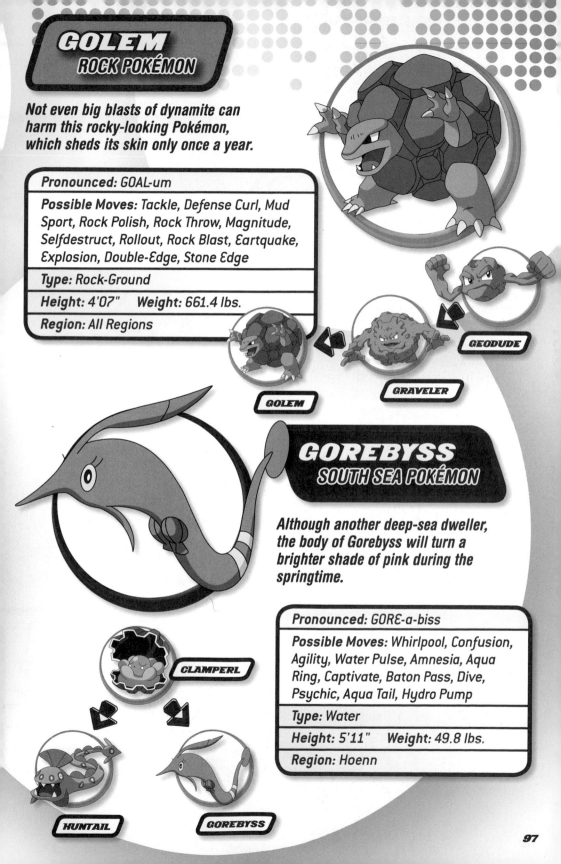

GEODUDE

GRAVELER

GOLEM

# GOREBYSS
## SOUTH SEA POKÉMON

Although another deep-sea dweller, the body of Gorebyss will turn a brighter shade of pink during the springtime.

CLAMPERL

**Pronounced:** GORE-a-biss

**Possible Moves:** Whirlpool, Confusion, Agility, Water Pulse, Amnesia, Aqua Ring, Captivate, Baton Pass, Dive, Psychic, Aqua Tail, Hydro Pump

**Type:** Water

**Height:** 5'11"    **Weight:** 49.8 lbs.

**Region:** Hoenn

HUNTAIL

GOREBYSS

# GRANBULL
## FAIRY POKÉMON

*Using its huge fangs to strike at its foe, Granbull may seem imposing, but most are known to be timid.*

| | |
|---|---|
| **Pronounced:** *GRAN-bull* | |
| **Possible Moves:** *Ice Fang, Fire Fang, Thunder Fang, Tackle, Scary Face, Tail Whip, Charm, Bite, Lick, Headbutt, Roar, Rage, Take Down, Payback, Crunch* | |
| **Type:** *Normal* | |
| **Height:** *4'07"* | **Weight:** *107.4 lbs.* |
| **Region:** *Johto* | |

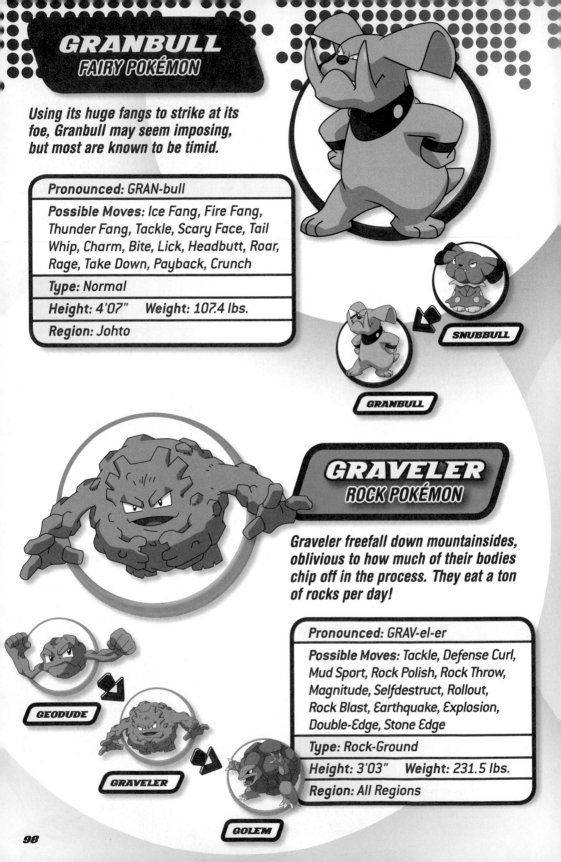

SNUBBULL

GRANBULL

# GRAVELER
## ROCK POKÉMON

*Graveler freefall down mountainsides, oblivious to how much of their bodies chip off in the process. They eat a ton of rocks per day!*

GEODUDE

GRAVELER

GOLEM

| | |
|---|---|
| **Pronounced:** *GRAV-el-er* | |
| **Possible Moves:** *Tackle, Defense Curl, Mud Sport, Rock Polish, Rock Throw, Magnitude, Selfdestruct, Rollout, Rock Blast, Earthquake, Explosion, Double-Edge, Stone Edge* | |
| **Type:** *Rock-Ground* | |
| **Height:** *3'03"* | **Weight:** *231.5 lbs.* |
| **Region:** *All Regions* | |

# GRIMER
## SLUDGE POKÉMON

When dirt and filth from a stream were exposed to the moon's X-rays, Grimer was born.

**Pronounced:** GRIMƐ-er

**Possible Moves:** Poison Gas, Pound, Harden, Mud-Slap, Disable, Minimize, Sludge, Mud Bomb, Fling, Screech, Sludge Bomb, Acid Armor, Gunk Shot, Memento

**Type:** Poison

**Height:** 2'11"    **Weight:** 66.1 lbs.

**Region:** Kanto

MUK

GRIMER

# GROTLE
## GROVE POKÉMON

Grotle likes to lay out in the sun. The berries that grow on its back can be eaten by other Pokémon.

**Pronounced:** GRAHT-ull

**Possible Moves:** Tackle, Withdraw, Absorb, Razor Leaf, Curse, Bite, Mega Drain, Leech Seed, Synthsis, Crunch, Giga Drain, Leaf Storm

**Type:** Grass

**Height:** 3'07"    **Weight:** 213.8 lbs.

**Region:** Sinnoh

TURTWIG

GROTLE

TORTERRA

# GROUDON
## CONTINENT POKÉMON
*Legendary Pokémon*

*After fighting Kyogre ages ago, Groudon now rests underground in a magma cavern.*

**Pronounced:**
GRAU-don

**Possible Moves:** Mud Shot, Scary Face, AncientPower, Slash, Bulk Up, Earthquake, Fire Blast, Rest, Fissure, SolarBeam, Earth Power, Eruption

**Type:** Ground

**Height:** 11'06"

**Weight:** 2094.4 lbs.

**Region:** Hoenn

**DOES NOT EVOLVE**

# GROVYLE
## WOOD GECKO POKÉMON

Grovyle attacks its foe by jumping from branch to branch in the deep jungles.

| | |
|---|---|
| **Pronounced:** GROW-vile | |
| **Possible Moves:** Pound, Leer, Absorb, Quick Attack, Fury Cutter, Pursuit, Screech, Leaf Blade, Agility, Slam, Detect, False Swipe, Leaf Storm | |
| **Type:** Grass | |
| **Height:** 2'11" | **Weight:** 47.6 lbs. |
| **Region:** Hoenn | |

TREECKO

SCEPTILE

GROVYLE

# GROWLITHE
## PUPPY POKÉMON

An extremely obedient Pokémon, Growlithe will wait patiently for orders by its Trainer.

| | |
|---|---|
| **Pronounced:** GROWL-ith | |
| **Possible Moves:** Bite, Roar, Ember, Leer, Odor Sleuth, Helping Hand, Flame Wheel, Reversal, Fire Fang, Take Down, Flamethrower, Agility, Crunch, Heat Wave, Flare Blitz | |
| **Type:** Fire | |
| **Height:** 2'04" | **Weight:** 41.9 lbs. |
| **Region:** Kanto | |

GROWLITHE

ARCANINE

# GRUMPIG
## MANIPULATE POKÉMON

Grumpig gains control over its enemies by dancing and using the black pearls around its neck to increase its psychic power.

| | |
|---|---|
| **Pronounced:** GRUM-pig | |
| **Possible Moves:** Splash, Psywave, Odor Sleuth, Psybeam, Psych Up, Confuse Ray, Magic Coat, Zen Headbutt, Rest, Snore, Payback, Psychic, Power Gem, Bounce | |
| **Type:** Psychic | |
| **Height:** 2'11" | **Weight:** 157.6 lbs. |
| **Region:** Hoenn | |

SPOINK

GRUMPIG

# GULPIN
## STOMACH POKÉMON

Gulpin's toxic digestive juices immediately dissolve anything it swallows, and since all of its body is stomach, that's saying a lot.

| | |
|---|---|
| **Pronounced:** GULL-pin | |
| **Possible Moves:** Pound, Yawn, Poison Gas, Sludge, Amnesia, Encore, Toxic, Stockpile, Spit Up, Swallow, Sludge Bomb, Gastro Acid, Wring Out, Gunk Shot | |
| **Type:** Poison | |
| **Height:** 1'04" | **Weight:** 22.7 lbs. |
| **Region:** Hoenn | |

GULPIN

SWALOT

# GYARADOS
## ATROCIOUS POKÉMON

This Pokémon will not stop its rage until every field and village around it has been razed.

| | |
|---|---|
| **Pronounced:** GAR-i-dose | |
| **Possible Moves:** Thrash, Bite, Dragon Rage, Leer, Twister, Ice Fang, Aqua Tail, Rain Dance, Hydro Pump, Dragon Dance, Hyper Beam | |
| **Type:** Water-Flying | |
| **Height:** 21'04"  **Weight:** 518.1 lbs. | |
| **Region:** All Regions | |

GYARADOS

MAGIKARP

# HAPPINY
## PLAYHOUSE POKÉMON

Happiny loves to carry around white rocks in its pouch to imitate Chansey.

| | |
|---|---|
| **Pronounced:** hap-PEE-nee | |
| **Possible Moves:** Pound, Charm, Copycat, Refresh, Sweet Kiss | |
| **Type:** Normal | |
| **Height:** 2'00"  **Weight:** 53.8 lbs. | |
| **Region:** Sinnoh | |

HAPPINY

CHANSEY

BLISSEY

# HARIYAMA
## ARM THRUST POKÉMON

Hariyama uses its arms—powerful enough to knock over trucks—to thrust, and it loves going up against bigger Pokémon.

**Pronounced:** HAR-ee-YAH-mah

**Possible Moves:** Brine, Tackle, Focus Energy, Sand-Attack, Arm Thrust, Vital Throw, Fake Out, Whirlwind, Knock Off, SmellingSalt, Belly Drum, Force Palm, Seismic Toss, Wake-Up Slap, Endure, Close Combat, Reversal

**Type:** Fighting

**Height:** 7'07"    **Weight:** 559.5 lbs.

**Region:** Hoenn

MAKUHITA

HARIYAMA

# HAUNTER
## GAS POKÉMON

It can hide in the darkness and inside walls to watch its prey and foes, then licks them to steal their life force.

**Pronounced:** HAWN-ter

**Possible Moves:** Hypnosis, Lick, Spite, Mean Look, Curse, Night Shade, Confuse Ray, Sucker Punch, Shadow Punch, Payback, Shadow Ball, Dream Eater, Dark Pulse, Destiny Bond, Nightmare

**Type:** Ghost-Poison

**Height:** 5'03"    **Weight:** 0.2 lbs.

**Region:** Kanto, Johto, and Sinnoh

GASTLY

HAUNTER

GENGAR

# HEATRAN
## LAVA DOME POKÉMON
### *Legendary Pokémon*

Its cross-shaped feet are perfect for helping it dig into the hard rock walls and cavern ceilings of the volcanic caves where it dwells.

**Pronounced:** HEE-tran

**Possible Moves:** AncientPower, Leer, Fire Fang, Metal Sound, Crunch, Scary Face, Lava Plume, Fire Spin, Iron Head, Earth Power, Heat Wave, Stone Edge, Magma Storm

**Type:** Fire-Steel

**Height:** 5'07"    **Weight:** 948.0 lbs.

**Region:** Sinnoh

DOES NOT EVOLVE

# HERACROSS
## SINGLE HORN POKÉMON

Because of the tremendous strength in its legs and claws, Heracross is strong enough to pick up and throw its foes great distances.

**Pronounced:** HAIR-uh-cross

**Possible Moves:** Night Slash, Tackle, Leer, Horn Attack, Endure, Fury Attack, Aerial Ace, Brick Break, Counter, Take Down, Close Combat, Reversal, Feint, Megahorn

**Type:** Bug-Fighting

**Height:** 4'11"    **Weight:** 119.0 lbs.

**Region:** Johto and Sinnoh

DOES NOT EVOLVE

# HIPPOPOTAS
## HIPPO POKÉMON

Hippopotas does not like getting wet. It prefers to cover itself with a layer of sand for protection.

**Pronounced:** HIP-po-puh-TOSS

**Possible Moves:** Tackle, Sand-Attack, Bite, Yawn, Take Down, Sand Tomb, Crunch, Earthquake, Double-Edge, Fissure

**Type:** Ground

**Height:** 2'07"    **Weight:** 109.1 lbs.

**Region:** Sinnoh

HIPPOPOTAS  HIPPOWDON

# HIPPOWDON
## HEAVYWEIGHT POKÉMON

Hippowdon can create powerful twisters by shooting out sand that it has stored in its body, and can crush cars in its powerful jaws.

**Pronounced:** hip-POW-donn

**Possible Moves:** Ice Fang, Fire Fang, Thunder Fang, Tackle, Sand-Attack, Bite, Yawn, Take Down, Sand Tomb, Crunch, Earthquake, Double-Edge, Fissure

**Type:** Ground

**Height:** 6'07"    **Weight:** 661.4 lbs.

**Region:** Sinnoh

HIPPOPOTAS  HIPPOWDON

# HITMONCHAN
## PUNCHING POKÉMON

Although it has to rest after three minutes of fighting, its punches can burst through concrete.

| | |
|---|---|
| **Pronounced:** HIT-moan-chan | |
| **Possible Moves:** Revenge, Comet Punch, Agility, Pursuit, Mach Punch, Bullet Punch, Feint, Vacuum Wave, ThunderPunch, Ice Punch, Fire Punch, Sky Uppercut, Mega Punch, Detect, Counter, Close Combat | |
| **Type:** Fighting | |
| **Height:** 4'07" | **Weight:** 110.7 lbs. |
| **Region:** Kanto | |

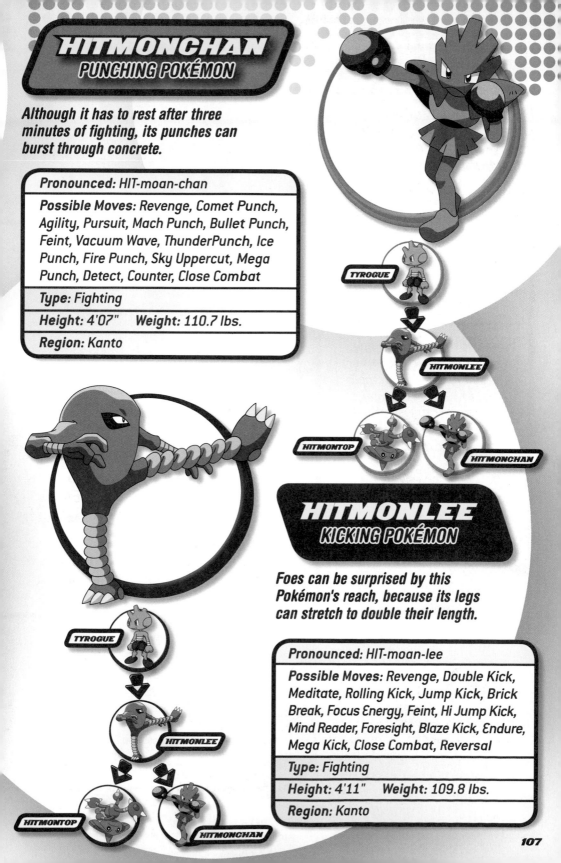

TYROGUE

HITMONLEE

HITMONTOP

HITMONCHAN

# HITMONLEE
## KICKING POKÉMON

Foes can be surprised by this Pokémon's reach, because its legs can stretch to double their length.

| | |
|---|---|
| **Pronounced:** HIT-moan-lee | |
| **Possible Moves:** Revenge, Double Kick, Meditate, Rolling Kick, Jump Kick, Brick Break, Focus Energy, Feint, Hi Jump Kick, Mind Reader, Foresight, Blaze Kick, Endure, Mega Kick, Close Combat, Reversal | |
| **Type:** Fighting | |
| **Height:** 4'11" | **Weight:** 109.8 lbs. |
| **Region:** Kanto | |

TYROGUE

HITMONLEE

HITMONTOP

HITMONCHAN

# HITMONTOP
## HANDSTAND POKÉMON

When Hitmontop spins like a whirling top, the power of its attack increases tenfold.

**Pronounced:**
HIT-mon-TOP

**Possible Moves:** Revenge, Rolling Kick, Focus Energy, Pursuit, Quick Attack, Triple Kick, Rapid Spin, Counter, Feint, Agility, Gyro Ball, Detect, Close Combat, Endeavor

**Type:** Fighting

**Height:** 4'07"

**Weight:** 105.8 lbs.

**Region:** Johto

TYROGUE

HITMONLEE

HITMONTOP

HITMONCHAN

# HO-OH
## RAINBOW POKÉMON
### Legendary Pokémon

*If you see the multi-colored Ho-oh, it is said that you will have eternal happiness.*

**Pronounced:** HOE-OH

**Possible Moves:** Whirlwind, Safeguard, Gust, Recover, Fire Blast, Sunny Day, Swift, Natural Gift, AncientPower, Extrasensory, Punishment, Future Sight, Sacred Fire, Calm Mind, Sky Power

**Type:** Fire-Flying

**Height:** 12'06"

**Weight:** 438.7 lbs.

**Region:** Johto

## DOES NOT EVOLVE

# HONCHKROW
## BIG BOSS POKÉMON

Honchkrow is a nocturnal Pokémon, and will travel with Murkrow in groups.

**Pronounced:**
HONCH-krow

**Possible Moves:** Astonish, Pursuit, Haze, Wing Attack, Swagger, Nasty Plot, Night Slash, Dark Pulse

**Type:** Dark-Flying

**Height:** 2'11"

**Weight:** 60.2 lbs.

**Region:** Sinnoh

MURKROW

HONCHKROW

# HOOTHOOT
## OWL POKÉMON

Even thought it has two feet, Hoothoot will only stand on one foot at a time while fighting.

**Pronounced:** HOOT-HOOT

**Possible Moves:** Tackle, Growl, Foresight, Hypnosis, Peck, Reflect, Confusion, Take Down, Air Slash, Zen Headbutt, Extrasensory, Psycho Shift, Roost, Dream Eater

**Type:** Normal-Flying

**Height:** 2'04"    **Weight:** 46.7 lbs.

**Region:** Johto and Sinnoh

HOOTHOOT

NOCTOWL

# HOPPIP
## COTTONWEED POKÉMON

Hoppip are carried by blowing winds, and when they arrive at a destination, it is said that spring is on the way.

**Pronounced:** HOP-pip

**Possible Moves:** Splash, Synthesis, Tail Whip, Tackle, PoisonPowder, Stun Spore, Sleep Powder, Bullet Seed, Leech Seed, Mega Drain, Cotton Spore, U-Turn, Worry Seed, Giga Drain, Bounce, Memento

**Type:** Grass-Flying

**Height:** 1'04"    **Weight:** 1.1 lbs.

**Region:** Johto

HOPPIP

SKIPLOOM

JUMPLUFF

# HORSEA
## DRAGON POKÉMON

When it senses danger, Horsea will spit out thick ink and usually rests in the shade of coral reefs.

| | |
|---|---|
| **Pronounced:** HORSE-ee | |
| **Possible Moves:** Bubble, SmokeScreen, Leer, Water Gun, Focus Energy, BubbleBeam, Agility, Twister, Brine, Hydro Pump, Dragon Dance, Dragon Pulse | |
| **Type:** Water | |
| **Height:** 1'04"    **Weight:** 17.6 lbs. | |
| **Region:** Kanto | |

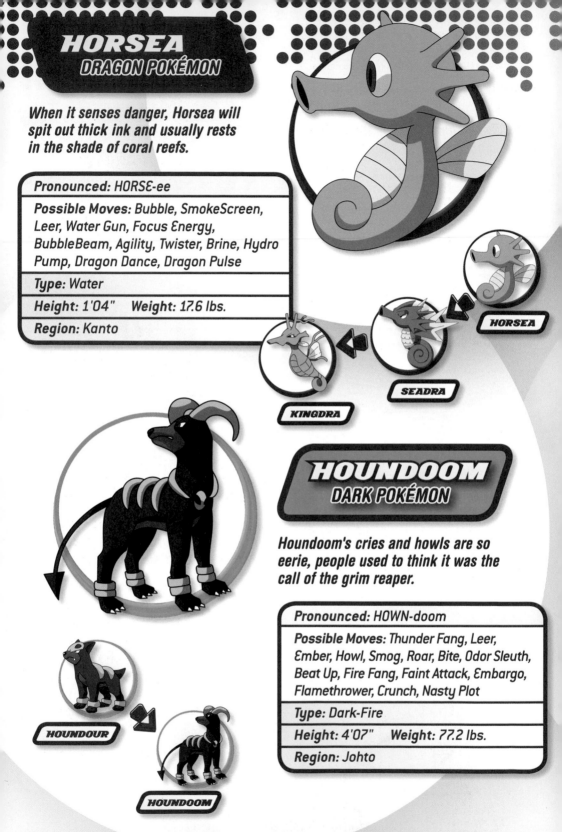

KINGDRA

SEADRA

HORSEA

# HOUNDOOM
## DARK POKÉMON

Houndoom's cries and howls are so eerie, people used to think it was the call of the grim reaper.

| | |
|---|---|
| **Pronounced:** HOWN-doom | |
| **Possible Moves:** Thunder Fang, Leer, Ember, Howl, Smog, Roar, Bite, Odor Sleuth, Beat Up, Fire Fang, Faint Attack, Embargo, Flamethrower, Crunch, Nasty Plot | |
| **Type:** Dark-Fire | |
| **Height:** 4'07"    **Weight:** 77.2 lbs. | |
| **Region:** Johto | |

HOUNDOUR

HOUNDOOM

# HOUNDOUR
## DARK POKÉMON

Houndour are pack Pokémon that can eloquently convey their feelings through the different pitch of their cries.

Pronounced: HOWN-dowr

Possible Moves: Leer, Ember, Howl, Smog, Roar, Bite, Odor Sleuth, Beat Up, Fire Fang, Faint Attack, Embargo, Flamethrower, Crunch, Nasty Plot

Type: Dark-Fire

Height: 2'00"    Weight: 23.8 lbs.

Region: Johto

HOUNDOUR

HOUNDOOM

# HUNTAIL
## DEEP SEA POKÉMON

Huntail will use its fish-shaped tail to lure in its prey from the deepest parts of the seas in which it lives.

Pronounced: HUN-tail

Possible Moves: Whirlpool, Bite, Screech, Water Pulse, Scary Face, Ice Fang, Brine, Baton Pass, Dive, Crunch, Aqua Tail, Hydro Pump

Type: Water

Height: 5'07"    Weight: 59.5 lbs.

Region: Hoenn

CLAMPERL

HUNTAIL

GOREBYSS

# HYPNO
## HYPNOSIS POKÉMON

Hypno is able to put anyone to sleep at anytime using its pendulum.

| | |
|---|---|
| **Pronounced:** HIP-no | |
| **Possible Moves:** Nightmare, Switcheroo, Pound, Hypnosis, Disable, Confusion, Headbutt, Poison Gas, Meditate, Psybeam, Psych Up, Swagger, Psychic, Nasty Plot, Zen Headbutt, Future Sight | |
| **Type:** Psychic | |
| **Height:** 5'03" | **Weight:** 166.7 lbs. |
| **Region:** Kanto | |

DROWZEE

HYPNO

# IGGLYBUFF
## BALLOON POKÉMON

It can be very hard to stop Igglybuff from bouncing once it starts.

| | |
|---|---|
| **Pronounced:** IG-lee-buff | |
| **Possible Moves:** Sing, Charm, Defense Curl, Pound, Sweet Kiss, Copycat | |
| **Type:** Normal | |
| **Height:** 1'00" | **Weight:** 2.2 lbs. |
| **Region:** Johto | |

IGGLYBUFF

JIGGLYPUFF

WIGGLYTUFF

## ILLUMISE
### FIREFLY POKÉMON

Illumise can guide Volbeat to draw signs with light in the night sky by using its sweet aroma.

| | |
|---|---|
| **Pronounced:** EE-loom-MEE-zay | |
| **Possible Moves:** Tackle, Sweet Scent, Charm, Moonlight, Quick Attack, Wish, Encore, Flatter, Helping Hand, Zen Headbutt, Bug Buzz, Covet | |
| **Type:** Bug | |
| **Height:** 2'00" | **Weight:** 39.0 lbs. |
| **Region:** Hoenn | |

*DOES NOT EVOLVE*

## INFERNAPE
### FLAME POKÉMON

Infernape's fire never goes out. This Pokémon also uses many different forms of martial arts to defeat its foe.

| | |
|---|---|
| **Pronounced:** in-FER-nape | |
| **Possible Moves:** Scratch, Leer, Ember, Taunt, Mash Punch, Fury Swipes, Flame Wheel, Feint, Punishment, Close Combat, Fire Spin, Calm Mind, Flame Blitz | |
| **Type:** Fire-Fighting | |
| **Height:** 3'11" | **Weight:** 121.3 lbs. |
| **Region:** Sinnoh | |

CHIMCHAR

MONFERNO

INFERNAPE

# IVYSAUR
## SEED POKÉMON

A sweet aroma is the signal that the bulb on its back will soon be in bloom.

**Pronounced:** ƐYƐ-vee-sore

**Possible Moves:** Tackle, Growl, Leech Seed, Vine Whip, PoisonPowder, Sleep Powder, Take Down, Razor Leaf, Sweet Scent, Growth, Double-Ɛdge, Worry Seed, Synthesis, SolarBeam

**Type:** Grass-Poison

**Height:** 3'03"    **Weight:** 28.7 lbs.

**Region:** Kanto

BULBASAUR

VENUSAUR

IVYSAUR

# JIGGLYPUFF
## BALLOON POKÉMON

By singing a lullaby, it can make everyone drowsy.

**Pronounced:** jig-lee-PUFF

**Possible Moves:** Sing, Defense Curl, Pound, Disable, Rollout, DoubleSlap, Rest, Body Slam, Gyro Ball, Wake-Up Slap, Mimic, Hyper Voice, Double-Ɛdge

**Type:** Normal

**Height:** 1'08"    **Weight:** 12.1 lbs.

**Region:** Kanto and Hoenn

IGGLYBUFF

JIGGLYPUFF

WIGGLYTUFF

## JIRACHI
### WISH POKÉMON
*Legendary Pokémon*

*Every thousand years, Jirachi has the ability to grant any wish for one week.*

**Pronounced:**
jer-AH-chi

**Possible Moves:** Wish, Confusion, Rest, Swift, Helping Hand, Psychic, Refresh, Rest, Zen Headbutt, Double-Edge, Gravity, Healing Wish, Future Sight, Cosmic Power, Last Resort, Doom Desire

**Type:** Steel-Psychic

**Height:** 1'00"

**Weight:** 2.4 lbs.

**Region:** Hoenn

## DOES NOT EVOLVE

# JOLTEON
## LIGHTNING POKÉMON

By raising the fur on its body, Jolteon looks like its covered in sharp needles, and can emit 10,000 volts of electricity.

| | |
|---|---|
| **Pronounced:** JOLT-ee-on | |
| **Possible Moves:** Tackle, Tail Whip, Helping Hand, Sand-Attack, ThunderShock, Quick Attack, Double Kick, Pin Missile, Thunder Fang, Last Resort, Thunder Wave, Agility, Thunder | |
| **Type:** Electric | |
| **Height:** 2'07" | **Weight:** 54.0 lbs. |
| **Region:** Kanto | |

EEVEE

JOLTEON

# JUMPLUFF
## COTTONWEED POKÉMON

Jumpluff scatters cotton spores while traveling by wind current around the world.

| | |
|---|---|
| **Pronounced:** JUM-pluff | |
| **Possible Moves:** Splash, Synthesis, Tail Whip, Tackle, PoisonPowder, Stun Spore, Sleep Powder, Bullet Seed, Leech Seed, Mega Drain, Cotton Spore, U-Turn, Worry Seed, Giga Drain, Bounce, Memento | |
| **Type:** Grass-Flying | |
| **Height:** 2'07" | **Weight:** 6.6 lbs. |
| **Region:** Johto | |

HOPPIP

SKIPLOOM

JUMPLUFF

# JYNX
## HUMAN SHAPE POKÉMON

Although it is impossible to understand Jynx, its cries do sound human.

| | |
|---|---|
| **Pronounced:** JINKS | |
| **Possible Moves:** Pound, Lick, Lovely Kiss, Powder Snow, DoubleSlap, Ice Punch, Mean Look, Fake Tears, Wake-Up Slap, Avalanche, Body Slam, Wring Out, Perish Song, Blizzard | |
| **Type:** Ice-Psychic | |
| **Height:** 4'07"    **Weight:** 89.5 lbs. | |
| **Region:** Kanto | |

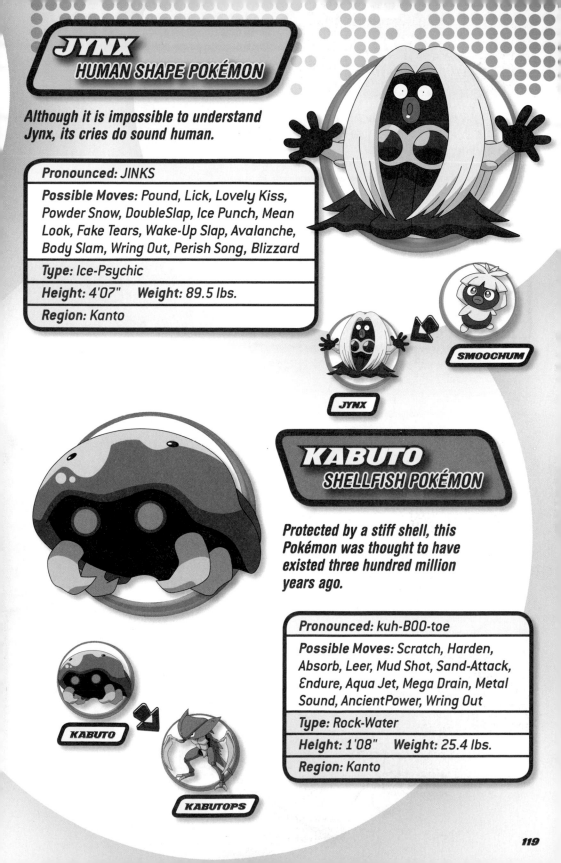

JYNX

SMOOCHUM

# KABUTO
## SHELLFISH POKÉMON

Protected by a stiff shell, this Pokémon was thought to have existed three hundred million years ago.

| | |
|---|---|
| **Pronounced:** kuh-BOO-toe | |
| **Possible Moves:** Scratch, Harden, Absorb, Leer, Mud Shot, Sand-Attack, Endure, Aqua Jet, Mega Drain, Metal Sound, AncientPower, Wring Out | |
| **Type:** Rock-Water | |
| **Height:** 1'08"    **Weight:** 25.4 lbs. | |
| **Region:** Kanto | |

KABUTO

KABUTOPS

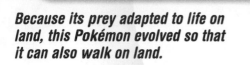

# KABUTOPS
## SHELLFISH POKÉMON

Because its prey adapted to life on land, this Pokémon evolved so that it can also walk on land.

**Pronounced:** kuh-BOO-tops

**Possible Moves:** Scratch, Harden, Absorb, Leer, Mud Shot, Sand-Attack, Endure, Aqua Jet, Mega Drain, Slash, Metal Sound, AncientPower, Wring Out, Night Slash

**Type:** Rock-Water

**Height:** 4'03"    **Weight:** 89.3 lbs.

**Region:** Kanto

KABUTO

KABUTOPS

# KADABRA
## PSYCHIC POKÉMON

If you see the shadow of this Pokémon, it is said to bring bad luck—and the alpha waves it emits can ruin precision devices.

**Pronounced:** kah-DA-bruh

**Possible Moves:** Teleport, Kinesis, Confusion, Disable, Miracle Eye, Psybeam, Reflect, Recover, Psycho Cut, Role Play, Psychic, Future Sight, Trick

**Type:** Psychic

**Height:** 4'03"    **Weight:** 124.6 lbs.

**Region:** All Regions

ABRA

KADABRA

ALAKAZAM

# KAKUNA
## COCOON POKÉMON

Kakuna is a master of camouflage, hiding in leaves and tree branches as it waits for evolution.

| | |
|---|---|
| Pronounced: ka-KOO-nuh | |
| Possible Moves: Harden | |
| Type: Bug-Poison | |
| Height: 2'00" | Weight: 22.0 lbs. |
| Region: Kanto | |

BEEDRILL

KAKUNA

WEEDLE

# KANGASKHAN
## PARENT POKÉMON

Kangaskhan will let its baby come out of its pouch only when it feels safe.

| |
|---|
| Pronounced: KANG-gus-con |
| Possible Moves: Comet Punch, Leer, Fake Out, Tail Whip, Bite, Mega Punch, Rage, Dizzy Punch, Crunch, Endure, Outrage, Double Hit, Sucker Punch, Reversal |
| Type: Normal |
| Height: 7'03"    Weight: 176.4 lbs. |
| Region: Kanto |

DOES NOT EVOLVE

121

# KECLEON
## COLOR SWAP POKÉMON

The pattern on Kecleon's belly will never change, but it does have the ability to change the color of the rest of its body.

| |
|---|
| **Pronounced:** KEH-clee-on |
| **Possible Moves:** Thief, Tail Whip, Astonish, Lick, Scratch, Bind, Faint Attack, Fury Swipes, Psybeam, Shadow Sneak, Slash, Screech, Substitute, Sucker Punch, Shadow Claw, AncientPower |
| **Type:** Normal |
| **Height:** 3'03"    **Weight:** 48.5 lbs. |
| **Region:** Hoenn |

DOES NOT EVOLVE

# KINGDRA
## DRAGON POKÉMON

Whenever Kingdra moves while on the seafloor, it creates giant whirlpools.

| |
|---|
| **Pronounced:** KING-dra |
| **Possible Moves:** Yawn, Bubble, SmokeScreen, Leer, Water Gun, Focus Energy, BubbleBeam, Agility, Twister, Brine, Hydro Pump, Dragon Dance, Dragon Pulse |
| **Type:** Water-Dragon |
| **Height:** 5'11"    **Weight:** 335.1 lbs. |
| **Region:** Johto |

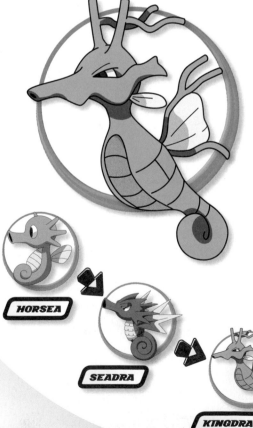

HORSEA

SEADRA

KINGDRA

# KINGLER
## PINCER POKÉMON

Kingler's big pincer is so heavy that it's hard for it to aim—but it is extremely strong.

| | |
|---|---|
| **Pronounced:** KING-ler | |
| **Possible Moves:** Mud Sport, Bubble, ViceGrip, Leer, Harden, BubbleBeam, Mud Shot, Metal Claw, Stomp, Protect, Guillotine, Slam, Brine, Crabhammer, Flail | |
| **Type:** Water | |
| **Height:** 4'03" | **Weight:** 132.3 lbs. |
| **Region:** Kanto | |

KRABBY

KINGLER

# KIRLIA
## EMOTION POKÉMON

When Kirlia is happy it will dance around, and is always "in tune" with its Trainer.

| | |
|---|---|
| **Pronounced:** KEERL-lee-ah | |
| **Possible Moves:** Growl, Confusion, Double Team, Teleport, Lucky Chant, Magical Leaf, Calm Mind, Psychic, Imprison, Future Sight, Charm, Hypnosis, Dream Eater | |
| **Type:** Psychic | |
| **Height:** 2'07" | **Weight:** 44.5 lbs. |
| **Region:** Hoenn | |

RALTS

KIRLIA

GARDEVOIR OR GALLADE

# KOFFING
## POISON GAS POKÉMON

The lighter-than-air gases that make up this Pokémon keep it aloft, but they smell terrible and can explode.

| | |
|---|---|
| **Pronounced:** CAWF-ing | |
| **Possible Moves:** Poison Gas, Tackle, Smog, SmokeScreen, Assurance, Selfdestruct, Sludge, Haze, Gyro Ball, Explosion, Sludge Bomb, Destiny Bond, Memento | |
| **Type:** Poison | |
| **Height:** 2'00" | **Weight:** 2.2 lbs. |
| **Region:** Kanto | |

KOFFING

WEEZING

# KRABBY
## RIVER CRAB POKÉMON

Krabby hides in holes it digs on beaches, and its pincers will grow back if they break.

| | |
|---|---|
| **Pronounced:** CRA-bee | |
| **Possible Moves:** Mud Sport, Bubble, ViceGrip, Leer, Harden, BubbleBeam, Mud Shot, Metal Claw, Stomp, Protect, Guillotine, Slam, Brine, Crabhammer, Flail | |
| **Type:** Water | |
| **Height:** 1'04" | **Weight:** 14.3 lbs. |
| **Region:** Kanto | |

KRABBY

KINGLER

# KRICKETOT
## CRICKET POKÉMON

Kricketot will communicate with each other by shaking their heads and knocking their antennae together.

| | |
|---|---|
| Pronounced: KRICK-eh-tot | |
| Possible Moves: Growl, Bite | |
| Type: Bug | |
| Height: 1'00" | Weight: 4.9 lbs. |
| Region: Sinnoh | |

KRICKETUNE

KRICKETOT

# KRICKETUNE
## CRICKET POKÉMON

Kricketune will show its emotion by creating melodies. When it cries, it will cross its arms in front of itself.

| | |
|---|---|
| Pronounced: KRICK-eh-toon | |
| Possible Moves: Growl, Bite, Fury Cutter, Leech Life, Sing, Focus Energy, X-Scissor, Screech, Bug Buzz, Perish, Song | |
| Type: Bug | |
| Height: 3'03" | Weight: 56.2 lbs. |
| Region: Sinnoh | |

KRICKETOT

KRICKETUNE

# KYOGRE
## SEA BASIN POKÉMON
### Legendary Pokémon

Kyogre has slumbered in a marine trench for ages, but when it awakes, it could cause downpours that would widen the oceans.

**Pronounced:**
kai-OH-gurr

**Possible Moves:** Water Pulse, Scary Face, AncientPower, Body Slam, Calm Mind, Ice Beam, Hydro Pump, Rest, Sheer Cold, Double-Edge, Aqua Tail, Water Spout

**Type:** Water

**Height:** 14'09"

**Weight:** 776.0 lbs.

**Region:** Hoenn

## DOES NOT EVOLVE

# LAIRON
## IRON ARMOR POKÉMON

To bulk up, Lairon digs up and eats iron ore. It also smashes its strong body against others to fight for territory.

**Pronounced:** LAIR-ron

**Possible Moves:** Tackle, Harden, Mud-Slap, Headbutt, Metal Claw, Iron Defense, Roar, Take Down, Iron Head, Protect, Metal Sound, Iron Tail, Double-Edge, Metal Burst

**Type:** Steel-Rock

**Height:** 2'11"     **Weight:** 264.6 lbs.

**Region:** Hoenn

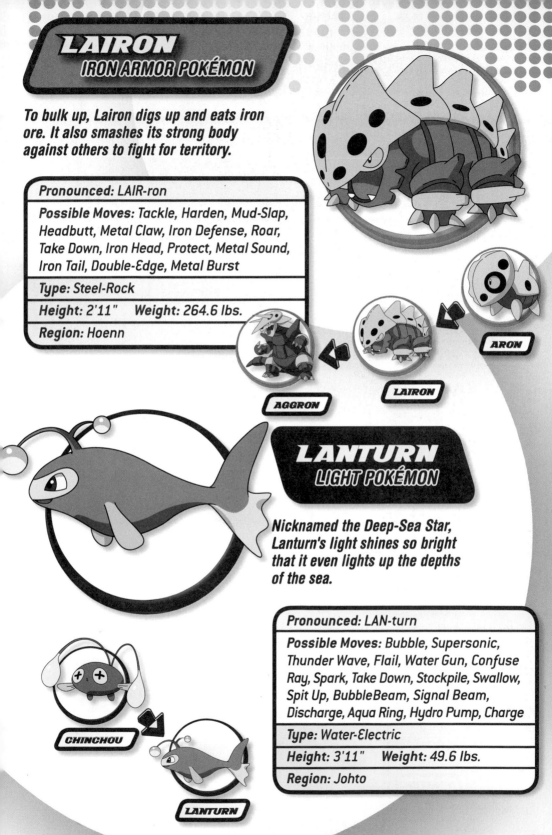

ARON

LAIRON

AGGRON

# LANTURN
## LIGHT POKÉMON

Nicknamed the Deep-Sea Star, Lanturn's light shines so bright that it even lights up the depths of the sea.

**Pronounced:** LAN-turn

**Possible Moves:** Bubble, Supersonic, Thunder Wave, Flail, Water Gun, Confuse Ray, Spark, Take Down, Stockpile, Swallow, Spit Up, BubbleBeam, Signal Beam, Discharge, Aqua Ring, Hydro Pump, Charge

**Type:** Water-Electric

**Height:** 3'11"     **Weight:** 49.6 lbs.

**Region:** Johto

CHINCHOU

LANTURN

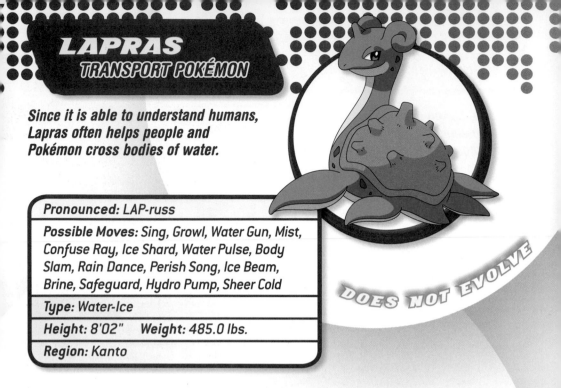

# LAPRAS
## TRANSPORT POKÉMON

*Since it is able to understand humans, Lapras often helps people and Pokémon cross bodies of water.*

**Pronounced:** LAP-russ

**Possible Moves:** Sing, Growl, Water Gun, Mist, Confuse Ray, Ice Shard, Water Pulse, Body Slam, Rain Dance, Perish Song, Ice Beam, Brine, Safeguard, Hydro Pump, Sheer Cold

**Type:** Water-Ice

**Height:** 8'02"  **Weight:** 485.0 lbs.

**Region:** Kanto

DOES NOT EVOLVE

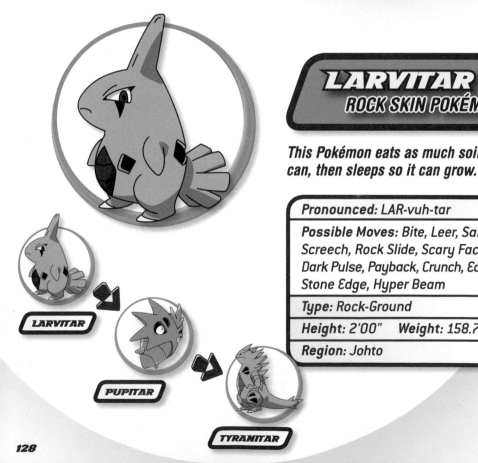

# LARVITAR
## ROCK SKIN POKÉMON

*This Pokémon eats as much soil as it can, then sleeps so it can grow.*

**Pronounced:** LAR-vuh-tar

**Possible Moves:** Bite, Leer, Sandstorm, Screech, Rock Slide, Scary Face, Thrash, Dark Pulse, Payback, Crunch, Earthquake, Stone Edge, Hyper Beam

**Type:** Rock-Ground

**Height:** 2'00"  **Weight:** 158.7 lbs.

**Region:** Johto

LARVITAR

PUPITAR

TYRANITAR

# LATIAS
## EON POKÉMON
### Legendary Pokémon

Latias can become invisible if it sits in the light the right way, thanks to the light-refracting down that covers its body.

**Pronounced:**
*LAT-ee-ahs*

**Possible Moves:** Psywave, Wish, Helping Hand, Safeguard, DragonBreath, Water Sport, Refresh, Mist Ball, Zen Headbutt, Recover, Psycho Shift, Charm, Healing Wish, Psychic, Dragon Pulse

**Type:** Dragon-Psychic

**Height:** 4'07"

**Weight:** 88.2 lbs.

**Region:** Hoenn

## DOES NOT EVOLVE

# LATIOS
## EON POKÉMON
### Legendary Pokémon

An extremely intelligent Pokémon, Latios can fly faster than a plane.

**Pronounced:**
LAT-ee-ose

**Possible Moves:** Psywave, Heal Block, Helping Hand, Safeguard, DragonBreath, Protect, Refresh, Luster Purge, Zen Headbutt, Recover, Psycho Shift, Dragon Dance, Memento, Psychic, Dragon Pulse

**Type:** Dragon-Psychic

**Height:** 6'07"

**Weight:** 132.3 lbs.

**Region:** Hoenn

## DOES NOT EVOLVE

# LEAFEON
## VERDANT POKÉMON

Leafon is always surrounded by clear air, and, like a plant, it uses photosynthesis.

Pronounced:
LEEF-ee-on

Possible Moves: Tackle, Tail Whip, Helping Hand, Sand-Attack, Razor Leaf, Quick Attack, Synthesis, Magical Leaf, Giga Drain, Last Resort, GrassWhistle, Sunny Day, Leaf Blade

Type: Grass

Height: 3'03"

Weight: 56.2 lbs.

Region: Sinnoh

EEVEE

LEAFEON

# LEDIAN
## FIVE START POKÉMON

Using starlight for energy, the patterns on Ledian's back will become bigger or smaller depending on the amount of energy it stores.

| | |
|---|---|
| **Pronounced:** LEH-dee-an | |
| **Possible Moves:** Tackle, Supersonic, Comet Punch, Light Screen, Reflect, Safeguard, Mach Punch, Baton Pass, Silver Wind, Agility, Swift, Double-Edge, Bug Buzz | |
| **Type:** Bug-Flying | |
| **Height:** 4'07" | **Weight:** 78.5 lbs. |
| **Region:** Johto | |

LEDYBA

LEDIAN

# LEDYBA
## FIVE START POKÉMON

Ledyba is so timid it will only move with a swarm of others, and communicates with other Ledyba by using its scent.

| | |
|---|---|
| **Pronounced:** LAY-dee-bah | |
| **Possible Moves:** Tackle, Supersonic, Comet Punch, Light Screen, Reflect, Safeguard, Mach Punch, Baton Pass, Silver Wind, Agility, Swift, Double-Edge, Bug Buzz | |
| **Type:** Bug-Flying | |
| **Height:** 3'03" | **Weight:** 23.8 lbs. |
| **Region:** Johto | |

LEDYBA

LEDIAN

## LICKILICKY
### LICKING POKÉMON

*Lickilicky battles by coiling foes in its large and long tongue, leaving them soaked with drool!*

**Pronounced:**
LICK-ee-LICK-ee

**Possible Moves:** Lick, Supersonic, Defense Curl, Knock Off, Wrap, Stomp, Disable, Slam, Rollout, Me First, Refresh, Screech, Power Whip, Wring Out, Gyro Ball

**Type:** Normal

**Height:** 5'07"

**Weight:** 308.6 lbs.

**Region:** Sinnoh

LICKITUNG

LICKILICKY

# LICKITUNG
## LICKING POKÉMON

*Lickitung uses its tongue to fight instead of its hands—it is covered with a sticky saliva that can grip anything.*

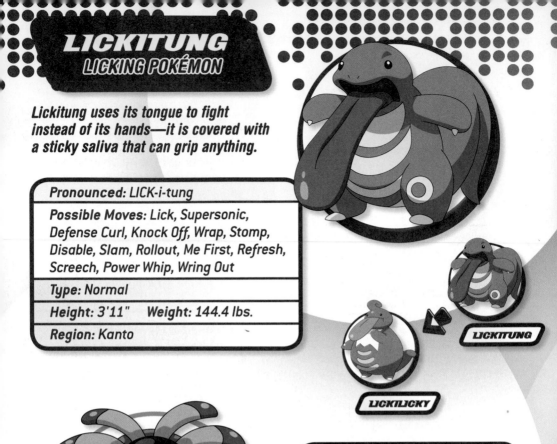

Pronounced: LICK-i-tung

Possible Moves: Lick, Supersonic, Defense Curl, Knock Off, Wrap, Stomp, Disable, Slam, Rollout, Me First, Refresh, Screech, Power Whip, Wring Out

Type: Normal

Height: 3'11"   Weight: 144.4 lbs.

Region: Kanto

LICKITUNG

LICKILICKY

# LILEEP
## SEA LILLY POKÉMON

*This Pokémon shares the same origin story as Anorith. Scientists found the fossilized Lileep on the sea floor, and reanimated it.*

Pronounced: LILL-leep

Possible Moves: Astonish, Constrict, Acid, Ingrain, Confuse Ray, Amnesia, Gastro Acid, AncientPower, Energy Ball, Stockpile, Spit Up, Swallow, Wring Out

Type: Rock-Grass

Height: 3'03"   Weight: 52.5 lbs.

Region: Hoenn

LILEEP

CRADILY

# LINOONE
## RUSHING POKÉMON

The trick to avoiding Linoone is to cut right or left if it is chasing you. Although it reaches speeds of up to 60 mph, it can only run in a straight line.

| |
|---|
| **Pronounced:** line-NOON |
| **Possible Moves:** Switcheroo, Tackle, Growl, Tail Whip, Headbutt, Sand-Attack, Odor Sleuth, Mud Sport, Fury Swipes, Covet, Slash, Rest, Belly Drum, Fling |
| **Type:** Normal |
| **Height:** 1'08"    **Weight:** 71.6 lbs. |
| **Region:** Hoenn |

ZIGZAGOON

LINOONE

# LOMBRE
## JOLLY POKÉMON

Lombre loves to play with fisher-man, often tugging on fishing lines to make people believe they've caught something.

| |
|---|
| **Pronounced:** LOM-brey |
| **Possible Moves:** Astonish, Growl, Absorb, Nature Power, Fake Out, Fury Swipes, Water Sport, Zen Headbutt, Uproar, Hydro Pump |
| **Type:** Water-Grass |
| **Height:** 3'11"    **Weight:** 71.6 lbs. |
| **Region:** Hoenn |

LOTAD

LOMBRE

LUDICOLO

# LOPUNNY
## RABBIT POKÉMON

Lopunny will use its ears to cloak itself when it senses danger. It is known to be a very vain Pokémon.

**Pronounced:** LAH-puh-nee

**Possible Moves:** Mirror Coat, Magic Coat, Splash, Pound, Defense Curl, Foresight, Endure, Return, Quick Attack, Jump Kick, Baton Pass, Agility, Dizzy Punch, Charm, Bounce, Healing Wish

**Type:** Normal

**Height:** 3'11"    **Weight:** 73.4 lbs.

**Region:** Sinnoh

BUNEARY

LOPUNNY

# LOTAD
## WATER WEED POKÉMON

Lotad looks like a water lily, but this sturdy Pokémon can ferry Pokémon that can't swim.

**Pronounced:** LOW-tad

**Possible Moves:** Astonish, Growl, Absorb, Nature Power, Mist, Natural Gift, Mega Drain, Zen Headbutt, Rain Dance, Energy Ball

**Type:** Water-Grass

**Height:** 1'08"    **Weight:** 5.7 lbs.

**Region:** Hoenn

LOTAD

LOMBRE

LUDICOLO

# LOUDRED
## BIG VOICE POKÉMON

To power up, Loudred will stamp its feet although it doesn't need to, since the shock waves generated when it cries are so powerful they can tip over vehicles.

**Pronounced:**
LOUD-red

**Possible Moves:** Pound, Uproar, Astonish, Howl, Bite, Supersonic, Stomp, Screech, Roar, Rest, Sleep Talk, Hyper Voice

**Type:** Normal

**Height:** 3'03"

**Weight:** 89.3 lbs.

**Region:** Hoenn

WHISMUR

LOUDRED

EXPLOUD

# LUCARIO
## AURA POKÉMON

Lucario is able to read thoughts by sensing the auras around others. It can also understand human speech.

**Pronounced:**
loo-CAR-ee-oh

**Possible Moves:** Dark Pulse, Quick Attack, Foresight, Detect, Metal Claw, Counter, Force Palm, Feint, Bone Rush, Metal Sound, Me First, Swords Dance, Aura Sphere, Close Combat, Dragon Pulse, ExtremeSpeed

**Type:** Fighting-Steel

**Height:** 3'11"

**Weight:** 119.0 lbs.

**Region:** Sinnoh

RIOLU

LUCARIO

# LUDICOLO
## CAREFREE POKÉMON

Ludicolo's muscles are filled with energy when it hears music, and then it can't help but dance.

| | |
|---|---|
| **Pronounced:** LOO-dee-KO-low | |
| **Possible Moves:** Astonish, Growl, Mega Drain, Nature Power | |
| **Type:** Water-Grass | |
| **Height:** 4'11" | |
| **Weight:** 121.3 lbs. | |
| **Region:** Hoenn | |

LOTAD

LOMBRE

LUDICOLO

# LUGIA
## DIVING POKÉMON
### Legendary Pokémon

*If Lugia used its wings, it could cause a forty day storm—thankfully, it rarely emerges from the deep-sea trenches it calls home.*

**Pronounced:**
LOO-gee-uh

**Possible Moves:** Whirlwind, Safeguard, Gust, Recover, Hydro Pump, Rain Dance, Swift, Natural Gift, AncientPower, Extrasensory, Punishment, Future Sight, Aeroblast, Calm Mind, Sky Power

**Type:** Psychic-Flying

**Height:** 17'01"

**Weight:** 476.2 lbs.

**Region:** Johto

## DOES NOT EVOLVE

# LUMINEON
## NEON POKÉMON

Lumineon can crawl along sea floors using the fins on its chest. It will flash the patterns on its tail fins to attract prey.

**Pronounced:** loo-MIN-ee-onn

**Possible Moves:** Pound, Water Gun, Attract, Rain Dance, Gust, Water Pulse, Captivate, Safeguard, Aqua Ring, Whirlpool, U-Turn, Bounce, Silver Wind

**Type:** Water

**Height:** 3'11"    **Weight:** 52.9 lbs.

**Region:** Sinnoh

LUMINEON

FINNEON

DOES NOT EVOLVE

# LUNATONE
## METEORITE POKÉMON

Lunatone will only become active on nights with a full moon—which would explain its crescent shape, and its affinity for everything moon-like.

**Pronounced:** LOO-nuh-tone

**Possible Moves:** Tackle, Harden, Confusion, Rock Throw, Hypnosis, Rock Polish, Psywave, Embargo, Cosmic Power, Heal Block, Psychic, Future Sight, Explosion

**Type:** Rock-Psychic

**Height:** 3'03"    **Weight:** 370.4 lbs.

**Region:** Hoenn

# LUVDISC
## RENDEZVOUS POKÉMON

When a couple finds the warm-sea dwelling Luvdisc, it is said they will enjoy eternal love.

**Pronounced:** LOVE-disk

**Possible Moves:** Tackle, Charm, Water Gun, Agility, Take Down, Lucky Chant, Attract, Sweet Kiss, Water Pulse, Aqua Ring, Captivate, Flail, Safeguard

**Type:** Water

**Height:** 2'00"    **Weight:** 19.2 lbs.

**Region:** Hoenn

DOES NOT EVOLVE

# LUXIO
## SPARK POKÉMON

Luxio can cause their foes to faint by letting loose with some spectacular high voltage electricity.

**Pronounced:** LUCKS-ee-oh

**Possible Moves:** Weather Ball, Poison Sting, Mega Drain, Magical Leaf, Sweet Scent

**Type:** Electric

**Height:** 2'11"    **Weight:** 67.2 lbs.

**Region:** Sinnoh

SHINX

LUXIO

LUXRAY

# LUXRAY
## GLEAM EYES POKÉMON

When Luxray's eyes turn gold, it can spot a prey hiding anywhere, including those trying to duck behind walls.

**Pronounced:** LUCKS-ray

**Possible Moves:** Headbutt, Leer, Focus Energy, Pursuit, Take Down, Scary Face, Assurance, AncientPower, Zen Headbutt, Screech, Head Smash

**Type:** Electric

**Height:** 4'07"    **Weight:** 92.6 lbs.

**Region:** Sinnoh

SHINX

LUXRAY

LUXIO

# MACHAMP
## SUPERPOWER POKÉMON

Machamp's four arms allow it to punch at ExtremeSpeeds.

**Pronounced:** MAH-champ

**Possible Moves:** Low Kick, Leer, Focus Energy, Karate Chop, Foresight, Seismic Toss, Revenge, Vital Throw, Submission, Wake-Up Slap, Cross Chop, Scary Face, DynamicPunch

**Type:** Fighting

**Height:** 5'03"    **Weight:** 286.6 lbs.

**Region:** All Regions

MACHOP

MACHOKE

MACHAMP

# MACHOKE
## SUPERPOWER POKÉMON

Machoke's strength can be out of control, so it wears a belt to help keep it in check.

**Pronounced:** MAH-choke

**Possible Moves:** Low Kick, Leer, Focus Energy, Focus Energy, Karate Chop, Foresight, Seismic Toss, Revenge, Vital Throw, Submission, Wake-Up Slap, Cross Chop, Scary Face, DynamicPunch

**Type:** Fighting

**Height:** 4'01"    **Weight:** 155.4 lbs.

**Region:** All Regions

MACHOP

MACHOKE

MACHAMP

# MACHOP
## SUPERPOWER POKÉMON

Machop trains in all types of martial arts to keep itself strong.

**Pronounced:** MAH-chop

**Possible Moves:** Low Kick, Leer, Focus Energy, Karate Chop, Foresight, Seismic Toss, Revenge, Vital Throw, Submission, Wake-Up Slap, Cross Chop, Scary Face, DynamicPunch

**Type:** Fighting

**Height:** 2'07"    **Weight:** 43.0 lbs.

**Region:** All Regions

MACHOP

MACHOKE

MACHAMP

# MAGBY
## LIVE COAL POKÉMON

As long as it's breathing yellow flames, Magby is healthy—even though its body temperature can reach one thousand degrees Fahrenheit.

| |
|---|
| **Pronounced:** MAG-bee |
| **Possible Moves:** Smog, Leer, Ember, SmokeScreen, Faint Attack, Fire Spin, Confuse Ray, Fire Punch, Lava Plume, Flamethrower, Sunny Day, Fire Blast |
| **Type:** Fire |
| **Height:** 2'04"    **Weight:** 47.2 lbs. |
| **Region:** Johto |

MAGBY

MAGMAR

MAGMORTAR

# MAGCARGO
## LAVA POKÉMON

Flames occasionally erupt fron Magcargo's shell, which is normal considering its body reaches temps of eighteen thousand degrees Fahrenheit.

| |
|---|
| **Pronounced:** mag-CAR-go |
| **Possible Moves:** Yawn, Smog, Ember, Rock Throw, Harden, Recover, Ancient-Power, Amnesia, Lava Plume, Rock Slide, Body Slam, Flamethrower |
| **Type:** Fire-Rock |
| **Height:** 2'07"    **Weight:** 121.3 lbs. |
| **Region:** Johto |

SLUGMA

MAGCARGO

# MAGIKARP
## FISH POKÉMON

Poor Magikarp! It is generally regarded as the weakest Pokémon ever. How it has managed to survive is a mystery.

| | |
|---|---|
| **Pronounced:** MAJ-i-karp | |
| **Possible Moves:** Splash, Tackle, Flail | |
| **Type:** Water | |
| **Height:** 2'11" | **Weight:** 22.0 lbs. |
| **Region:** All Regions | |

**GYARADOS**

**MAGIKARP**

**MAGBY**

**MAGMAR**

**MAGMORTAR**

# MAGMAR
## SPITFIRE POKÉMON

Covered in flames that shimmer like the sun, this Pokémon was born in a volcano.

| | |
|---|---|
| **Pronounced:** MAG-mar | |
| **Possible Moves:** Smog, Leer, Ember, SmokeScreen, Faint Attack, Fire Spin, Confuse Ray, Fire Punch, Lava Plume, Flamethrower, Sunny Day, Fire Blast | |
| **Type:** Fire | |
| **Height:** 4'03" | **Weight:** 98.1 lbs. |
| **Region:** Kanto | |

# MAGMORTAR
## BLAST POKÉMON

Magmortar can blast fireballs of over thirty-six hundred degrees Fahrenheit from the ends of its arms.

**Pronounced:**
MAG-mor-tur

**Possible Moves:**
ThunderPunch, Smog, Leer, Ember, SmokeScreen, Feint Attack, Fire Spin, Confuse Ray, Fire Punch, Lava Plume, Flamethrower, Sunny Day, Fire Blast, Hyper Beam

**Type:** Fire

**Height:** 5'03"

**Weight:** 149.9 lbs.

**Region:** Sinnoh

MAGBY

MAGMAR

MAGMORTAR

# MAGNEMITE
## MAGNET POKÉMON

Feeding on electricity, it uses its sides to make electromagnetic waves that enable it to fly.

**Pronounced:** MAG-nuh-mite

**Possible Moves:** Metal Sound, Tackle, ThunderShock, Supersonic, SonicBoom, Thunder Wave, Spark, Lock-On, Magnet Bomb, Screech, Discharge, Mirror Shot, Magnet Rise, Gyro Ball, Zap Cannon

**Type:** Electric-Steel

**Height:** 1'00"    **Weight:** 13.2 lbs.

**Region:** Johto, Kanto, and Hoenn

MAGNEMITE

MAGNETON

MAGNEZONE

# MAGNETON
## MAGNET POKÉMON

Look closely—did you know Magneton is three Magnemites stuck together by magnets? A group of these can set off a magnetic storm!

**Pronounced:** MAG-nuh-tun

**Possible Moves:** Tri Power, Metal Sound, Tackle, ThunderShock, Supersonic, SonicBoom, Thunder Wave, Spark, Lock-On, Magnet Bomb, Screech, Discharge, Mirror Shot, Magnet Rise, Gyro Ball, Zap Cannon

**Type:** Electric-Steel

**Height:** 3'03"    **Weight:** 132.3 lbs.

**Region:** Johto, Kanto, and Hoenn

MAGNEMITE

MAGNETON

MAGNEZONE

# MAGNEZONE
## MAGNET AREA POKÉMON

With three Magnezone, which evolved from exposure to special magnetic fields, you can generate magnetism.

**Pronounced:**
MAG-nuh-zone

**Possible Moves:** Mirror Coat, Barrier, Metal Sound, Tackle, ThunderShock, Supersonic, SonicBoom, Thunder Wave, Spark, Lock-On, Magnet Bomb, Screech, Discharge, Mirror Shot, Magnet Rise, Gyro Ball, Zap Cannon

**Type:** Electric-Steel

**Height:** 3'11"

**Weight:** 396.8 lbs.

**Region:** Sinnoh

MAGNEMITE

MAGNETON

MAGNEZONE

# MAKUHITA
## GUTS POKÉMON

You're likely to find a lot of snapped trees near this Pokémon—it slams into them to toughen up its body.

**Pronounced:** MAK-oo-HƐƐ-ta

**Possible Moves:** Tackle, Focus Energy, Sand-Attack, Arm Thrust, Vital Throw, Fake Out, Whirlwind, Knock Off, SmellingSalt, Belly Drum, Force Palm, Seismic Toss, Wake-Up Slap, Endure, Close Combat, Reversal

**Type:** Fighting

**Height:** 3'03"    **Weight:** 190.5 lbs.

**Region:** Hoenn

MAKUHITA

HARIYAMA

# MAMOSWINE
## TWIN TUSK POKÉMON

The Mamoswine population decreased shortly after the ice age. Its tusks are made of ice.

**Pronounced:** MAMO-swine

**Possible Moves:** AncientPower, Peck, Odor Sleuth, Mud Sport, Powder Snow, Mud-Slap, Endure, Mud Bomb, Hail, Ice Fang, Take Down, Double Hit, Earthquake, Mist, Blizzard, Scary Face

**Type:** Ice-Ground

**Height:** 8'02"    **Weight:** 641.5 lbs.

**Region:** Sinnoh

SWINUB

PILOSWINE

MAMOSWINE

# MANAPHY
## SEAFARING POKÉMON
*Legendary Pokémon*

*Because water makes up eighty percent of its body, this Pokémon is greatly affected by weather changes in its environment. It will also swim great distances to return to its birthplace.*

**Pronounced:**
man-UH-fee

**Possible Moves:** Tail Glow, Bubble, Water Sport, Charm, Supersonic, BubbleBeam, Acid Armor, Whirlpool, Water Pulse, Aqua Ring, Dive, Rain Dance, Heart Swap

**Type:** Water

**Height:** 1'00"

**Weight:** 3.1 lbs.

**Region:** Sinnoh

## DOES NOT EVOLVE

# MANECTRIC
## DISCHARGE POKÉMON

Manectric creates a lighting-bolt thundercloud by discharging electricity through its mane.

**Pronounced:** mane-EK-trick

**Possible Moves:** Fire Fang, Tackle, Thunder Wave, Leer, Howl, Quick Attack, Spark, Odor Sleuth, Bite, Thunder Fang, Roar, Discharge, Charge, Thunder

**Type:** Electric

**Height:** 4'11"    **Weight:** 88.6 lbs.

**Region:** Hoenn

ELECTRIKE

MANECTRIC

# MANKEY
## PIG MONKEY POKÉMON

Mankey lives with groups of other Mankey on treetops. If one Mankey gets angry, the whole group will follow suit.

MANKEY

PRIMEAPE

**Pronounced:** MANK-ee

**Possible Moves:** Covet, Scratch, Low Kick, Leer, Focus Energy, Fury Swipes, Karate Chop, Seismic Toss, Screech, Assurance, Swagger, Cross Chop, Thrash, Punishment, Close Combat

**Type:** Fighting

**Height:** 1'08"    **Weight:** 61.7 lbs.

**Region:** Kanto

# MANTINE
## KITE POKÉMON

These docile Pokémon can be seen swimming in unison when the sea is calm—it almost seems as if they are flying.

Pronounced: MAN-tine

Possible Moves: Psybeam, Bullet Seed, Signal Beam, Tackle, Bubble, Supersonic, BubbleBeam, Headbutt, Agility, Wing Attack, Water Pulse, Take Down, Confuse Ray, Bounce, Aqua Ring, Hydro Pump

Type: Water-Flying

Height: 6'11"    Weight: 485.0 lbs.

Region: Johto

MANTYKE

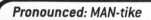

MANTINE

# MANTYKE
## KITE POKÉMON

The patterns on Mantyke's back will be different in every region. It uses the antennae on its head to detect subtle changes in the ocean's currents.

Pronounced: MAN-tike

Possible Moves: Tackle, Bubble, Supersonic, BubbleBeam, Headbutt, Agility, Wing Attack, Water Pulse, Take Down, Confuse Ray, Bounce, Aqua Ring, Hydro Pump

Type: Water-Flying

Height: 3'03"    Weight: 143.3 lbs.

Region: Sinnoh

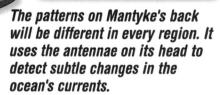

MANTYKE

MANTINE

# MAREEP
## WOOL POKÉMON

Mareep is not prone to being petted, especially since its fluffy coat immediately doubles in size due to stored static electricity.

Pronounced: mah-REEP

Possible Moves: Tackle, Growl, ThunderShock, Thunder Wave, Cotton Spore, Charge, Discharge, Signal Beam, Light Screen, Power Gem, Thunder

Type: Electric

Height: 2'00"    Weight: 17.2 lbs.

Region: Johto

MAREEP

FLAAFFY

AMPHAROS

# MARILL
## AQUA MOUSE POKÉMON

When it dives underwater, Marill use its oil-filled tail as a float, and eats plants from the river bottom.

Pronounced: MARE-rull

Possible Moves: Tackle, Defense Curl, Tail Whip, Water Gun, Rollout, BubbleBeam, Aqua Ring, Double-Edge, Rain Dance, Aqua Tail, Hydro Pump

Type: Water

Height: 1'04"    Weight: 18.7 lbs.

Region: Johto, Hoenn, and Sinnoh

AZURILL

MARILL

AZUMARILL

154

# MAROWAK
## BONE KEEPER POKÉMON

Marowak uses bones that it has held since birth as weapons.

**Pronounced:** MAR-row-ack

**Possible Moves:** Growl, Tail Whip, Bone Club, Headbutt, Leer, Focus Energy, Bonemerang, Rage, False Swipe, Thrash, Fling, Bone Rush, Endeavor

**Type:** Ground

**Height:** 3'03"    **Weight:** 99.2 lbs.

**Region:** Kanto

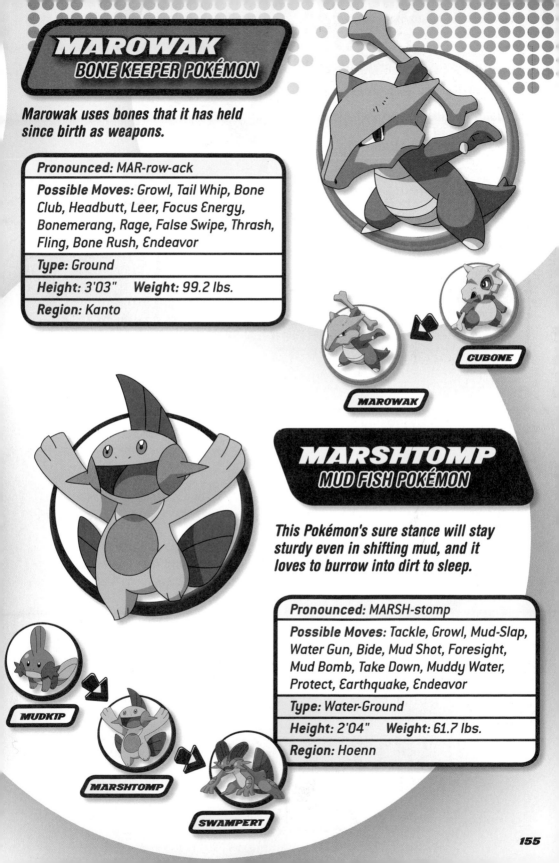

CUBONE

MAROWAK

# MARSHTOMP
## MUD FISH POKÉMON

This Pokémon's sure stance will stay sturdy even in shifting mud, and it loves to burrow into dirt to sleep.

**Pronounced:** MARSH-stomp

**Possible Moves:** Tackle, Growl, Mud-Slap, Water Gun, Bide, Mud Shot, Foresight, Mud Bomb, Take Down, Muddy Water, Protect, Earthquake, Endeavor

**Type:** Water-Ground

**Height:** 2'04"    **Weight:** 61.7 lbs.

**Region:** Hoenn

MUDKIP

MARSHTOMP

SWAMPERT

155

# MASQUERAIN
## EYEBALL POKÉMON

Masquerain uses its four eye-patterned wings to fly and hover in any direction.

**Pronounced:** mas-ker-RAIN

**Possible Moves:** Ominous Wind, Bubble, Quick Attack, Sweet Scent, Water Sport, Gust, Scary Face, Stun Spore, Silver Wind, Air Slash, Whirlwind, Bug Buzz

**Type:** Bug-Flying

**Height:** 2'07"　　**Weight:** 7.9 lbs.

**Region:** Hoenn

SURSKIT

MASQUERAIN

DOES NOT EVOLVE

# MAWILE
## DECEIVER POKÉMON

The huge set of jaws formed by horns on Mawile's head can chew through iron beams.

**Pronounced:** MAW-while

**Possible Moves:** Astonish, Fake Tears, Bite, Sweet Scent, ViceGrip, Faint Attack, Baton Pass, Crunch, Iron Defense, Sucker Punch, Stockpile, Swallow, Spit Up, Iron Head

**Type:** Steel

**Height:** 2'00"　　**Weight:** 25.4 lbs.

**Region:** Hoenn

# MEDICHAM
## MEDITATE POKÉMON

Medicham hones its sixth sense with a disciplined routine of daily meditation.

**Pronounced:** MED-uh-cham

**Possible Moves:** Fire Punch, Thunderpunch, Ice Punch, Bide, Meditate, Confusion, Detect, Hidden Power, Mind Reader, Feint, Calm Mind, Force Palm, Hi Jump Kick, Psych Up, Power Trick, Reversal, Recover

**Type:** Fighting-Psychic

**Height:** 4'03"    **Weight:** 69.4 lbs.

**Region:** Hoenn

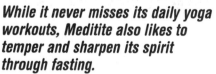

MEDITITE    MEDICHAM

# MEDITITE
## MEDITATE POKÉMON

While it never misses its daily yoga workouts, Meditite also likes to temper and sharpen its spirit through fasting.

**Pronounced:** MED-uh-tite

**Possible Moves:** Bide, Meditate, Confusion, Detect, Hidden Power, Mind Reader, Feint, Calm Mind, Force Palm, Hi Jump Kick, Psych Up, Power Trick, Reversal, Recover

**Type:** Fighting-Psychic

**Height:** 2'00"    **Weight:** 24.7 lbs.

**Region:** Hoenn

MEDITITE    MEDICHAM

# MEGANIUM
## HERB POKÉMON

Meganium has the ability to bring dead plants and flowers back to life! All it has to do is breathe onto them.

**Pronounced:**
meg-GAY-nee-um

**Possible Moves:** Tackle, Growl, Razor Leaf, PoisonPowder, Synthesis, Reflect, Magical Leaf, Natural Gift, Petal Dance, Sweet Scent, Light Screen, Body Slam, Safeguard, Aromatherapy, SolarBeam

**Type:** Grass

**Height:** 5'11"

**Weight:** 221.6 lbs.

**Region:** Johto

CHIKORITA

BAYLEEF

MEGANIUM

# MEOWTH
## SCRATCH CAT POKÉMON

*Meowth is mostly nocturnal, but its eyes will glitter brightly if it sees something shiny.*

**Pronounced:**
me-OUTH

**Possible Moves:** Scratch, Growl, Bite, Fake Out, Fury Swipes, Screech, Faint Attack, Taunt, Pay Day, Slash, Nasty Plot, Assurance, Captivate, Night Slash

**Type:** Normal

**Height:** 1'04"

**Weight:** 9.3 lbs.

**Region:** Kanto

MEOWTH

PERSIAN

# MESPRIT

*Also known as The Being of Emotion, Mesprit is said to have taught humans the nobility of pain, sorrow, and joy.*

**Pronounced:**
MES-prit

**Possible Moves:** Rest, Imprison, Protect, Confusion, Lucky Chant, Future Sight, Charm, Extrasensory, Copycat, Natural Gift, Healing Wish

**Type:** Psychic

**Height:** 1'00"

**Weight:** 0.7 lbs.

**Region:** Sinnoh

**DOES NOT EVOLVE**

160

# METAGROSS
## IRON LEG POKÉMON

By combining two Metang, the quad-brained Metagross has the smarts of a supercomputer.

**Pronounced:**
MET-uh-gross

**Possible Moves:** Magnet Rise, Take Down, Metal Claw, Confusion, Scary Face, Pursuit, Bullet Punch, Psychic, Iron Defense, Agility, Hammer Arm, Meteor Mash, Zen Headbutt, Hyper Beam

**Type:** Steel-Psychic

**Height:** 5'03"

**Weight:** 1212.5 lbs.

**Region:** Hoenn

BELDUM

METANG

METAGROSS

# METANG
## IRON CLAW POKÉMON

Metang's body is so strong that not even a jet plane could scratch it. Its body is formed by the combination of two Beldum.

| | |
|---|---|
| **Pronounced:** met-TANG | |
| **Possible Moves:** Magnet Rise, Take Down, Metal Claw, Confusion, Scary Face, Pursuit, Bullet Punch, Psychic, Iron Defense, Agility, Meteor Mash, Zen Headbutt, Hyper Beam | |
| **Type:** Steel-Psychic | |
| **Height:** 3'11" **Weight:** 446.4 lbs. | |
| **Region:** Hoenn | |

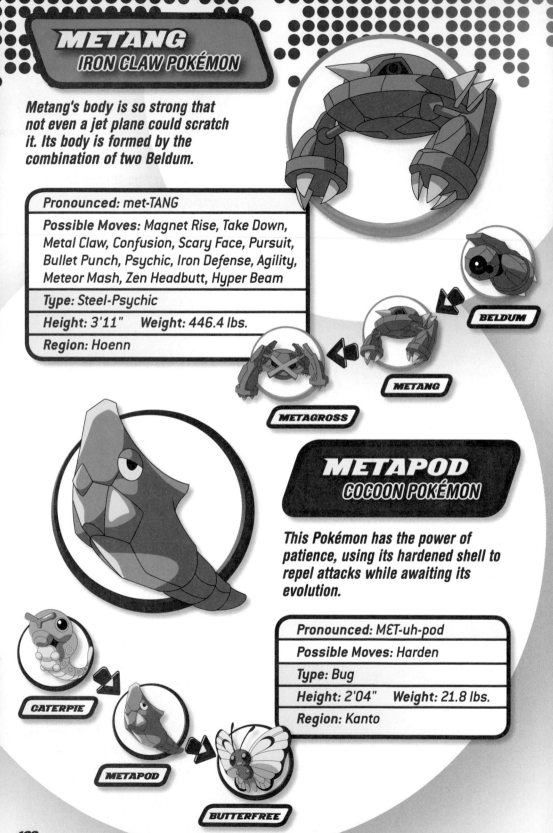

BELDUM

METANG

METAGROSS

# METAPOD
## COCOON POKÉMON

This Pokémon has the power of patience, using its hardened shell to repel attacks while awaiting its evolution.

| | |
|---|---|
| **Pronounced:** MET-uh-pod | |
| **Possible Moves:** Harden | |
| **Type:** Bug | |
| **Height:** 2'04" **Weight:** 21.8 lbs. | |
| **Region:** Kanto | |

CATERPIE

METAPOD

BUTTERFREE

# MEW
## NEW SPECIES POKÉMON
*Legendary Pokémon*

**Because Mew can learn and use any Pokémon move, it is thought to be ancestrally linked to all Pokémon.**

**Pronounced:**
*MYU*

**Possible Moves:** Pound, Transform, Mega Punch, Metronome, Psychic, Barrier, AncientPower, Amnesia, Me First, Baton Pass, Nasty Plot, Aura Sphere

**Type:** Psychic

**Height:** 1'04"

**Weight:** 8.8 lbs.

**Region:** Kanto

## DOES NOT EVOLVE

# MEWTWO
## GENETIC POKÉMON
### Legendary Pokémon

Mewtwo was created when scientists recombined Mew's genes. It has the most savage heart of all Pokémon.

**Pronounced:**
*MYU-too*

**Possible Moves:** *Confusion, Disable, Barrier, Swift, Future Sight, Psych Up, Miracle Eye, Mist, Psycho Cut, Amnesia, Power Swap, Guard Swap, Psychic, Me First, Recover, Safeguard, Aura Sphere*

**Type:** Psychic

**Height:** 6'07"

**Weight:** 269.0 lbs.

**Region:** Kanto

## DOES NOT EVOLVE

# MIGHTYENA
## BITE POKÉMON

This Pokémon chases down its prey in a pack, and is very obedient to a skilled Trainer.

| | |
|---|---|
| **Pronounced:** MY-tee-EH-nah | |
| **Possible Moves:** Tackle, Howl, Sand-Attack, Bite, Odor Sleuth, Roar, Swagger, Assurance, Scary Face, Taunt, Embargo, Take Down, Thief, Sucker Punch | |
| **Type:** Dark | |
| **Height:** 3'03"  **Weight:** 81.6 lbs. | |
| **Region:** Hoenn | |

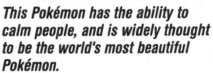

# MILOTIC
## TENDER POKÉMON

This Pokémon has the ability to calm people, and is widely thought to be the world's most beautiful Pokémon.

| | |
|---|---|
| **Pronounced:** my-LOW-tic | |
| **Possible Moves:** Water Gun, Wrap, Water Sport, Refresh, Water Pulse, Twister, Recover, Captivate, Aqua Tail, Rain Dance, Hydro Pump, Attract, Safeguard, Aqua Ring | |
| **Type:** Water | |
| **Height:** 20'04"  **Weight:** 357.1 lbs. | |
| **Region:** Hoenn | |

# MILTANK
## MILK COW POKÉMON

*By drinking Miltank's milk, kids will become healthy adults.*

**Pronounced:** MILL-tank

**Possible Moves:** Tackle, Growl, Defense Curl, Stomp, Milk Drink, Bide, Rollout, Body Slam, Zen Headbutt, Captivate, Gyro Ball, Heal Bell, Wake-Up Slap

**Type:** Normal

**Height:** 3'11"    **Weight:** 166.4 lbs.

**Region:** Johto

*DOES NOT EVOLVE*

# MIME JR.
## MIME POKÉMON

*Mime Jr. can imitate its foes and mesmerize them, allowing it to escape.*

**Pronounced:** mime-JOON-yur

**Possible Moves:** Tickle, Barrier, Confusion, Copycat, Meditate, Encore, DoubleSlap, Mimic, Light Screen, Reflect, Psybeam, Substitute, Recycle, Trick, Psychic, Role Play, Baton Pass, Safeguard

**Type:** Psychic

**Height:** 2'00"    **Weight:** 28.7 lbs.

**Region:** Sinnoh

MIME JR.

MR. MIME

# MINUN
## CHEERING POKÉMON

Minun is another cheerleader Pokémon, like Plusle. If its friends are losing, its body lets off more and more sparks.

DOES NOT EVOLVE

| | |
|---|---|
| **Pronounced:** MIE-nun | |
| **Possible Moves:** Growl, Thunder Wave, Quick Attack, Helping Hand, Spark, Encore, Charm, Copycat, Swift, Fake Tears, Charge, Thunder, Baton Pass, Agility, Trump Card, Nasty Plot | |
| **Type:** Electric | |
| **Height:** 1'04" | **Weight:** 9.3 lbs. |
| **Region:** Hoenn | |

MISDREAVUS

MISMAGIUS

# MISDREAVUS
## SCREECH POKÉMON

Misdreavus feeds on fear, which it instills in the unsuspecting with its banshee-like cry.

| | |
|---|---|
| **Pronounced:** mis-DREE-vuss | |
| **Possible Moves:** Growl, Psywave, Spite, Astonish, Confuse Ray, Mean Look, Psybeam, Pain Split, Payback, Shadow Ball, Perish Song, Grudge | |
| **Type:** Ghost | |
| **Height:** 2'04" | **Weight:** 2.2 lbs. |
| **Region:** Johto | |

# MISMAGIUS
## MAGICAL POKÉMON

While most of Mismagius' chants can cause pain and headaches, some of them are known to bring happiness.

**Pronounced:**
mis-MAG-ee-us

**Possible Moves:** Lucky Chant, Magical Leaf, Growl, Psywave, Spite, Astonish

**Type:** Ghost

**Height:** 2'11"

**Weight:** 9.7 lbs.

**Region:** Sinnoh

MISDREAVUS

MISMAGIUS

The appearance of Moltres, a Legendary Pokémon, usually heralds the fact that spring is on its way.

**Pronounced:** MOLE-trace

**Possible Moves:** Wing Attack, Ember, Fire Spin, Agility, Endure, AncientPower, Flamethrower, Safeguard, Air Slash, Roost, Heat Wave, SolarBeam, Sky Power, Sunny Day

**Type:** Fire-Flying

**Height:** 6'07"

**Weight:** 132.3 lbs.

**Region:** Kanto

**DOES NOT EVOLVE**

# MONFERNO
## PLAYFUL POKÉMON

Monferno has been known to strategically use the fire on its tail to make itself appear larger.

**Pronounced:**
mon-FERN-oh

**Possible Moves:** Scratch, Leer, Ember, Taunt, Mach Punch, Fury Swipes, Flame Wheel, Faint, Torment, Close Combat, Fire Spin, Slack Off, Flare Blitz

**Type:** Fire-Fighting

**Height:** 2'11"

**Weight:** 48.5 lbs.

**Region:** Sinnoh

CHIMCHAR

MONFERNO

INFERNAPE

# MOTHIM
## MOTH POKÉMON

Mothim are always in search of honey. They're on the go so much that they won't take the time to make nests. Sometimes, this Pokémon will even steal honey from Combee.

**Pronounced:**
MAH-thum

**Possible Moves:** Tackle, Protect, Hidden Power, Confusion, Gust, PoisonPowder, Psybeam, Camouflage, Silver Wind, Air Slash, Psychic, Bug Buzz

**Type:** Bug-Flying

**Height:** 2'11"

**Weight:** 51.4 lbs.

**Region:** Sinnoh

BURMY ♂

MOTHIM

## MR. MIME
### BARRIER POKÉMON

By using certain pantomime gestures, Mr. Mime can build invisible solid walls.

Pronounced: MIS-ter mime

Possible Moves: Magical Leaf, Power Swap, Guard Swap, Barrier, Confusion, Copycat, Meditate, Encore, DoubleSlap, Mimic, Light Screen, Reflect, Psybeam, Substitute, Recycle, Trick, Psychic, Role Play, Baton Pass, Safeguard

Type: Psychic

Height: 4'03"    Weight: 120.1 lbs.

Region: Kanto and Sinnoh

MIME JR.

MR. MIME

## MUDKIP
### MUD FISH POKÉMON

Mudkip uses its strength to lift heavy boulders. The fin on top of its head can sense the flow of water.

Pronounced: MUD-kip

Possible Moves: Tackle, Growl, Mud-Slap, Water Gun, Bide, Foresight, Mud Sport, Take Down, Whirlpool, Protect, Hydro Pump, Endeavor

Type: Water

Height: 1'04"    Weight: 16.8 lbs.

Region: Hoenn

MUDKIP

MARSHTOMP

SWAMPERT

# MUK
## SLUDGE POKÉMON

The fluid that comes out of Muk is so toxic it can kill plants and trees instantly.

**Pronounced:** MUCK

**Possible Moves:** Poison Gas, Pound, Harden, Mud-Slap, Disable, Minimize, Sludge, Mud Bomb, Fling, Screech, Sludge Bomb, Acid Armor, Gunk Shot, Memento

**Type:** Poison

**Height:** 3'11"    **Weight:** 66.1 lbs.

**Region:** Kanto

GRIMER

MUK

# MUNCHLAX
## BIG EATER POKÉMON

Munchlax can swallow its food whole and eats the equivalent of its body weight every day. It hoards food, too. Sometimes, it hides spare food in its long hair, and then forgets its there.

**Pronounced:** MUNCH-lacks

**Possible Moves:** Metronome, Odor Sleuth, Tackle, Defense Curl, Amnesia, Lick, Recycle, Screech, Stockpile, Swallow, Body Slam, Fling, Rollout, Natural Gift, Last Resort

**Type:** Normal

**Height:** 2'00"    **Weight:** 231.5 lbs.

**Region:** Sinnoh

MUNCHLAX

SNORLAX

# MURKROW
## DARKNESS POKÉMON

Night travelers know to avoid ominous Murkrow. This Pokémon is rumored to bring bad luck to those that it lures into the forests.

| | |
|---|---|
| **Pronounced:** MUR-crow | |
| **Possible Moves:** Peck, Astonish, Pursuit, Haze, Wing Attack, Night Shade, Assurance, Taunt, Faint Attack, Mean Look, Sucker Punch | |
| **Type:** Dark-Flying | |
| **Height:** 1'08"    **Weight:** 4.6 lbs. | |
| **Region:** Johto and Sinnoh | |

MURKROW

HONCHKROW

# NATU
## TINY BIRD POKÉMON

Natu is so agile that it can pick food from cacti without hitting buds or spines, even though it seems to skip while it moves.

| | |
|---|---|
| **Pronounced:** NAH-too | |
| **Possible Moves:** Peck, Leer, Night Shade, Teleport, Lucky Chant, Miracle Eye, Me First, Confuse Ray, Wish, Psycho Shift, Future Sight, Ominous Wind, Power Swap, Guard Swap, Psychic | |
| **Type:** Psychic-Flying | |
| **Height:** 0'08"    **Weight:** 4.4 lbs. | |
| **Region:** Johto | |

NATU

XATU

# NIDOKING
## DRILL POKÉMON

*Talk about might—the tail on this ferocious Pokémon can snap a telephone pole like a toothpick.*

| | |
|---|---|
| **Pronounced:** nee-doe-KING | |
| **Possible Moves:** Peck, Focus Energy, Double Kick, Poison Sting, Thrash, Earth Power, Megahorn | |
| **Type:** Poison-Ground | |
| **Height:** 4'07" | **Weight:** 136.7 lbs. |
| **Region:** Kanto | |

NIDORAN ♂

NIDORINO

NIDOKING

# NIDOQUEEN
## DRILL POKÉMON

*This queen is a deadly protector of its young—it will defend a lair with its life, and it is formidable, with iron-hard scales all over its body.*

| | |
|---|---|
| **Pronounced:** nee-doe-QUEEN | |
| **Possible Moves:** Scratch, Tail Whip, Double Kick, Poison Sting, Body Slam, Earth Power, SuperPower | |
| **Type:** Poison-Ground | |
| **Height:** 4'03" | **Weight:** 132.3 lbs. |
| **Reglon:** Kanto | |

NIDORAN ♀

NIDORINA

NIDOQUEEN

# NIDORAN ♀
## POISON PIN POKÉMON

Nidoran ♀ doesn't like to fight, and it doesn't need to either—one pinprick of its poisonous barbs can be fatal.

**Pronounced:** nee-door-ANN

**Possible Moves:** Growl, Scratch, Tail Whip, Double Kick, Poison Sting, Fury Swipes, Bite, Helping Hand, Toxic Spikes, Flatter, Crunch, Captivate, Poison Fang

**Type:** Poison

**Height:** 1'04"    **Weight:** 15.4 lbs.

**Region:** Kanto

NIDORAN ♀

NIDORINA

NIDOQUEEN

# NIDORAN ♂
## POISON PIN POKÉMON

How does a Nidoran ♂ know when prey is around? It raises its ears above the grass line. It keeps enemies away with the toxic horn on its head.

**Pronounced:** nee-door-ANN

**Possible Moves:** Leer, Peck, Focus Energy, Double Kick, Poison Sting, Fury Attack, Horn Attack, Helping Hand, Toxic Spikes, Flatter, Poison Jab, Captivate, Horn Drill

**Type:** Poison

**Height:** 1'08"    **Weight:** 19.8 lbs.

**Region:** Kanto

NIDORAN ♂

NIDORINO

NIDOKING

# NIDORINA
## POISON PIN POKÉMON

When it senses danger, the barbs on its body are raised. You can tell the sex of these Pokémon by the size of the barbs— the Nidorina grows them slower and shorter than the Nidorino.

| Pronounced: nee-door-EE-nuh |
| --- |
| **Possible Moves:** Growl, Scratch, Tail Whip, Double Kick, Poison Sting, Fury Swipes, Bite, Helping Hand, Toxic Spikes, Flatter, Crunch, Captivate, Poison Fang |
| **Type:** Poison |
| **Height:** 2'07"    **Weight:** 44.1 lbs. |
| **Region:** Kanto |

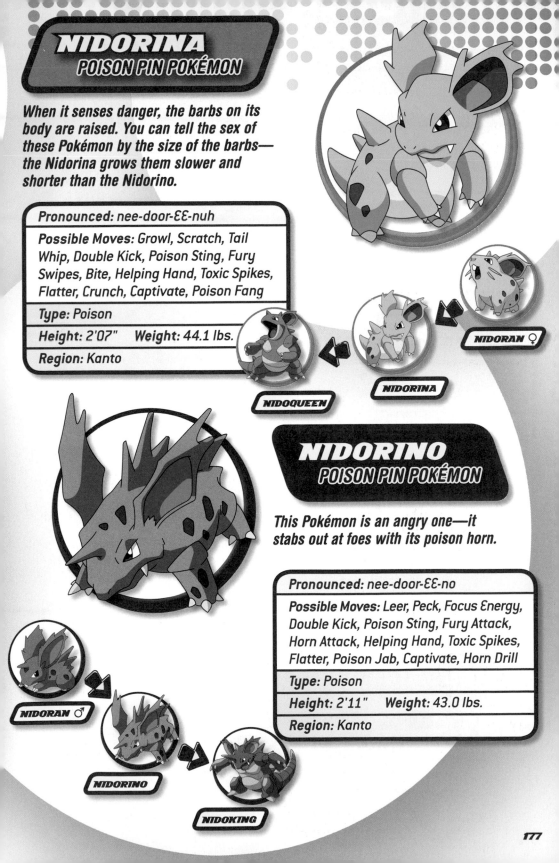

NIDORAN ♀

NIDORINA

NIDOQUEEN

# NIDORINO
## POISON PIN POKÉMON

This Pokémon is an angry one—it stabs out at foes with its poison horn.

| Pronounced: nee-door-EE-no |
| --- |
| **Possible Moves:** Leer, Peck, Focus Energy, Double Kick, Poison Sting, Fury Attack, Horn Attack, Helping Hand, Toxic Spikes, Flatter, Poison Jab, Captivate, Horn Drill |
| **Type:** Poison |
| **Height:** 2'11"    **Weight:** 43.0 lbs. |
| **Region:** Kanto |

NIDORAN ♂

NIDORINO

NIDOKING

# NINCADA
## TRAINEE POKÉMON

The underground-dwelling Nincada uses its antennae on top of its head (instead of its eyes) to sense its surroundings.

| | |
|---|---|
| **Pronounced:** nin-KAH-da | |
| **Possible Moves:** Scratch, Harden, Leech Life, Sand-Attack, Fury Swipes, Mind Reader, False Swipe, Mud-Slap, Metal Claw, Dig | |
| **Type:** Bug-Ground | |
| **Height:** 1'08"    **Weight:** 12.1 lbs. | |
| **Region:** Hoenn | |

SHEDINJA     OR     NINJASK

NINCADA

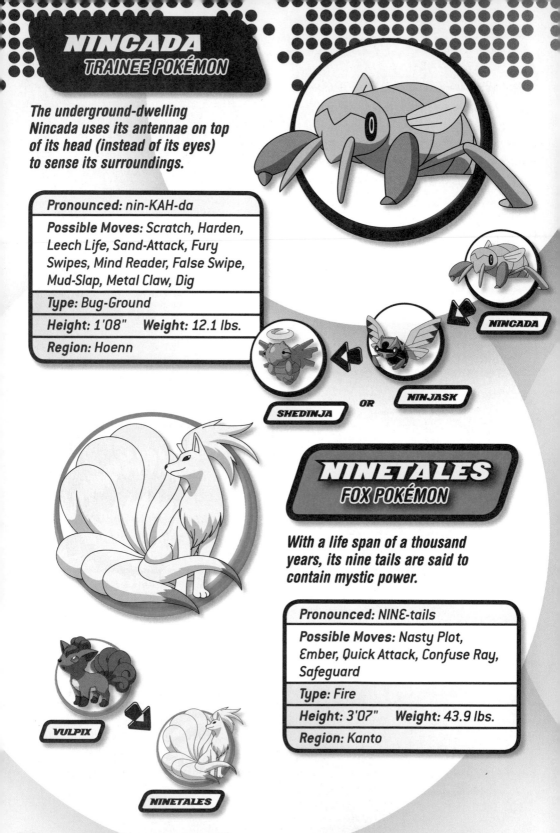

# NINETALES
## FOX POKÉMON

With a life span of a thousand years, its nine tails are said to contain mystic power.

| | |
|---|---|
| **Pronounced:** NINE-tails | |
| **Possible Moves:** Nasty Plot, Ember, Quick Attack, Confuse Ray, Safeguard | |
| **Type:** Fire | |
| **Height:** 3'07"    **Weight:** 43.9 lbs. | |
| **Region:** Kanto | |

VULPIX

NINETALES

# NINJASK
## NINJA POKÉMON

You can usually find this Pokémon around tree sap, but look fast—it moves so quickly that it is virtually unnoticeable.

**Pronounced:** NIN-jask

**Possible Moves:** Bug Bite, Scratch, Harden, Leech Life, Sand-Attack, Fury Swipes, Mind Reader, Double Team, Fury Cutter, Screech, Swords Dance, Slash, Agility, Baton Pass, X-Scissor

**Type:** Bug-Flying

**Height:** 2'07"    **Weight:** 26.5 lbs.

**Region:** Hoenn

NINJASK

NINCADA

# NOCTOWL
## OWL POKÉMON

Even in the most minimal levels of light, Noctowl can use its super-sharp eyesight to find objects.

**Pronounced:** NAHK-towl

**Possible Moves:** Sky Power, Tackle, Growl, Foresight, Hypnosis, Peck, Reflect, Confusion, Take Down, Air Slash, Zen Headbutt, Extrasensory, Psycho Shift, Roost, Dream Eater

**Type:** Normal-Flying

**Height:** 5'03"    **Weight:** 89.9 lbs.

**Region:** Johto and Sinnoh

HOOTHOOT

NOCTOWL

# NOSEPASS
## COMPASS POKÉMON

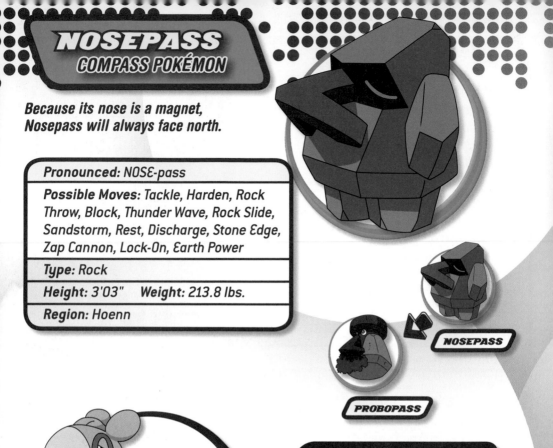

*Because its nose is a magnet, Nosepass will always face north.*

**Pronounced:** NOSE-pass

**Possible Moves:** Tackle, Harden, Rock Throw, Block, Thunder Wave, Rock Slide, Sandstorm, Rest, Discharge, Stone Edge, Zap Cannon, Lock-On, Earth Power

**Type:** Rock

**Height:** 3'03"      **Weight:** 213.8 lbs.

**Region:** Hoenn

NOSEPASS

PROBOPASS

# NUMEL
## NUMB POKÉMON

**Numel wouldn't slow down were it not for its humped back, which stores extremely hot magma. When raining, the magma cools and Numel slows to a crawl.**

NUMEL

CAMERUPT

**Pronounced:** NUM-mull

**Possible Moves:** Growl, Tackle, Ember, Magnitude, Focus Energy, Take Down, Amnesia, Lava Plume, Earth Power, Earthquake, Flamethrower, Double-Edge

**Type:** Fire-Ground

**Height:** 2'04"      **Weight:** 52.9 lbs.

**Region:** Hoenn

# NUZLEAF
## WILY POKÉMON

If you happen to be in the deep forests Nuzleaf inhabits, and you hear the sound of its grass flute, it will make you uneasy.

**Pronounced:** NUZ-leaf

**Possible Moves:** Razor Leaf, Pound, Harden, Growth, Nature Power, Fake Out, Torment, Faint Attack, Razor Wind, Swagger, Extrasensory

**Type:** Grass-Dark

**Height:** 3'03"    **Weight:** 61.7 lbs.

**Region:** Hoenn

SHIFTRY

NUZLEAF

SEEDOT

# OCTILLERY
## JET POKÉMON

Octillery uses its suction cups to grip its prey, which it finds among gaps in sea floor boulders.

**Pronounced:** ock-TILL-er-ree

**Possible Moves:** Gunk Shot, Rock Blast, Water Gun, Constrict, Psybeam, Aurora Beam, BubbleBeam, Focus Energy, Octazooka, Bullet Seed, Wring Out, Signal Beam, Ice Beam, Hyper Beam

**Type:** Water

**Height:** 2'11"    **Weight:** 62.8 lbs.

**Region:** Johto and Sinnoh

REMORAID

OCTILLERY

# ODDISH
## WEED POKÉMON

Oddish can plant its feet in the ground during the day, and gather the seeds at night with its feet.

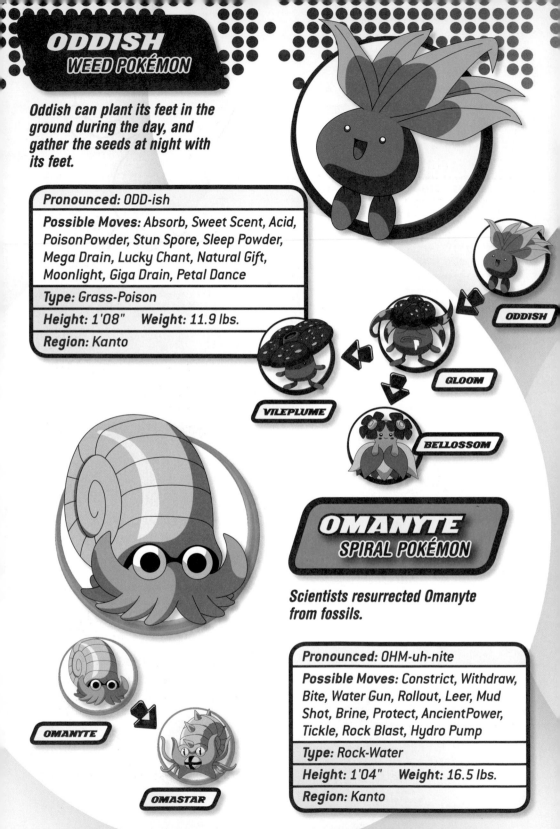

| | |
|---|---|
| **Pronounced:** ODD-ish | |
| **Possible Moves:** Absorb, Sweet Scent, Acid, PoisonPowder, Stun Spore, Sleep Powder, Mega Drain, Lucky Chant, Natural Gift, Moonlight, Giga Drain, Petal Dance | |
| **Type:** Grass-Poison | |
| **Height:** 1'08"  **Weight:** 11.9 lbs. | |
| **Region:** Kanto | |

ODDISH

GLOOM

VILEPLUME

BELLOSSOM

# OMANYTE
## SPIRAL POKÉMON

Scientists resurrected Omanyte from fossils.

| | |
|---|---|
| **Pronounced:** OHM-uh-nite | |
| **Possible Moves:** Constrict, Withdraw, Bite, Water Gun, Rollout, Leer, Mud Shot, Brine, Protect, AncientPower, Tickle, Rock Blast, Hydro Pump | |
| **Type:** Rock-Water | |
| **Height:** 1'04"  **Weight:** 16.5 lbs. | |
| **Region:** Kanto | |

OMANYTE

OMASTAR

# OMASTAR
## SPIRAL POKÉMON

Because its shell is so large, this Pokémon was thought to be extinct.

**Pronounced:** AHM-uh-star

**Possible Moves:** Constrict, Withdraw, Bite, Water Gun, Rollout, Leer, Mud Shot, Brine, Protect, AncientPower, Spike Cannon, Tickle, Rock Blast, Hydro Pump

**Type:** Rock-Water

**Height:** 3'03"   **Weight:** 77.2 lbs.

**Region:** Kanto

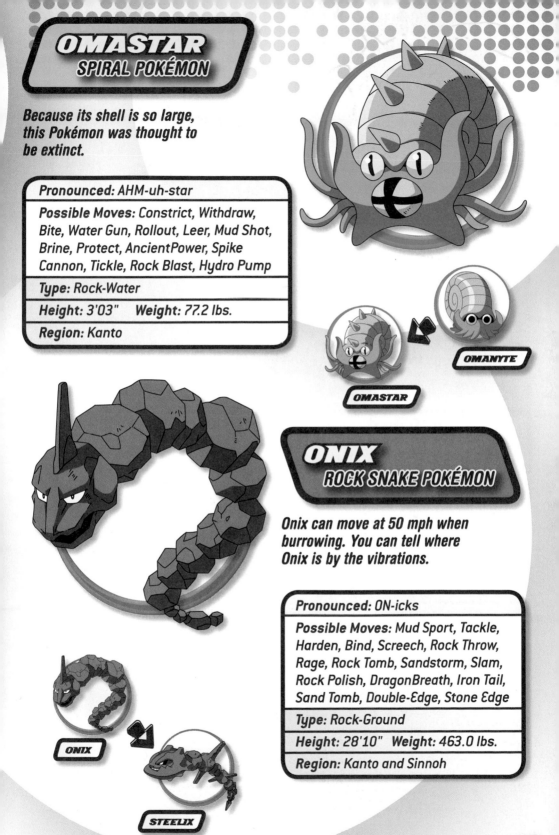

OMANYTE

OMASTAR

# ONIX
## ROCK SNAKE POKÉMON

Onix can move at 50 mph when burrowing. You can tell where Onix is by the vibrations.

**Pronounced:** ON-icks

**Possible Moves:** Mud Sport, Tackle, Harden, Bind, Screech, Rock Throw, Rage, Rock Tomb, Sandstorm, Slam, Rock Polish, DragonBreath, Iron Tail, Sand Tomb, Double-Edge, Stone Edge

**Type:** Rock-Ground

**Height:** 28'10"   **Weight:** 463.0 lbs.

**Region:** Kanto and Sinnoh

ONIX

STEELIX

# PACHIRISU
## ELECTRIC SQUIRREL POKÉMON

Pachirisu lives atop trees and will make electricified fur balls that it hides along with berries it collects. For defense, it shoots electricity from its tail.

**Pronounced:** patch-ee-REE-su

**Possible Moves:** Growl, Bide, Quick Attack, Charm, Spark, Endure, Swift, Sweet Kiss, Discharge, Super Fang, Last Resort

**Type:** Electric

**Height:** 1'04"

**Weight:** 8.6 lbs.

**Region:** Sinnoh

**DOES NOT EVOLVE**

*This mythological creature from the Sinnoh Region is rumored to live in a gap in the spatial dimension, and has the ability to distort space.*

**Pronounced:**
PAL-kee-uh

**Possible Moves:** Dragon-Breath, Scary Face, Water Pulse, AncientPower, Dragon Claw, Spacial Rend, Heal Block, Earth Power, Slash, Aqua Tail, Aura Sphere

**Type:** Water-Dragon

**Height:** 13'09"

**Weight:** 740.8 lbs.

**Region:** Sinnoh

## DOES NOT EVOLVE

# PARAS
## MUSHROOM POKÉMON

Paras grows mushrooms on its back (called tochukaso), and they grow along with Paras.

| | |
|---|---|
| **Pronounced:** PAR-iss | |
| **Possible Moves:** Scratch, Stun Spore, PoisonPowder, Leech Life, Spore, Slash, Growth, Giga Drain, Aromatherapy, X-Scissor | |
| **Type:** Bug-Grass | |
| **Height:** 1'00"   **Weight:** 11.9 lbs. | |
| **Region:** Kanto | |

# PARASECT
## MUSHROOM POKÉMON

The mushroom on its back eventually outgrows Parasect and scatters poisonous spores.

| | |
|---|---|
| **Pronounced:** PAR-i-sect | |
| **Possible Moves:** Cross Poison, Scratch, Stun Spore, PoisonPowder, Leech Life, Spore, Slash, Growth, Giga Drain, Aromatherapy, X-Scissor | |
| **Type:** Bug-Grass | |
| **Height:** 3'03"   **Weight:** 65.0 lbs. | |
| **Region:** Kanto | |

# PELIPPER
## WATER BIRD POKÉMON

Pelipper will gather up prey in its mouth by dipping its large bill in the water. Pelipper also delivers mail in its bill to other Pokémon.

| | |
|---|---|
| **Pronounced:** PEL-ip-purr | |
| **Possible Moves:** Growl, Water Gun, Water Sport, Wing Attack, Supersonic, Mist, Water Pulse, Payback, Protect, Roost, Stockpile, Swallow, Spit Up, Fling, Tailwind, Hydro Pump | |
| **Type:** Water-Flying | |
| **Height:** 3'11"   **Weight:** 61.7 lbs. | |
| **Region:** Hoenn and Sinnoh | |

WINGULL

PELIPPER

# PERSIAN
## CLASSY CAT POKÉMON

A very snobby Pokémon, the jewel on its head is usually the topic of conversation.

| | |
|---|---|
| **Pronounced:** PURR-shin | |
| **Possible Moves:** Switcheroo, Scratch, Growl, Bite, Fake Out, Fury Swipes, Screech, Faint Attack, Taunt, Power Gem, Slash, Nasty Plot, Assurance, Captivate, Night Slash | |
| **Type:** Normal | |
| **Height:** 3'03"   **Weight:** 70.5 lbs. | |
| **Region:** Kanto | |

MEOWTH

PERSIAN

# PHANPY
## LONG NOSE POKÉMON

Diminutive and cute, Phanpy is still capable of lifting an adult onto its back.

**Pronounced:**
FAN-pee

**Possible Moves:** Odor Sleuth, Tackle, Growl, Defense Curl, Flail, Take Down, Rollout, Natural Gift, Slam, Endure, Charm, Last Resort, Double-Edge

**Type:** Ground

**Height:** 1'08"

**Weight:** 73.9 lbs.

**Region:** Johto

PHANPY

DONPHAN

# PHIONE
## SEA DRIFTER POKÉMON
*Legendary Pokémon*

**See that small bubble on Phione's head? It inflates that sac to drift on the ocean surface in warm seas and look for food.**

**Pronounced:** *fee-OWN-ay*

**Possible Moves:** Bubble, Water Sport, Charm, Supersonic, BubbleBeam, Acid Armor, Whirlpool, Water Pulse, Aqua Ring, Dive, Rain Dance

**Type:** Water

**Height:** 1'04"

**Weight:** 6.8 lbs.

**Region:** Sinnoh

## DOES NOT EVOLVE

# PICHU
## TINY MOUSE POKÉMON

Pichu can only store small amounts of electricity in its cheeks, but it does play with others by touching tails and discharging power. Ouch!

| | |
|---|---|
| **Pronounced:** PEE-choo | |
| **Possible Moves:** ThunderShock, Charm, Tail Whip, Thunder Wave, Sweet Kiss, Nasty Plot | |
| **Type:** Electric | |
| **Height:** 1'00"  **Weight:** 4.4 lbs. | |
| **Region:** Johto, Kanto, and Sinnoh | |

PICHU

RAICHU

PIKACHU

# PIDGEOT
## BIRD POKÉMON

Pidgeot commands the winds by whipping them up with its wings, bending even stout trees.

| | |
|---|---|
| **Pronounced:** pid-JEE-ot | |
| **Possible Moves:** Tackle, Sand-Attack, Gust, Quick Attack, Whirlwind, Twister, FeatherDance, Agility, Wing Attack, Roost, Tailwind, Mirror Move, Air Slash | |
| **Type:** Normal-Flying | |
| **Height:** 4'11"  **Weight:** 87.1 lbs. | |
| **Region:** Kanto | |

PIDGEY

PIDGEOTTO

PIDGEOT

# PIDGEOTTO
## BIRD POKÉMON

This Pokémon is very territorial, taking down prey with razor-sharp claws.

| | |
|---|---|
| **Pronounced:** pid-JYO-toe | |
| **Possible Moves:** Tackle, Sand-Attack, Gust, Quick Attack, Whirlwind, Twister, FeatherDance, Agility, Wing Attack, Roost, Tailwind, Mirror Move, Air Slash | |
| **Type:** Normal-Flying | |
| **Height:** 3'07"    **Weight:** 66.1 lbs. | |
| **Region:** Kanto | |

PIDGEOT

PIDGEOTTO

PIDGEY

# PIDGEY
## TINY BIRD POKÉMON

Pidgey is a flyer, not a fighter—but it will defend itself with ferocity when attacked.

| | |
|---|---|
| **Pronounced:** PID-jee | |
| **Possible Moves:** Tackle, Sand-Attack, Gust, Quick Attack, Whirlwind, Twister, FeatherDance, Agility, Wing Attack, Roost, Tailwind, Mirror Move, Air Slash | |
| **Type:** Normal-Flying | |
| **Height:** 1'00"    **Weight:** 4.0 lbs. | |
| **Region:** Kanto | |

PIDGEY

PIDGEOTTO

PIDGEOT

# PIKACHU
## MOUSE POKÉMON

This forest-dwelling Pokémon stores electricity in the pouches of its cheeks. One of them has been Ash's constant companion through the years.

**Pronounced:**
PƐƐK-uh-chew

**Possible Moves:** Thunder-Shock, Growl, Tail Whip, Thunder Wave, Quick Attack, Double Team, Slam, Thunderbolt, Feint, Agility, Discharge, Light Screen, Thunder

**Type:** Electric

**Height:** 1'04"

**Weight:** 13.2 lbs.

**Region:** All Regions

PICHU

PIKACHU

RAICHU

# PILOSWINE
## SWINE POKÉMON

Piloswine uses its sensitive nose to check its surroundings because it can't see through its hairy coat.

**Pronounced:** PILE-oh-swine

**Possible Moves:** AncientPower, Peck, Odor Sleuth, Mud Sport, Powder Snow, Mud-Slap, Endure, Mud Bomb, Icy Wind, Ice Fang, Take Down, Fury Attack, Earthquake, Mist, Blizzard, Amnesia

**Type:** Ice-Ground

**Height:** 3'07"    **Weight:** 123.0 lbs.

**Region:** Johto

MAMOSWINE

PILOSWINE

SWINUB

# PINECO
## BAGWORM POKÉMON

Its pinecone-shaped shell protects it from other Pokémon that try to peck it by mistake.

**Pronounced:** PINE-co

**Possible Moves:** Tackle, Protect, Selfdestruct, Take Down, Rapid Spin, Bide, Natural Gift, Spikes, Payback, Explosion, Iron Defense, Gyro Ball, Double-Edge

**Type:** Bug

**Height:** 2'00"    **Weight:** 15.9 lbs.

**Region:** Johto

PINECO

FORRETRESS

193

# PINSIR
## STAG BEETLE POKÉMON

Pinsir can rip its prey in half with its pincers, and usually tosses what it can't tear—and tosses it far!

| | |
|---|---|
| **Pronounced:** PIN-sir | |
| **Possible Moves:** ViceGrip, Focus Energy, Bind, Seismic Toss, Harden, Revenge, Brick Break, Vital Throw, X-Scissor, Thrash, Swords Dance, Submission, Guillotine, SuperPower | |
| **Type:** Bug | |
| **Height:** 4'11" | **Weight:** 121.3 lbs. |
| **Region:** Kanto | |

*DOES NOT EVOLVE*

# PIPLUP
## PENGUIN POKÉMON

Piplup can dive in icy northern waters for ten minutes at a time. Seems like a lot of trouble, but Piplup is too proud to accept food from humans.

| | |
|---|---|
| **Pronounced:** PIP-plup | |
| **Possible Moves:** Pound, Growl, Bubble, Water Sport, Peck, Bite, BubbleBeam, Fury Attack, Brine, Whirlpool, Mist, Drill Peck, Hydro Pump | |
| **Type:** Water | |
| **Height:** 1'04" | **Weight:** 11.5 lbs. |
| **Region:** Sinnoh | |

PIPLUP

PRINPLUP

EMPOLEON

## CHEERING POKÉMON

Plusle is the cheerleader of Pokémon, cheering on friends with pom-poms made of sparks. It drains power from telephone poles.

Pronounced: PLUS-ull

Possible Moves: Growl, Thunder Wave, Quick Attack, Helping Hand, Spark, Encore, Fake Tears, Copycat, Swift, Charge, Thunder, Baton Pass, Agility, Last Resort, Nasty Plot

Type: Electric

Height: 1'04"   Weight: 9.3 lbs.

Region: Hoenn

*DOES NOT EVOLVE*

## POLITOED
### FROG POKÉMON

This natural leader rallies others to its cause. When it cries, Poliwag seem to obey it.

Pronounced: POL-ee-toad

Possible Moves: BubbleBeam, Hypnosis, DoubleSlap, Perish Song, Bounce, Swagger

Type: Water

Height: 3'07"   Weight: 74.7 lbs.

Region: Johto

POLIWAG

POLIWHIRL

POLITOED

# POLIWAG
## TADPOLE POKÉMON

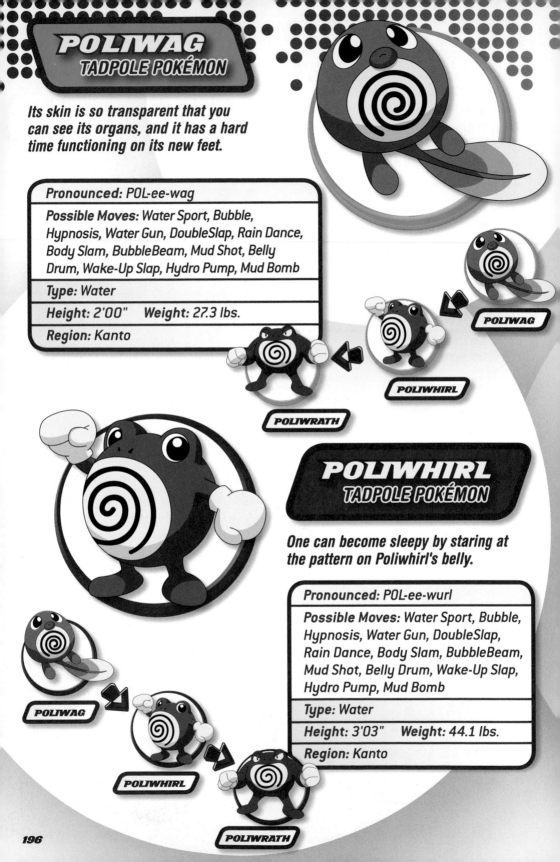

Its skin is so transparent that you can see its organs, and it has a hard time functioning on its new feet.

**Pronounced:** POL-ee-wag

**Possible Moves:** Water Sport, Bubble, Hypnosis, Water Gun, DoubleSlap, Rain Dance, Body Slam, BubbleBeam, Mud Shot, Belly Drum, Wake-Up Slap, Hydro Pump, Mud Bomb

**Type:** Water

**Height:** 2'00"    **Weight:** 27.3 lbs.

**Region:** Kanto

POLIWAG

POLIWHIRL

POLIWRATH

# POLIWHIRL
## TADPOLE POKÉMON

One can become sleepy by staring at the pattern on Poliwhirl's belly.

**Pronounced:** POL-ee-wurl

**Possible Moves:** Water Sport, Bubble, Hypnosis, Water Gun, DoubleSlap, Rain Dance, Body Slam, BubbleBeam, Mud Shot, Belly Drum, Wake-Up Slap, Hydro Pump, Mud Bomb

**Type:** Water

**Height:** 3'03"    **Weight:** 44.1 lbs.

**Region:** Kanto

POLIWAG

POLIWHIRL

POLIWRATH

# POLIWRATH
## TADPOLE POKÉMON

Having great muscles, this Pokémon can swim for long periods of time, and frequents the warmer oceans.

| | |
|---|---|
| **Pronounced:** POL-ee-rath | |
| **Possible Moves:** BubbleBeam, Hypnosis, DoubleSlap, Submission, Dynamicpunch, Mind Reader | |
| **Type:** Water-Fighting | |
| **Height:** 4'03" | **Weight:** 119.0 lbs. |
| **Region:** Kanto | |

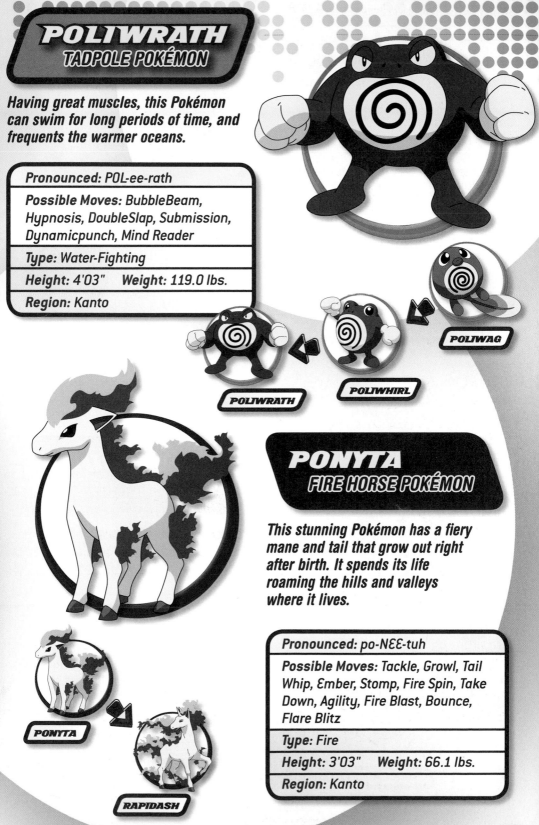

POLIWRATH

POLIWHIRL

POLIWAG

# PONYTA
## FIRE HORSE POKÉMON

This stunning Pokémon has a fiery mane and tail that grow out right after birth. It spends its life roaming the hills and valleys where it lives.

| | |
|---|---|
| **Pronounced:** po-NEE-tuh | |
| **Possible Moves:** Tackle, Growl, Tail Whip, Ember, Stomp, Fire Spin, Take Down, Agility, Fire Blast, Bounce, Flare Blitz | |
| **Type:** Fire | |
| **Height:** 3'03" | **Weight:** 66.1 lbs. |
| **Region:** Kanto | |

PONYTA

RAPIDASH

197

# POOCHYENA
## BITE POKÉMON

Poochyena never gives up, chasing down foes until they are utterly exhausted.

| | |
|---|---|
| **Pronounced:** POO-chee-EH-nah | |
| **Possible Moves:** Tackle, Howl, Sand-Attack, Bite, Odor Sleuth, Roar, Swagger, Assurance, Scary Face, Taunt, Embargo, Take Down, Sucker Punch | |
| **Type:** Dark | |
| **Height:** 1'08" | **Weight:** 30.0 lbs. |
| **Region:** Hoenn | |

POOCHYENA

MIGHTYENA

# PORYGON
## VIRTUAL POKÉMON

This Pokémon can travel through electronic space and was the first artificially created Pokémon.

| | |
|---|---|
| **Pronounced:** POR-eh-gon | |
| **Possible Moves:** Tackle, Conversion, Sharpen, Psybeam, Agility, Recover, Magnet Rise, Signal Beam, Recycle, Discharge, Lock-On, Tri Power, Magic Coat, Zap Cannon | |
| **Type:** Normal | |
| **Height:** 2'07" | **Weight:** 80.5 lbs. |
| **Region:** Kanto | |

PORYGON

PORYGON 2

PORYGON-Z

# PORYGON 2
## VIRTUAL POKÉMON

Porygon-2 can actually work in space thanks to planetary development software loaded into it.

Pronounced: POR-eh-gon-too

**Possible Moves:** Conversion 2, Tackle, Conversion, Defense Curl, Psybeam, Agility, Recover, Magnet Rise, Signal Beam, Recycle, Discharge, Lock-On, Tri Power, Magic Coat, Zap Cannon, Hyper Beam

Type: Normal

Height: 2'00"     Weight: 71.6 lbs.

Region: Johto

PORYGON-Z

PORYGON2

PORYGON

# PORYGON-Z
## VIRTUAL POKÉMON

The additional software that was loaded into Porygon-Z to make it better actually caused it to act in odd and unexpected ways.

Pronounced: POR-eh-gon-zee

**Possible Moves:** Trick Room, Conversion 2, Tackle, Conversion, Nasty Plot, Psybeam, Agility, Recover, Magnet Rise, Signal Beam, Embargo, Discharge, Lock-On, Tri Attack, Magic Coat, Zap Cannon, Hyper Beam

Type: Normal

Height: 2'11"     Weight: 75.0 lbs.

Region: Sinnoh

PORYGON

PORYGON 2

PORYGON-Z

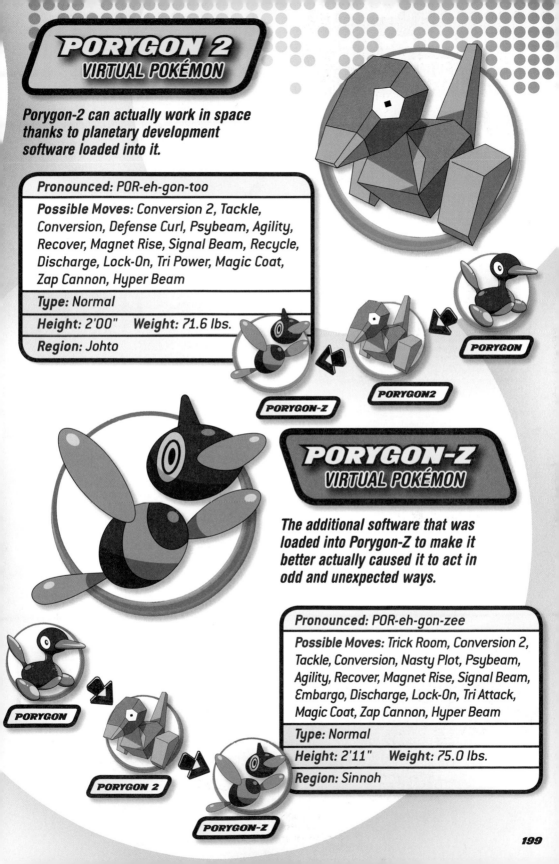

# PRIMEAPE
## PIG MONKEY POKÉMON

*If you look into its eyes, your choices are flight or fight. Either way, Primeape will deliver a ferocious beating.*

| | |
|---|---|
| **Pronounced:** PRIMƐ-ape | |
| **Possible Moves:** Fling, Scratch, Low Kick, Leer, Focus Energy, Fury Swipes, Karate Chop, Seismic Toss, Screech, Assurance, Rage, Swagger, Cross Chop, Thrash, Punishment, Close Combat | |
| **Type:** Fighting | |
| **Height:** 3'03"   **Weight:** 70.5 lbs. | |
| **Region:** Kanto | |

**MANKEY**

**PRIMEAPE**

# PRINPLUP
## PENGUIN POKÉMON

*Prinplup looks for prey in icy waters and will use its wings to break the thickest of trees. It's a loner Pokémon, because each one believes it is the most important one among its kind.*

| | |
|---|---|
| **Pronounced:** PRIN-plup | |
| **Possible Moves:** Tackle, Growl, Bubble, Water Sport, Peck, Metal Chew, Bite, BubbleBeam, Fury Attack, Brine, Whirlpool, Mist, Drill Peck, Hydro Pump | |
| **Type:** Water | |
| **Height:** 2'07"   **Weight:** 50.7 lbs. | |
| **Region:** Sinnoh | |

**PIPLUP**

**PRINPLUP**

**EMPOLEON**

# PROBOPASS
## COMPASS POKÉMON

You can feel the magnetism from this Pokémon on all fronts. It controls three small units called Mini Units.

**Pronounced:**
PRO-bo-pass

**Possible Moves:** Magnet Rise, Gravity, Tackle, Iron Defense, Magnet Bomb, Block, Thunder Wave, Rock Slide, Sandstorm, Rest, Discharge, Stone Edge, Zap Cannon, Lock-On, Earth Power

**Type:** Rock-Steel

**Height:** 4'07"

**Weight:** 749.6 lbs.

**Region:** Sinnoh

NOSEPASS

PROBOPASS

# PSYDUCK
## DUCK POKÉMON

*When its headaches become unbearable, it will use weird powers—but it never remembers them later.*

**Pronounced:**
SYƐ-duck

**Possible Moves:** Water Sport, Scratch, Tail Whip, Water Gun, Disable, Confusion, Water Pulse, Fury Swipes, Screech, Psych Up, Zen Headbutt, Amnesia, Hydro Pump

**Type:** Water

**Height:** 2'07"

**Weight:** 43.2 lbs.

**Region:** All Regions

PSYDUCK

GOLDUCK

# PUPITAR
## HARD SHELL POKÉMON

*By building up gases in its body, Pupitar can shoot itself up like a rocket.*

Pronounced: PUP-i-tar

**Possible Moves:** Bite, Leer, Sandstorm, Screech, Rock Slide, Scary Face, Thrash, Dark Pulse, Payback, Crunch, Earthquake, Stone Edge, Hyper Beam

Type: Rock-Ground

Height: 3'11"    Weight: 335.1 lbs.

Region: Johto

LARVITAR

PUPITAR

TYRANITAR

# PURUGLY
## TIGER CAT POKÉMON

*Purugly will make itself appear bulkier by squeezing its two tails around its waist, and is known to take over other Pokémon's nests.*

Pronounced: prr-UG-lee

**Possible Moves:** Fake Out, Scratch, Growl, Hypnosis, Faint Attack, Fury Swipes, Charm, Assist, Captivate, Slash, Swagger, Body Slam, Attract

Type: Normal

Height: 3'03"    Weight: 96.6 lbs.

Region: Sinnoh

GLAMEOW

PURUGLY

# QUAGSIRE
## WATER FISH POKÉMON

Quagsire is a sluggard that waits for prey to enter its mouth. It doesn't even care if it knocks its head on boats or river rocks.

**Pronounced:** KWAG-sire

**Possible Moves:** Water Gun, Tail Whip, Mud Sport, Mud Shot, Slam, Mud Bomb, Amnesia, Yawn, Earthquake, Rain Dance, Mist, Haze, Muddy Water

**Type:** Water    Ground

**Height:** 4'07"    **Weight:** 165.3 lbs.

**Region:** Johto and Sinnoh

WOOPER

QUAGSIRE

# QUILAVA
## VOLCANO POKÉMON

When Quilava gets ready to fight, the flames around it will burn more intently, intimidating even the most stalwart foes.

**Pronounced:** kwil-LA-va

**Possible Moves:** Tackle, Leer, SmokeScreen, SmokeScreen, Ember, Quick Attack, Flame Wheel, Defense Curl, Swift, Lava Plume, Flamethrower, Rollout, Double-Edge, Eruption

**Type:** Fire

**Height:** 2'11"    **Weight:** 41.9 lbs.

**Region:** Johto

CYNDAQUIL

QUILAVA

TYPHLOSION

# QWILFISH
## BALLOON POKÉMON

Although not a very good swimmer due to its corpulent form, it is still capable of using its poison spines to defeat its foes.

DOES NOT EVOLVE

| | |
|---|---|
| **Pronounced:** KWIL-fish | |
| **Possible Moves:** Spikes, Tackle, Poison Sting, Harden, Minimize, Water Gun, Rollout, Toxic Spikes, Stockpile, Spit Up, Revenge, Brine, Pin Missile, Take Down, Aqua Tail, Poison Jab, Destiny Bond, Hydro Pump | |
| **Type:** Water | Poison |
| **Height:** 1'08" | **Weight:** 8.6 lbs. |
| **Region:** Johto | |

# RAICHU
## MOUSE POKÉMON

Raichu is actually affected by having too much electricity in its body. It becomes aggressive if too much electricity is stored in its body, and can release one hundred thousand volts at a time.

| | |
|---|---|
| **Pronounced:** RYE-chew | |
| **Possible Moves:** ThunderShock, Tail Whip, Quick Attack, Thunderbolt | |
| **Type:** Electric | |
| **Height:** 2'07" | **Weight:** 66.1 lbs. |
| **Region:** All Regions | |

PICHU

PIKACHU

RAICHU

# RAIKOU
## THUNDER POKÉMON
### Legendary Pokémon

Using the rain clouds on its back, Raikou can shoot thunderbolts from them.

**Pronounced:**
*RYE-coo*

**Possible Moves:** *Bite, Leer, ThunderShock, Roar, Quick Attack, Spark, Reflect, Crunch, Thunder Fang, Discharge, Extrasensory, Thunder, Calm Mind*

**Type:** Electric

**Height:** 6'03"

**Weight:** 392.4 lbs.

**Region:** Johto

## DOES NOT EVOLVE

# RALTS
## FEELING POKÉMON

Cheerful people are more likely to see Ralts, which can sense emotions by using the horn on its head.

| | |
|---|---|
| **Pronounced:** RALTS | |
| **Possible Moves:** Growl, Confusion, Double Team, Teleport, Lucky Chant, Magical Leaf, Calm Mind, Psychic, Imprison, Future Sight, Charm, Hypnosis, Dream Eater | |
| **Type:** Psychic | |
| **Height:** 1'04"  **Weight:** 14.6 lbs. | |
| **Region:** Hoenn | |

RALTS

KIRLIA

GARDEVOIR

GALLADE

# RAMPARDOS
## HEADBUTT POKÉMON

Rampardos can take down forests with a headbutt that has enough power to knock over even the sturdiest of objects.

| | |
|---|---|
| **Pronounced:** ram-PAR-dose | |
| **Possible Moves:** Headbutt, Leer, Focus Energy, Pursuit, Take Down, Scary Face, Assurance, AncientPower, Zen Headbutt, Screech, Head Smash | |
| **Type:** Rock | |
| **Height:** 5'03"  **Weight:** 226.0 lbs. | |
| **Region:** Sinnoh | |

CRANIDOS

RAMPARDOS

# RAPIDASH
## FIRE HORSE POKÉMON

A very fast Pokémon, Rapidash can run at nearly 150 mph. It reaches this speed with only ten steps from a dead standstill.

| | |
|---|---|
| **Pronounced:** RAP-i-dash | |
| **Possible Moves:** Poison Jab, Megahorn, Quick Attack, Growl, Tail Whip, Ember, Stomp, Fire Spin, Take Down, Agility, Fire Blast, Fury Attack, Bounce, Flare Blitz | |
| **Type:** Fire | |
| **Height:** 5'07"    **Weight:** 209.4 lbs. | |
| **Region:** Kanto and Sinnoh | |

PONYTA

RAPIDASH

# RATICATE
## MOUSE POKÉMON

The teeth on this Pokémon aren't just for decoration. It whittles its fangs by gnawing on hard material, and its teeth have the power to gnaw through cinderblock walls.

RATTATA

RATICATE

| | |
|---|---|
| **Pronounced:** RAT-i-kate | |
| **Possible Moves:** Swords Dance, Tackle, Tail Whip, Quick Attack, Focus Energy, Bite, Pursuit, Hyper Fang, Sucker Punch, Scary Face, Crunch, Assurance, Super Fang, Double-Edge, Endeavor | |
| **Type:** Normal | |
| **Height:** 2'04"    **Weight:** 40.8 lbs. | |
| **Region:** Kanto | |

## RATTATA
### MOUSE POKÉMON

Rattata is a survivor, able to live in almost any environment or extreme. Don't let its small size fool you.

**Pronounced:**
ruh-TA-tah

**Possible Moves:** Tackle, Tail Whip, Quick Attack, Focus Energy, Bite, Pursuit, Hyper Fang, Sucker Punch, Crunch, Assurance, Super Fang, Double-Edge, Endeavor

**Type:** Normal

**Height:** 1'00"

**Weight:** 7.7 lbs.

**Region:** Kanto

RATTATA

RATICATE

# RAYQUAZA
## SKY HIGH POKÉMON
### Legendary Pokémon

Rayquaza lives high above the ozone layer and is rarely seen by anyone.

**Pronounced:**
ray-KWAZ-uh

**Possible Moves:** Twister, Scary Face, AncientPower, Dragon Claw, Dragon Dance, Crunch, Fly, Rest, ExtremeSpeed, Hyper Beam, Dragon Pulse, Outrage

**Type:** Dragon-Flying

**Height:** 23'00"

**Weight:** 455.2 lbs.

**Region:** Hoenn

**DOES NOT EVOLVE**

# REGICE
## ICEBERG POKÉMON
### Legendary Pokémon

Regice can control air measured at -328 degrees Fahrenheit, and its body is encased in ice.

**Pronounced:**
REDGE-ice

**Possible Moves:** Explosion, Icy Wind, Curse, SuperPower, AncientPower, Amnesia, Charge Beam, Lock-On, Zap Cannon, Ice Beam, Hammer Arm, Hyper Beam

**Type:** Ice

**Height:** 5'11"

**Weight:** 385.8 lbs.

**Region:** Hoenn

## DOES NOT EVOLVE

# REGIGIGAS
## COLOSSAL POKÉMON
### Legendary Pokémon

*According to legend, this mighty Pokémon towed continents with ropes.*

**Pronounced:**
REDGE-ee-gee-gus

**Possible Moves:** Fire Punch, Ice Punch, Thunderpunch, Mega Punch, Knock Off, Confuse Ray, Stomp, SuperPower, Zen Headbutt, Crush Grip, Giga Impact

**Type:** Normal

**Height:** 12'02"

**Weight:** 925.9 lbs.

**Region:** Sinnoh

## DOES NOT EVOLVE

# REGIROCK
## ROCK PEAK POKÉMON
### Legendary Pokémon

Regirock can repair itself in any battle by picking up rocks and attaching them to itself.

**Pronounced:**
REDGE-ee-rock

**Possible Moves:** Explosion, Rock Throw, Curse, Super-Power, AncientPower, Iron Defense, Charge Beam, Lock-On, Zap Cannon, Stone Edge, Hammer Arm, Hyper Beam

**Type:** Rock

**Height:** 5'07"

**Weight:** 507.1 lbs.

**Region:** Hoenn

**DOES NOT EVOLVE**

# REGISTEEL
## IRON POKÉMON
### Legendary Pokémon

Registeel's body has been tempered underground for tens of thousands of years, so its body cannot be scratched.

**Pronounced:**
REDGE-ee-steel

**Possible Moves:** Explosion, Metal Claw, Curse, SuperPower, AncientPower, Iron Defense, Amnesia, Charge Beam, Lock-On, Zap Cannon, Iron Head, Flash Cannon, Hammer Arm, Hyper Beam

**Type:** Steel

**Height:** 6'03"

**Weight:** 451.9 lbs.

**Region:** Hoenn

**DOES NOT EVOLVE**

# RELICANTH
## LONGEVITY POKÉMON

This rare Pokémon was discovered during a deep-sea exploration and has remained unchanged for over one hundred million years.

| | |
|---|---|
| **Pronounced:** REL-uh-canth | |
| **Possible Moves:** Tackle, Harden, Water Gun, Rock Tomb, Yawn, Take Down, Mud Sport, AncientPower, Double-Edge, Dive, Rest, Hydro Pump, Head Smash | |
| **Type:** Water-Rock | |
| **Height:** 3'03" | **Weight:** 51.6 lbs. |
| **Region:** Hoenn | |

*DOES NOT EVOLVE*

# REMORAID
## JET POKÉMON

Remoraid clings to Mantine to feed on their food scraps. It can also shoot down flying prey with forceful squirts from its mouth.

| | |
|---|---|
| **Pronounced:** REM-oh-rade | |
| **Possible Moves:** Water Gun, Lock-On, Psybeam, Aurora Beam, BubbleBeam, Focus Energy, Bullet Seed, Water Pulse, Signal Beam, Ice Beam, Hyper Beam | |
| **Type:** Water | |
| **Height:** 2'00" | **Weight:** 26.5 lbs. |
| **Region:** Johto and Sinnoh | |

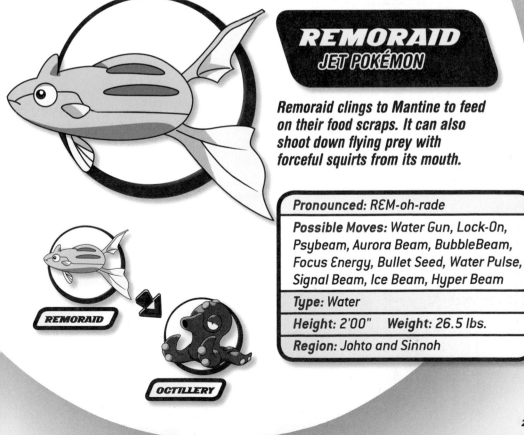

REMORAID

OCTILLERY

# RHYDON
## DRILL POKÉMON

Rhydon can use the horn on its head to barrel through thick rock. It is slightly smarter than Rhyhorn.

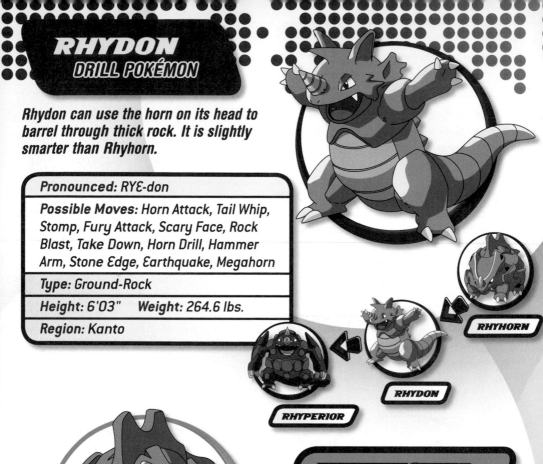

**Pronounced:** RYE-don

**Possible Moves:** Horn Attack, Tail Whip, Stomp, Fury Attack, Scary Face, Rock Blast, Take Down, Horn Drill, Hammer Arm, Stone Edge, Earthquake, Megahorn

**Type:** Ground-Rock

**Height:** 6'03"    **Weight:** 264.6 lbs.

**Region:** Kanto

RHYHORN

RHYDON

RHYPERIOR

# RHYHORN
## SPIKES POKÉMON

Covered in thick hide and able to take down buildings, this Pokémon is not known for its smarts.

**Pronounced:** RYE-horn

**Possible Moves:** Horn Attack, Tail Whip, Stomp, Fury Attack, Scary Face, Rock Blast, Take Down, Horn Drill, Stone Edge, Earthquake, Megahorn

**Type:** Ground-Rock

**Height:** 3'03"    **Weight:** 253.5 lbs.

**Region:** Kanto

RHYHORN

RHYDON

RHYPERIOR

# RHYPERIOR
## DRILL POKÉMON

Rhyperior uses its muscles to shoot rocks (and sometimes Geodude) through holes in its palms.

**Pronounced:** RYƐ-peer-ee-urr

**Possible Moves:** Poison Jab, Horn Attack, Tail Whip, Stomp, Fury Attack, Scary Face, Rock Blast, Take Down, Horn Drill, Hammer Arm, Stone Edge, Earthquake, Megahorn, Rock Wrecker

**Type:** Ground    Rock

**Height:** 7'10"    **Weight:** 623.5 lbs.

**Region:** Sinnoh

RHYHORN

RHYDON

RHYPERIOR

# RIOLU
## EMANATION POKÉMON

Riolu is very agile. It may look small, but it's extremely powerful. You can gauge its emotion from the aura that projects from its body.

**Pronounced:** ree-OH-loo

**Possible Moves:** Quick Attack, Foresight, Endure, Counter, Force Palm, Feint, Reversal, Screech, Copycat

**Type:** Fighting

**Height:** 2'04"    **Weight:** 44.5 lbs.

**Region:** Sinnoh

RIOLU

LUCARIO

# ROSELIA
## THORN POKÉMON

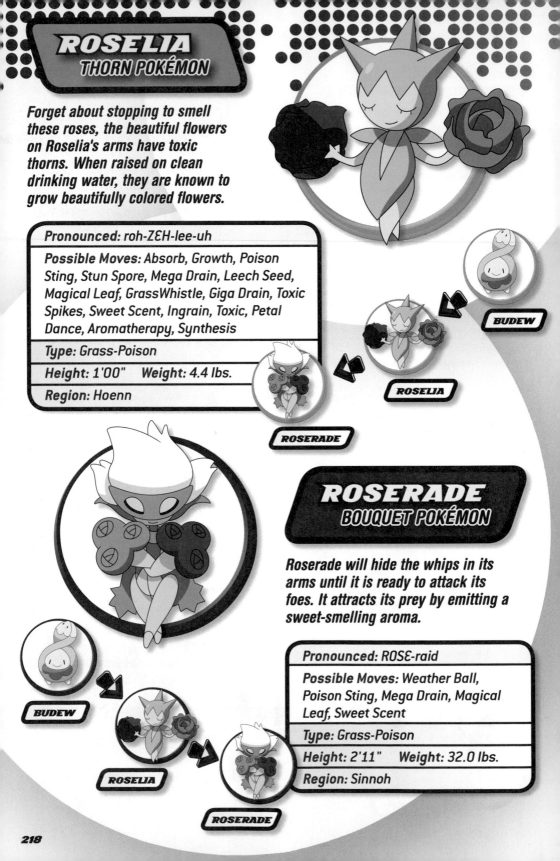

Forget about stopping to smell these roses, the beautiful flowers on Roselia's arms have toxic thorns. When raised on clean drinking water, they are known to grow beautifully colored flowers.

Pronounced: roh-ZEH-lee-uh

Possible Moves: Absorb, Growth, Poison Sting, Stun Spore, Mega Drain, Leech Seed, Magical Leaf, GrassWhistle, Giga Drain, Toxic Spikes, Sweet Scent, Ingrain, Toxic, Petal Dance, Aromatherapy, Synthesis

Type: Grass-Poison

Height: 1'00"    Weight: 4.4 lbs.

Region: Hoenn

BUDEW

ROSELIA

ROSERADE

# ROSERADE
## BOUQUET POKÉMON

Roserade will hide the whips in its arms until it is ready to attack its foes. It attracts its prey by emitting a sweet-smelling aroma.

Pronounced: ROSE-raid

Possible Moves: Weather Ball, Poison Sting, Mega Drain, Magical Leaf, Sweet Scent

Type: Grass-Poison

Height: 2'11"    Weight: 32.0 lbs.

Region: Sinnoh

BUDEW

ROSELIA

ROSERADE

# ROTOM
## PLASMA POKÉMON
### Legendary Pokémon

This destructive little Pokémon gets into electronic devices and causes lots of damage, which is easy for Rotom since it is composed of plasma.

**Pronounced:**
ROW-tom

**Possible Moves:** Trick, Astonish, Thunder Wave, ThunderShock, Confuse Ray, Uproar, Double Team, Shock Wave, Ominous Wind, Substitute, Charge, Discharge

**Type:** Electric-Ghost

**Height:** 1'00"

**Weight:** 0.7 lbs.

**Region:** Sinnoh

**DOES NOT EVOLVE**

# SABLEYE
## DARKNESS POKÉMON

Sableye's eyes have been transformed into gemstones as a result of its steady diet of gems. It loves the darkness of caves.

**Pronounced:** SAY-bull-eye

**Possible Moves:** Leer, Scratch, Foresight, Night Shade, Astonish, Fury Swipes, Fake Out, Detect, Shadow Sneak, Knock Off, Faint Attack, Punishment, Shadow Claw, Power Gem, Confuse Ray, Zen Headbutt, Shadow Ball, Mean Look

**Type:** Dark-Ghost

**Height:** 1'08"    **Weight:** 24.3 lbs.

**Region:** Hoenn

*DOES NOT EVOLVE*

# SALAMENCE
## DRAGON POKÉMON

Because its pre-evolved form, Bagon, always dreamed of flying, Salamence's cellular structure changed: It grew wings and is able to fly.

BAGON

SHELGON

SALAMENCE

**Pronounced:** SAL-uh-mence

**Possible Moves:** Fire Fang, Thunder Fang, Rage, Bite, Leer, Headbutt, Focus Energy, Ember, Protect, DragonBreath, Zen Headbutt, Scary Face, Fly, Crunch, Dragon Claw, Double-Edge

**Type:** Dragon-Flying

**Height:** 4'11"    **Weight:** 226.2 lbs.

**Region:** Hoenn

# SANDSHREW
## MOUSE POKÉMON

This Pokémon curls into a defensive ball when attacked, and survives in mostly arid areas.

| | |
|---|---|
| **Pronounced:** SAND-shroo | |
| **Possible Moves:** Scratch, Defense Curl, Sand-Attack, Poison Sting, Rapid Spin, Swift, Fury Swipes, Rollout, Fury Cutter, Sand Tomb, Slash, Gyro Ball, Sandstorm | |
| **Type:** Ground | |
| **Height:** 2'00" | **Weight:** 26.5 lbs. |
| **Region:** Kanto | |

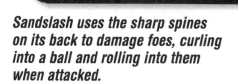

SANDSLASH

SANDSHREW

# SANDSLASH
## MOUSE POKÉMON

Sandslash uses the sharp spines on its back to damage foes, curling into a ball and rolling into them when attacked.

| | |
|---|---|
| **Pronounced:** SAND-slash | |
| **Possible Moves:** Scratch, Defense Curl, Sand-Attack, Poison Sting, Rapid Spin, Swift, Fury Swipes, Rollout, Crush Claw, Fury Cutter, Sand Tomb, Slash, Gyro Ball, Sandstorm | |
| **Type:** Ground | |
| **Height:** 3'03" | **Weight:** 65.0 lbs. |
| **Region:** Kanto | |

SANDSHREW

SANDSLASH

# SCEPTILE
## FOREST POKÉMON

Unmatched in jungle combat, Sceptile can take down trees using the razor-sharp leaves on its arms.

**Pronounced:**
SEP-tile

**Possible Moves:** Night Slash, Pound, Leer, Absorb, Quick Attack, X-Scissor, Pursuit, Screech, Leaf Blade, Agility, Slam, Detect, False Swipe, Leaf Storm

**Type:** Grass

**Height:** 5'07"

**Weight:** 115.1 lbs.

**Region:** Hoenn

TREECKO

GROVYLE

SCEPTILE

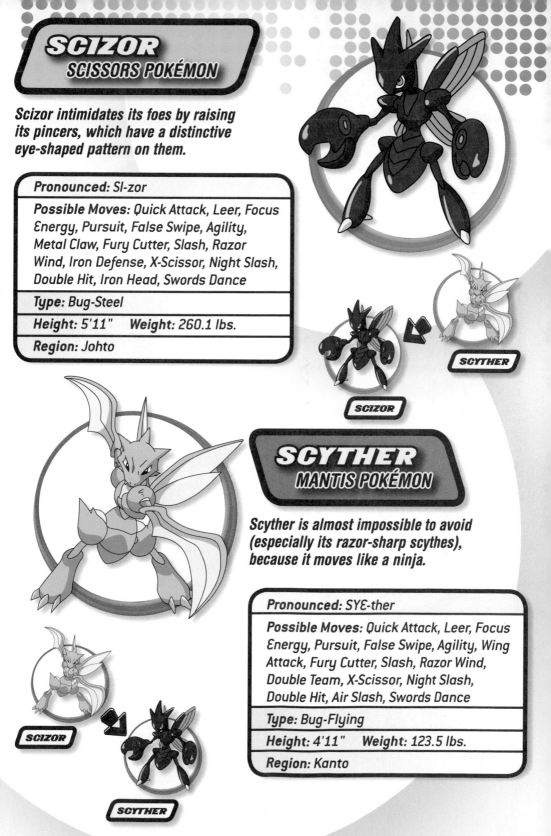

# SCIZOR
## SCISSORS POKÉMON

Scizor intimidates its foes by raising its pincers, which have a distinctive eye-shaped pattern on them.

| | |
|---|---|
| **Pronounced:** | SI-zor |

**Possible Moves:** Quick Attack, Leer, Focus Energy, Pursuit, False Swipe, Agility, Metal Claw, Fury Cutter, Slash, Razor Wind, Iron Defense, X-Scissor, Night Slash, Double Hit, Iron Head, Swords Dance

**Type:** Bug-Steel

**Height:** 5'11"     **Weight:** 260.1 lbs.

**Region:** Johto

SCYTHER

SCIZOR

# SCYTHER
## MANTIS POKÉMON

Scyther is almost impossible to avoid (especially its razor-sharp scythes), because it moves like a ninja.

**Pronounced:** SYE-ther

**Possible Moves:** Quick Attack, Leer, Focus Energy, Pursuit, False Swipe, Agility, Wing Attack, Fury Cutter, Slash, Razor Wind, Double Team, X-Scissor, Night Slash, Double Hit, Air Slash, Swords Dance

**Type:** Bug-Flying

**Height:** 4'11"     **Weight:** 123.5 lbs.

**Region:** Kanto

SCIZOR

SCYTHER

# SEADRA
## DRAGON POKÉMON

Located in its fins and bones are ingredients used to make medicine—but its spine is used purely for protection.

| | |
|---|---|
| **Pronounced:** SEE-druh | |
| **Possible Moves:** Bubble, SmokeScreen, Leer, Water Gun, Focus Energy, BubbleBeam, Agility, Twister, Brine, Hydro Pump, Dragon Dance, Dragon Pulse | |
| **Type:** Water | |
| **Height:** 3'11" | **Weight:** 55.1 lbs. |
| **Region:** Kanto | |

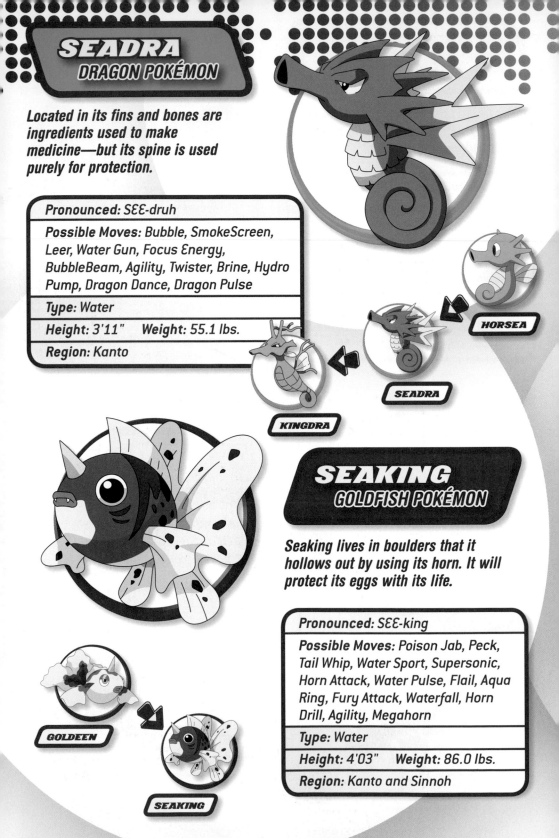

HORSEA

SEADRA

KINGDRA

# SEAKING
## GOLDFISH POKÉMON

Seaking lives in boulders that it hollows out by using its horn. It will protect its eggs with its life.

| | |
|---|---|
| **Pronounced:** SEE-king | |
| **Possible Moves:** Poison Jab, Peck, Tail Whip, Water Sport, Supersonic, Horn Attack, Water Pulse, Flail, Aqua Ring, Fury Attack, Waterfall, Horn Drill, Agility, Megahorn | |
| **Type:** Water | |
| **Height:** 4'03" | **Weight:** 86.0 lbs. |
| **Region:** Kanto and Sinnoh | |

GOLDEEN

SEAKING

# SEALEO
## BALL ROLL POKÉMON

Sealeo can learn different smells and textures by constantly spinning things on its nose.

| | |
|---|---|
| **Pronounced:** SEEL-ee-oh | |
| **Possible Moves:** Powder Snow, Growl, Water Gun, Encore, Ice Ball, Body Slam, Aurora Beam, Hail, Swagger, Rest, Snore, Blizzard, Sheer Cold | |
| **Type:** Ice-Water | |
| **Height:** 3'07" | **Weight:** 193.1 lbs. |
| **Region:** Hoenn | |

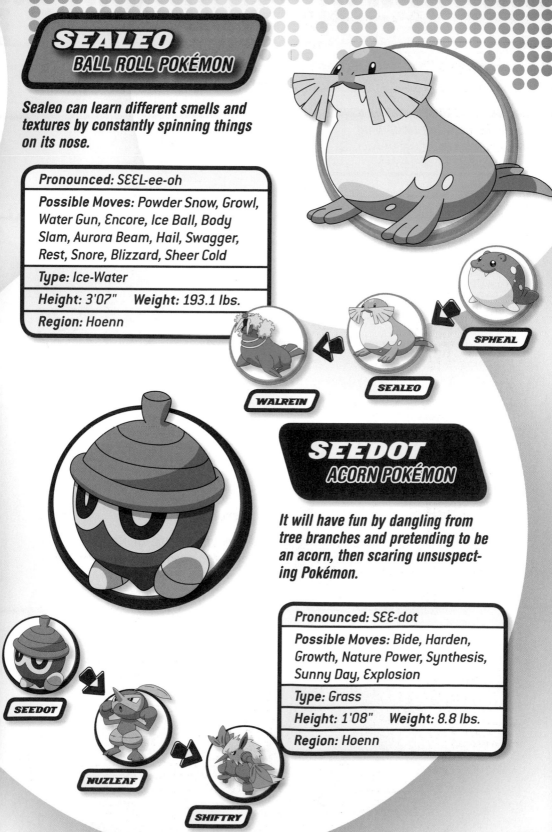

WALREIN SEALEO SPHEAL

# SEEDOT
## ACORN POKÉMON

It will have fun by dangling from tree branches and pretending to be an acorn, then scaring unsuspecting Pokémon.

| | |
|---|---|
| **Pronounced:** SEE-dot | |
| **Possible Moves:** Bide, Harden, Growth, Nature Power, Synthesis, Sunny Day, Explosion | |
| **Type:** Grass | |
| **Height:** 1'08" | **Weight:** 8.8 lbs. |
| **Region:** Hoenn | |

SEEDOT NUZLEAF SHIFTRY

# SEEL
## SEA LION POKÉMON

The point on Seel's head is used to break ice while swimming below icebergs.

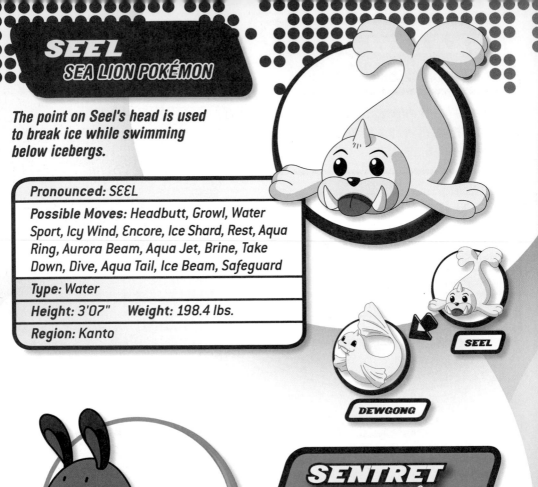

**Pronounced:** SEEL

**Possible Moves:** Headbutt, Growl, Water Sport, Icy Wind, Encore, Ice Shard, Rest, Aqua Ring, Aurora Beam, Aqua Jet, Brine, Take Down, Dive, Aqua Tail, Ice Beam, Safeguard

**Type:** Water

**Height:** 3'07"    **Weight:** 198.4 lbs.

**Region:** Kanto

DEWGONG    SEEL

# SENTRET
## SCOUT POKÉMON

Cautious by nature, Sentret will stand on its tail to scan wide areas for foes.

**Pronounced:** SEN-tret

**Possible Moves:** Scratch, Foresight, Defense Curl, Quick Attack, Fury Swipes, Helping Hand, Follow Me, Slam, Rest, Sucker Punch, Amnesia, Baton Pass, Me First, Hyper Voice

**Type:** Normal

**Height:** 2'07"    **Weight:** 13.2 lbs.

**Region:** Johto

SENTRET    FURRET

# SEVIPER
## FANG SNAKE POKÉMON

Seviper uses rocks to sharpen its tail for battle. Its greatest rival is Zangoose.

| |
|---|
| **Pronounced:** seh-VIƐ-per |
| **Possible Moves:** Wrap, Lick, Bite, Poison Tail, Screech, Glare, Crunch, Poison Fang, Swagger, Haze, Night Slash, Poison Jab, Wring Out |
| **Type:** Poison |
| **Height:** 8'10"  **Weight:** 115.7 lbs. |
| **Region:** Hoenn |

DOES NOT EVOLVE

# SHARPEDO
## BRUTAL POKÉMON

Sharpedo have been clocked swimming at 75 mph, and their fangs, which can rip through sheet iron, are one of the reasons that this Pokémon is known as the Bully of the Sea.

| |
|---|
| **Pronounced:** shar-PEƐ-do |
| **Possible Moves:** Leer, Bite, Rage, Focus Energy, Scary Face, Ice Fang, Screech, Swagger, Assurance, Crunch, Slash, Aqua Jet, Taunt, Agility, Skull Bash, Night Slash |
| **Type:** Water-Dark |
| **Height:** 5'11"  **Weight:** 195.8 lbs. |
| **Region:** Hoenn |

CARVANHA

SHARPEDO

# SHEDINJA
## SHED POKÉMON

Shedinja came to life from a discarded bug shell; it is said that if you look into the crack on its back, it can steal your soul.

**Pronounced:** sheh-DIN-ja

**Possible Moves:** Scratch, Harden, Leech Life, Sand-Attack, Fury Swipes, Mind Reader, Spite, Confuse Ray, Shadow Sneak, Grudge, Heal Block, Shadow Ball

**Type:** Bug-Ghost

**Height:** 2'07"　　**Weight:** 2.6 lbs.

**Region:** Hoenn

NINCADA

SHEDINJA

# SHELGON
## ENDURANCE POKÉMON

Shelgon's shell acts like a cocoon and will peel off the day it evolves.

**Pronounced:** SHELL-gon

**Possible Moves:** Rage, Bite, Leer, Headbutt, Focus Energy, Ember, Protect, DragonBreath, Zen Headbutt, Scary Face, Crunch, Dragon Claw, Double-Edge

**Type:** Dragon

**Height:** 3'07"　　**Weight:** 243.6 lbs.

**Region:** Hoenn

BAGON

SHELGON

SALAMENCE

# SHELLDER
## BIVALVE POKÉMON

By opening and closing its two shells it can swim backward, and its large tongue always hangs out.

| |
|---|
| **Pronounced:** SHELL-der |
| **Possible Moves:** Tackle, Withdraw, Supersonic, Icicle Spear, Protect, Leer, Clamp, Ice Shard, Aurora Beam, Whirlpool, Iron Defense, Brine, Ice Beam |
| **Type:** Water |
| **Height:** 1'00"   **Weight:** 8.8 lbs. |
| **Region:** Kanto |

CLOYSTER

SHELLDER

# SHELLOS (EAST)
## SEA SLUG POKÉMON

Like Gastrodon, Shellos will look quite different depending upon where it lives.

| |
|---|
| **Pronounced:** SHELL-oss |
| **Possible Moves:** Mud-Slap, Mud Sport, Harden, Water Pulse, Mud Bomb, Hidden Power, Rain Dance, Body Slam, Muddy Water, Recover |
| **Type:** Water |
| **Height:** 1'00"   **Weight:** 13.9 lbs. |
| **Region:** Sinnoh |

SHELLOS
(EAST SEA)

GASTRODON
(EAST SEA)

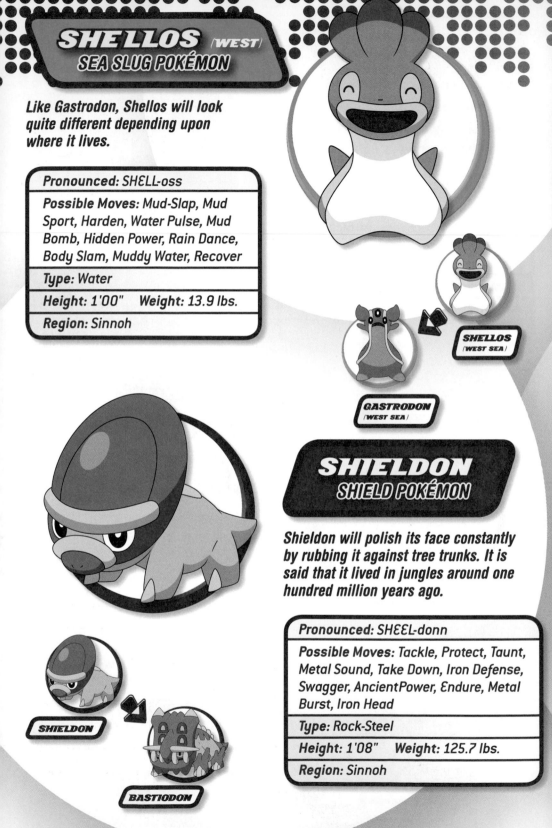

# SHELLOS (WEST)
## SEA SLUG POKÉMON

Like Gastrodon, Shellos will look quite different depending upon where it lives.

| | |
|---|---|
| **Pronounced:** SHELL-oss | |
| **Possible Moves:** Mud-Slap, Mud Sport, Harden, Water Pulse, Mud Bomb, Hidden Power, Rain Dance, Body Slam, Muddy Water, Recover | |
| **Type:** Water | |
| **Height:** 1'00" | **Weight:** 13.9 lbs. |
| **Region:** Sinnoh | |

SHELLOS (WEST SEA)

GASTRODON (WEST SEA)

# SHIELDON
## SHIELD POKÉMON

Shieldon will polish its face constantly by rubbing it against tree trunks. It is said that it lived in jungles around one hundred million years ago.

| | |
|---|---|
| **Pronounced:** SHEEL-donn | |
| **Possible Moves:** Tackle, Protect, Taunt, Metal Sound, Take Down, Iron Defense, Swagger, AncientPower, Endure, Metal Burst, Iron Head | |
| **Type:** Rock-Steel | |
| **Height:** 1'08" | **Weight:** 125.7 lbs. |
| **Region:** Sinnoh | |

SHIELDON

BASTIODON

# SHIFTRY
## WICKED POKÉMON

Shiftry uses its leafy fan to whip up winds of one hundred feet per second that take down houses.

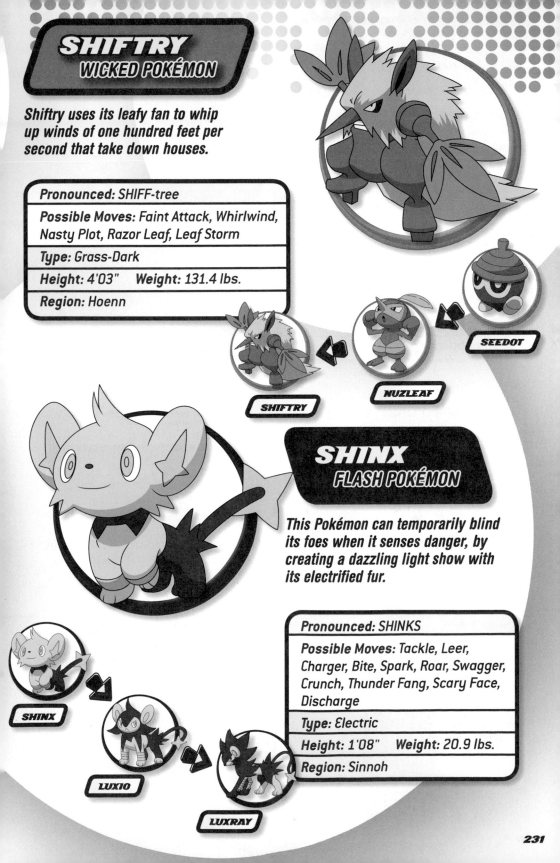

**Pronounced:** SHIFF-tree

**Possible Moves:** Faint Attack, Whirlwind, Nasty Plot, Razor Leaf, Leaf Storm

**Type:** Grass-Dark

**Height:** 4'03"     **Weight:** 131.4 lbs.

**Region:** Hoenn

SEEDOT

SHIFTRY

NUZLEAF

# SHINX
## FLASH POKÉMON

This Pokémon can temporarily blind its foes when it senses danger, by creating a dazzling light show with its electrified fur.

**Pronounced:** SHINKS

**Possible Moves:** Tackle, Leer, Charger, Bite, Spark, Roar, Swagger, Crunch, Thunder Fang, Scary Face, Discharge

**Type:** Electric

**Height:** 1'08"     **Weight:** 20.9 lbs.

**Region:** Sinnoh

SHINX

LUXIO

LUXRAY

# SHROOMISH
## MUSHROOM POKÉMON

If you inhale the poison that Shroomish emits from the top of its head, you will be wracked with pain.

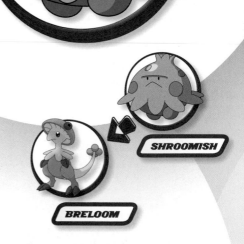

| Pronounced: SHROOM-ish |
|---|
| **Possible Moves:** Absorb, Tackle, Stun Spore, Leech Seed, Mega Drain, Headbutt, PoisonPowder, Worry Seed, Growth, Giga Drain, Seed Bomb, Spore |
| **Type:** Grass |
| **Height:** 1'04"   **Weight:** 9.9 lbs. |
| **Region:** Hoenn |

BRELOOM

SHROOMISH

DOES NOT EVOLVE

# SHUCKLE
## MOLD POKÉMON

Shuckle stores berries in its shell, which eventually ferment into delicious juice.

| Pronounced: SHUCK-kull |
|---|
| **Possible Moves:** Withdraw, Constrict, Bide, Encore, Safeguard, Wrap, Rest, Gastro Acid, Power Trick |
| **Type:** Bug-Rock |
| **Height:** 2'00"   **Weight:** 45.2 lbs. |
| **Region:** Johto |

Shuppet thrives on vengeful emotions, and will often hide in the houses of people who want revenge on someone or something.

| | |
|---|---|
| **Pronounced:** SHUP-pett | |
| **Possible Moves:** Knock Off, Screech, Night Shade, Curse, Spite, Shadow Sneak, Will-O-Wisp, Faint Attack, Shadow Ball, Sucker Punch, Embargo, Snatch, Grudge, Trick | |
| **Type:** Ghost | |
| **Height:** 2'00" | **Weight:** 5.1 lbs. |
| **Region:** Hoenn | |

BANETTE    SHUPPET

# SILCOON
## COCOON POKÉMON

Silcoon will stay motionless until it evolves, and anchors itself by using silk from its body to wrap itself up in twigs.

| | |
|---|---|
| **Pronounced:** sill-COON | |
| **Possible Moves:** Harden | |
| **Type:** Bug | |
| **Height:** 2'00" | **Weight:** 22.0 lbs. |
| **Region:** Hoenn and Sinnoh | |

WURMPLE

SILCOON

BEAUTIFLY

# SKARMORY
## ARMOR BIRD POKÉMON

Even though Skarmory's body is covered in iron armor, it can fly at over 180 mph.

| | |
|---|---|
| **Pronounced:** SKAR-more-ree | |
| **Possible Moves:** Leer, Peck, Sand-Attack, Swift, Agility, Fury Attack, Air Cutter, Spikes, Metal Sound, Steel Wing, Air Slash, Slash, Night Slash | |
| **Type:** Steel-Flying | |
| **Height:** 5'07"    **Weight:** 111.3 lbs. | |
| **Region:** Johto | |

DOES NOT EVOLVE

# SKIPLOOM
## COTTONWEED POKÉMON

Skiploom will float in the sky to absorb as much sunlight as it can, and will bloom when the weather is warm.

| | |
|---|---|
| **Pronounced:** SKIP-loom | |
| **Possible Moves:** Splash, Synthesis, Tail Whip, Tackle, PoisonPowder, Stun Spore, Sleep Powder, Bullet Seed, Leech Seed, Mega Drain, Cotton Spore, U-Turn, Worry Seed, Giga Drain, Bounce, Memento | |
| **Type:** Grass-Flying | |
| **Height:** 2'00"    **Weight:** 2.2 lbs. | |
| **Region:** Johto | |

HOPPIP

SKIPLOOM

JUMPLUFF

# SKITTY
## KITTEN POKÉMON

Skitty will run in circles chasing its own tail. It will look for any excuse to chase moving objects—or Pokémon.

| | |
|---|---|
| **Pronounced:** SKIT-tee | |
| **Possible Moves:** Fake Out, Growl, Tail Whip, Tackle, Attract, Sing, Copycat, DoubleSlap, Assist, Charm, Faint Attack, Wake-Up Slap, Covet, Heal Bell, Double-Edge, Captivate | |
| **Type:** Normal | |
| **Height:** 2'00" | **Weight:** 24.3 lbs. |
| **Region:** Hoenn | |

DELCATTY

SKITTY

# SKORUPI
## SCORPIAN POKÉMON

Skorupi will bury itself in sand to surprise its prey. Once its prey is in its claws, Skorupi will inject it with poison.

| | |
|---|---|
| **Pronounced:** sco-ROO-pee | |
| **Possible Moves:** Bite, Poison Sting, Leer, Pin Missile, Acupressure, Knock Off, Scary Face, Toxic Spikes, Poison Fang, Crunch, Cross Poison | |
| **Type:** Poison-Bug | |
| **Height:** 2'07" | **Weight:** 26.5 lbs. |
| **Region:** Sinnoh | |

SKORUPI

DRAPION

# SKUNTANK
## SKUNK POKÉMON

Skuntank is able to spray its stench hundreds of feet away, and the longer it lingers, the worse it will smell.

**Pronounced:** SKUN-tank

**Possible Moves:** Scratch, Focus Energy, Poison Gas, Screech, Fury Swipes, SmokeScreen, Toxic, Slash, Night Slash, Flamethrower, Memento, Explosion

**Type:** Poison-Dark

**Height:** 3'03"    **Weight:** 83.8 lbs.

**Region:** Sinnoh

STUNKY

SKUNTANK

# SLAKING
## LAZY POKÉMON

Although dubbed The World's Laziest Pokémon, Slaking is actually storing energy for attacks.

**Pronounced:** SLAH-king

**Possible Moves:** Scratch, Yawn, Encore, Slack Off, Faint Attack, Amnesia, Covet, Swagger, Counter, Flail, Fling, Punishment, Hammer Arm

**Type:** Normal

**Height:** 6'07"    **Weight:** 287.7 lbs.

**Region:** Hoenn

SLAKOTH

VIGOROTH

SLAKING

# SLAKOTH
## SLACKER POKÉMON

*Just looking at this Pokémon can make you sleepy, and no wonder—it spends all day lounging around.*

| |
|---|
| **Pronounced:** SLAH-koth |
| **Possible Moves:** Scratch, Yawn, Encore, Slack Off, Faint Attack, Amnesia, Covet, Counter, Flail |
| **Type:** Normal |
| **Height:** 2'07"  **Weight:** 52.9 lbs. |
| **Region:** Hoenn |

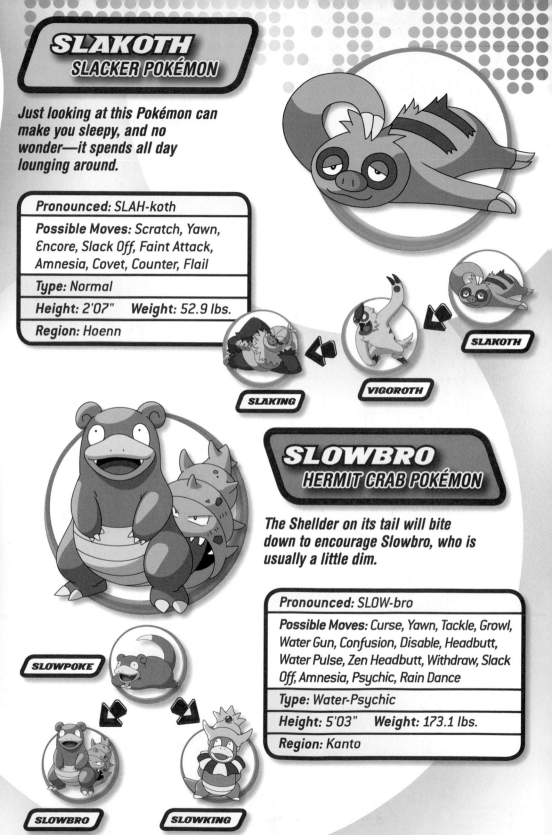

SLAKING

VIGOROTH

SLAKOTH

# SLOWBRO
## HERMIT CRAB POKÉMON

*The Shellder on its tail will bite down to encourage Slowbro, who is usually a little dim.*

| |
|---|
| **Pronounced:** SLOW-bro |
| **Possible Moves:** Curse, Yawn, Tackle, Growl, Water Gun, Confusion, Disable, Headbutt, Water Pulse, Zen Headbutt, Withdraw, Slack Off, Amnesia, Psychic, Rain Dance |
| **Type:** Water-Psychic |
| **Height:** 5'03"  **Weight:** 173.1 lbs. |
| **Region:** Kanto |

SLOWPOKE

SLOWBRO

SLOWKING

# SLOWKING
## ROYAL POKÉMON

Unlike Slowbro and Slowpoke, when bitten by the Shellder on its tail, Slowking's intelligence rises to that of well-known scientists.

| |
|---|
| **Pronounced:** SLOW-king |
| **Possible Moves:** Hidden Power, Curse, Yawn, Tackle, Growl, Water Gun, Confusion, Disable, Headbutt, Water Pulse, Zen Headbutt, Nasty Plot, Swagger, Psychic, Trump Card, Psych Up |
| **Type:** Water-Psychic |
| **Height:** 6'07"   **Weight:** 175.3 lbs. |
| **Region:** Johto |

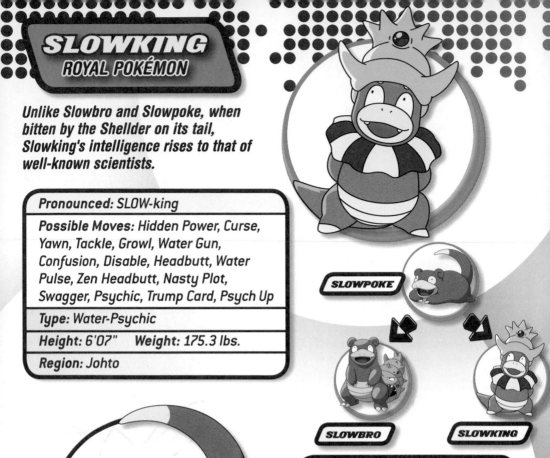

SLOWPOKE

SLOWBRO

SLOWKING

# SLOWPOKE
## DOPEY POKÉMON

Even though it's very slow, it has figured out how to use its tail (which doesn't register pain) to fish.

| |
|---|
| **Pronounced:** SLOW-poke |
| **Possible Moves:** Curse, Yawn, Tackle, Growl, Water Gun, Confusion, Disable, Headbutt, Water Pulse, Zen Headbutt, Slack Off, Amnesia, Psychic, Rain Dance |
| **Type:** Water-Psychic |
| **Height:** 3'11"   **Weight:** 79.4 lbs. |
| **Region:** Kanto |

SLOWPOKE

SLOWBRO

SLOWKING

# SLUGMA
## LAVA POKÉMON

This Pokémon needs to move constantly or the magma in its body will cool and harden.

| | |
|---|---|
| **Pronounced:** SLUG-ma | |
| **Possible Moves:** Yawn, Smog, Ember, Rock Throw, Harden, Recover, AncientPower, Amnesia, Lava Plume, Rock Slide, Body Slam, Flamethrower, Earth Power | |
| **Type:** Fire | |
| **Height:** 2'04" | **Weight:** 77.2 lbs. |
| **Region:** Johto | |

MAGCARGO    SLUGMA

DOES NOT EVOLVE

# SMEARGLE
## PAINTER POKÉMON

Using its tail like a paintbrush to claim its territory, Smeargle is capable of over five thousand different marks.

| | |
|---|---|
| **Pronounced:** SMEAR-gull | |
| **Possible Moves:** Sketch | |
| **Type:** Normal | |
| **Height:** 3'11" | **Weight:** 127.9 lbs. |
| **Region:** Johto | |

# SMOOCHUM
## KISS POKÉMON

Smoochum's lips will remember all the good and bad things it likes and dislikes.

**Pronounced:** SMOO-chum

**Possible Moves:** Pound, Lick, Sweet Kiss, Powder Snow, Confusion, Sing, Mean Look, Fake Tears, Lucky Chant, Avalanche, Psychic, Copycat, Perish Song, Blizzard

**Type:** Ice-Psychic

**Height:** 1'04"    **Weight:** 13.2 lbs.

**Region:** Johto

SMOOCHUM

JYNX

# SNEASEL
## SHARP CLAW POKÉMON

Using its hooked claws to defeat its prey, Sneasel will stop at nothing—even after the prey is incapable of moving.

**Pronounced:** SNEE-zul

**Possible Moves:** Scratch, Leer, Taunt, Quick Attack, Screech, Faint Attack, Fury Swipes, Agility, Icy Wind, Slash, Beat Up, Metal Claw, Ice Shard

**Type:** Dark-Ice

**Height:** 2'11"    **Weight:** 61.7 lbs.

**Region:** Johto and Sinnoh

SNEASEL

WEAVILE

# SNORLAX
## SLEEPING POKÉMON

Snorlax will eat anything—even rotten food—and feasts all day, stopping only to sleep.

Pronounced: SNORE-lacks

**Possible Moves:** Tackle, Defense Curl, Amnesia, Lick, Belly Drum, Yawn, Rest, Snore, Sleep Talk, Body Slam, Block, Rollout, Crunch, Giga Impact

**Type:** Normal

**Height:** 6'11"    **Weight:** 1014.1 lbs.

**Region:** Kanto and Sinnoh

SNORLAX

MUNCHLAX

# SNORUNT
## SNOW HAT POKÉMON

If a Snorunt appears at a home, it is said that the house will prosper. It lives in snowy countries.

Pronounced: SNOW-runt

**Possible Moves:** Powder Snow, Leer, Double Team, Bite, Icy Wind, Headbutt, Protect, Ice Fang, Crunch, Ice Shard, Hail, Blizzard

**Type:** Ice

**Height:** 2'04"    **Weight:** 37.0 lbs.

**Region:** Hoenn

SNORUNT

GLALIE

FROSLASS

# SNOVER
## FROST TREE POKÉMON

Having only had minor contact with humans, Snover tends to be curious. It lives on snowy mountains and grows berries around its belly every spring.

Pronounced: SNOW-vurr

Possible Moves: Powder Snow, Leer, Razor Leaf, Icy Wind, GrassWhistle, Swagger, Mist, Ice Shard, Ingrain, Wood Hammer, Blizzard, Sheer Cold

Type: Grass-Ice

Height: 3'03"  Weight: 111.3 lbs.

Region: Sinnoh

ABOMASNOW

SNOVER

# SNUBBULL
## FAIRY POKÉMON

Although considered cute by some women, most small creatures will flee from its scary face.

Pronounced: SNUB-bull

Possible Moves: Ice Fang, Fire Fang, Thunder Fang, Tackle, Scary Face, Tail Whip, Charm, Bite, Lick, Headbutt, Roar, Rage, Take Down, Payback, Crunch

Type: Normal

Height: 2'00"  Weight: 17.2 lbs.

Region: Johto

SNUBBULL

GRANBULL

# SOLROCK
## METEORITE POKÉMON

Unlike the moonish Lunatone, Solrock is rumored to be more sun-oriented, and gives off a sunlight-like glow while spinning.

| | |
|---|---|
| **Pronounced:** SOL-rock | |
| **Possible Moves:** Tackle, Harden, Confusion, Rock Throw, Fire Spin, Rock Polish, Psywave, Embargo, Cosmic Power, Heal Block, Rock Slide, SolarBeam, Explosion | |
| **Type:** Rock-Psychic | |
| **Height:** 3'11" | **Weight:** 339.5 lbs. |
| **Region:** Hoenn | |

DOES NOT EVOLVE

# SPEAROW
## TINY BIRD POKÉMON

Fast and furious, Spearow can spot prey in the grass and use its strong beak to pick it out.

| | |
|---|---|
| **Pronounced:** SPEER-oh | |
| **Possible Moves:** Peck, Growl, Leer, Fury Attack, Pursuit, Aerial Ace, Mirror Move, Agility, Assurance, Roost, Drill Peck | |
| **Type:** Normal-Flying | |
| **Height:** 1'00" | **Weight:** 4.4 lbs. |
| **Region:** Kanto | |

SPEAROW

FEAROW

# SPHEAL
## CLAP POKÉMON

Because Spheal's body is shaped like a ball, it can roll across frozen ice floes to reach the shore.

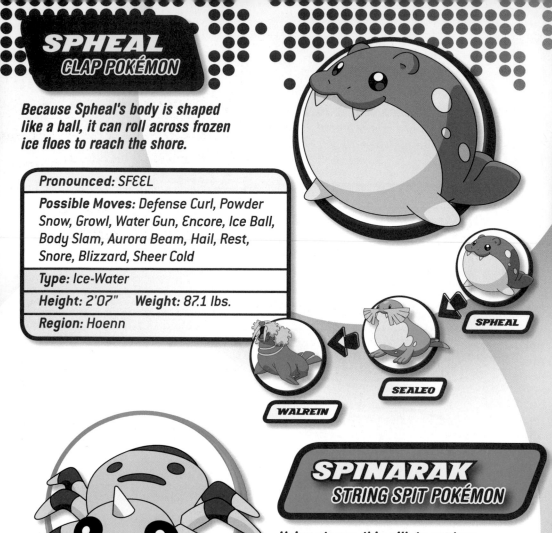

**Pronounced:** SFEEL

**Possible Moves:** Defense Curl, Powder Snow, Growl, Water Gun, Encore, Ice Ball, Body Slam, Aurora Beam, Hail, Rest, Snore, Blizzard, Sheer Cold

**Type:** Ice-Water

**Height:** 2'07"    **Weight:** 87.1 lbs.

**Region:** Hoenn

SPHEAL

SEALEO

WALREIN

# SPINARAK
## STRING SPIT POKÉMON

Using strong, thin silk to capture its prey, Spinarak will wait motionlessly for hours on end for its prey to arrive.

SPINARAK

ARIADOS

**Pronounced:** SPIN-uh-rack

**Possible Moves:** Poison Sting, String Shot, Scary Face, Constrict, Leech Life, Night Shade, Shadow Sneak, Fury Swipes, Sucker Punch, Spider Web, Agility, Pin Missile, Psychic, Poison Jab

**Type:** Bug-Poison

**Height:** 1'08"    **Weight:** 18.7 lbs.

**Region:** Johto

# SPINDA
## SPOT PANDA POKÉMON

*The way this Pokémon walks—
by teetering back and forth—
makes it a difficult target to hit.
Every Spinda has a unique
pattern of spots.*

**Pronounced:**
SPIN-dah

**Possible Moves:** Tackle,
Uproar, Copycat, Faint
Attack, Psybeam, Hypnosis,
Dizzy Punch, Sucker Punch,
Teeter Dance, Psych Up,
Double-Edge, Flail, Thrash

**Type:** Normal

**Height:** 3'07"

**Weight:** 11.0 lbs.

**Region:** Hoenn

*DOES NOT EVOLVE*

# SPIRITOMB
## FORBIDDEN POKÉMON

Spiritomb, which is a combination of over one hundred different spirits, was punished half a century ago by being bound to something called an Odd Keystone.

**Pronounced:**
SPIRI-toom

**Possible Moves:** Curse, Pursuit, Confuse Ray, Spite, Shadow Sneak, Faint Attack, Hypnosis, Dream Eater, Ominous Wind, Sucker Punch, Nasty Plot, Memento, Dark Pulse

**Type:** Ghost-Dark

**Height:** 3'03"

**Weight:** 238.1 lbs.

**Region:** Sinnoh

**DOES NOT EVOLVE**

# SPOINK
## BOUNCE POKÉMON

Spoink bounces constantly on its spring-like tail, which also keeps its heart beating.

| | |
|---|---|
| **Pronounced:** SPOINK | |
| **Possible Moves:** Splash, Psywave, Odor Sleuth, Psybeam, Psych Up, Confuse Ray, Magic Coat, Zen Headbutt, Rest, Snore, Payback, Psychic, Power Gem, Bounce | |
| **Type:** Psychic | |
| **Height:** 2'04" | **Weight:** 67.5 lbs. |
| **Region:** Hoenn | |

GRUMPIG

SPOINK

# SQUIRTLE
## WATER POKÉMON

Striking regularly with spouts of water, Squirtle can be tricky to see, since it hides within its shell a lot.

| | |
|---|---|
| **Pronounced:** SKWIR-tuhl | |
| **Possible Moves:** Tackle, Tail Whip, Bubble, Withdraw, Water Gun, Bite, Rapid Spin, Protect, Water Pulse, Aqua Tail, Skull Bash, Rain Dance, Hydro Pump | |
| **Type:** Water | |
| **Height:** 1'08" | **Weight:** 19.8 lbs. |
| **Region:** Kanto | |

SQUIRTLE

WARTORTLE

BLASTOISE

# STANTLER
## BIG HORN POKÉMON

*You can easily become entranced by the patterns on the majestic antlers of this Pokémon.*

**Pronounced:** STAN-tler

**Possible Moves:** Tackle, Leer, Astonish, Hypnosis, Stomp, Sand-Attack, Take Down, Confuse Ray, Calm Mind, Role Play, Zen Headbutt, Imprison, Captivate, Me First

**Type:** Normal

**Height:** 4'07"   **Weight:** 157.0 lbs.

**Region:** Johto

DOES NOT EVOLVE

# STARAPTOR
## PREDATOR POKÉMON

*Since it has strong legs and wings, Staraptor thinks nothing of challenging foes bigger than itself.*

**Pronounced:** star-RAPT-orr

**Possible Moves:** Tackle, Growl, Quick Attack, Wing Attack, Double Team, Endeavor, Whirlwind, Aerial Ace, Take Down, Close Combat, Agility, Brave Bird

**Type:** Normal-Flying

**Height:** 3'11"   **Weight:** 54.9 lbs.

**Region:** Sinnoh

STARLY

STARAVIA

STARAPTOR

# STARAVIA
## STARLING POKÉMON

While searching for Bug-type Pokémon, Staravia will fly around in flocks. But if they meet up with another flock, a territorial battle will erupt.

**Pronounced:** star-AY-vee-ah

**Possible Moves:** Tackle, Growl, Quick Attack, Wing Attack, Double Team, Endeavor, Whirlwind, Aerial Ace, Take Down, Agility, Brave Bird

**Type:** Normal-Flying

**Height:** 2'00"

**Weight:** 34.2 lbs.

**Region:** Sinnoh

STARLY

STARAVIA

STARAPTOR

# STARLY
## STARLING POKÉMON

Though small, Starly can flap their wings with great power. They always travel en masse, because they are small enough to be vulnerable on their own.

**Pronounced:** STAR-lee

**Possible Moves:** Tackle, Growl, Quick Attack, Wing Attack, Double Team, Endeavor, Whirlwind, Aerial Ace, Take Down, Agility, Brave Bird

**Type:** Normal-Flying

**Height:** 1'00"  **Weight:** 4.4 lbs.

**Region:** Sinnoh

STARAPTOR

STARAVIA

STARLY

# STARMIE
## MYSTERIOUS POKÉMON

The red core in the center of Starmie can send mysterious radio signals into the night sky.

**Pronounced:** STAR-me

**Possible Moves:** Water Gun, Rapid Spin, Recover, Swift, Confuse Ray

**Type:** Water-Psychic

**Height:** 3'07"  **Weight:** 176.4 lbs.

**Region:** Kanto

STARYU

STARMIE

# STARYU
## STAR FISH POKÉMON

*If it is torn or damaged in battle, the rest of Staryu can grow back—as long as the red core of its body (which flashes at midnight) stays intact.*

**Pronounced:** STAR-you

**Possible Moves:** Tackle, Harden, Water Gun, Agility, Recover, Camouflage, Swift, BubbleBeam, Minimize, Gyro Ball, Light Screen, Power Gem, Cosmic Power, Hydro Pump

**Type:** Water

**Height:** 2'07"    **Weight:** 76.1 lbs.

**Region:** Kanto

STARYU

STARMIE

# STEELIX
## IRON SNAKE POKÉMON

*Steelix has a body that is harder than any metal. It can chew through boulders and see in the dark.*

**Pronounced:** STEE-licks

**Possible Moves:** Thunder Fang, Ice Fang, Fire Fang, Mud Sport, Tackle, Harden, Bind, Screech, Rock Throw, Rage, Rock Tomb, Sandstorm, Slam, Rock Polish, DragonBreath, Iron Tail, Crunch, Double-Edge, Stone Edge

**Type:** Steel-Ground

**Height:** 30'02"   **Weight:** 881.8 lbs.

**Region:** Johto and Sinnoh

ONIX

SLEELIX

# STUNKY
## SKUNK POKÉMON

To keep away foes, Stunky will spray a noxious stench that emits from its rear. One word comes to mind—ewwwwww!

| | |
|---|---|
| **Pronounced:** STUNK-ee | |
| **Possible Moves:** Scratch, Focus Energy, Poison Gas, Screech, Fury Swipes, SmokeScreen, Toxic, Slash, Night Slash, Memento, Explosion | |
| **Type:** Poison-Dark | |
| **Height:** 1'04" | **Weight:** 42.3 lbs. |
| **Region:** Sinnoh | |

STUNKY

SKUNTANK

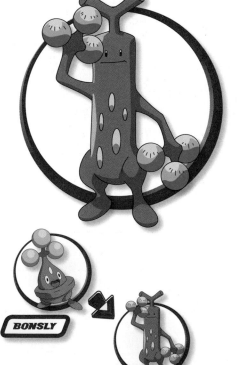

# SUDOWOODO
## IMITATION POKÉMON

Despite its stalwart wooden appearance, Sudowoodo is more closely related to rocks and stones than trees—which would explain why it seems to disappear when it rains.

BONSLY

SUDOWOODO

| | |
|---|---|
| **Pronounced:** SOO-doe-WOO-doe | |
| **Possible Moves:** Wood Hammer, Copycat, Flail, Low Kick, Rock Throw, Mimic, Block, Faint Attack, Rock Tomb, Rock Slide, Slam, Sucker Punch, Double-Edge, Hammer Arm | |
| **Type:** Rock | |
| **Height:** 3'11" | **Weight:** 83.8 lbs. |
| **Region:** Johto and Sinnoh | |

# SUICUNE
## AURORA POKÉMON
### Legendary Pokémon

Suicune will dash around the world on the north winds, purifying foul waters.

**Pronounced:** SWEE-koon

**Possible Moves:** Bite, Leer, BubbleBeam, Rain Dance, Gust, Aurora Beam, Mist, Mirror Coat, Ice Fang, Tailwind, Extrasensory, Hydro Pump, Calm Mind

**Type:** Water

**Height:** 6'07"

**Weight:** 412.3 lbs.

**Region:** Johto

## DOES NOT EVOLVE

# SUNFLORA
## SUN POKÉMON

Sunflora uses warm sunlight for energy, and will constantly travel to find it.

**Pronounced:** sun-FLORA

**Possible Moves:** Absorb, Pound, Growth, Mega Drain, Ingrain, GrassWhistle, Leech Seed, Bullet Seed, Worry Seed, Razor Leaf, Petal Dance, Sunny Day, SolarBeam, Leaf Storm

**Type:** Grass

**Height:** 2'07"   **Weight:** 18.7 lbs.

**Region:** Johto

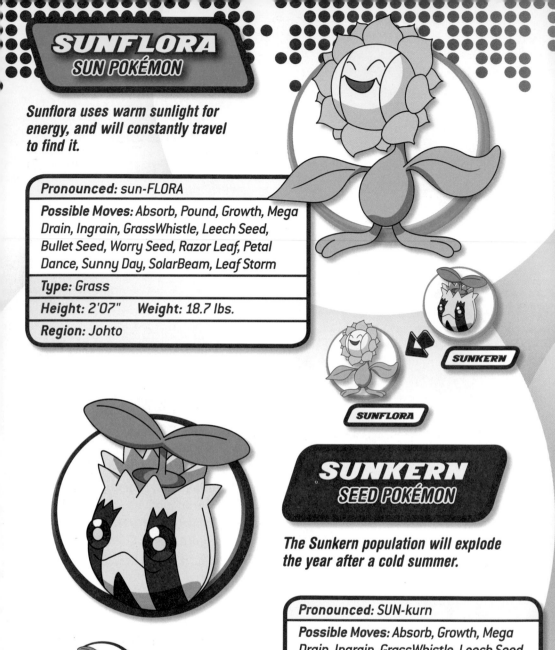

SUNKERN

SUNFLORA

# SUNKERN
## SEED POKÉMON

The Sunkern population will explode the year after a cold summer.

**Pronounced:** SUN-kurn

**Possible Moves:** Absorb, Growth, Mega Drain, Ingrain, GrassWhistle, Leech Seed, Endeavor, Worry Seed, Razor Leaf, Synthesis, Sunny Day, Giga Drain, Seed Bomb

**Type:** Grass

**Height:** 1'00"   **Weight:** 4.0 lbs.

**Region:** Johto

SUNKERN

SUNFLORA

# SURSKIT
## POUND SKATER POKÉMON

Surskit emits a sweet scent from the tip of its head. It looks like it's skating on water.

**Pronounced:** SUR-skit

**Possible Moves:** Bubble, Quick Attack, Sweet Scent, Water Sport, BubbleBeam, Agility, Mist, Haze, Baton Pass

**Type:** Bug-Water

**Height:** 1'08"    **Weight:** 3.7 lbs.

**Region:** Hoenn

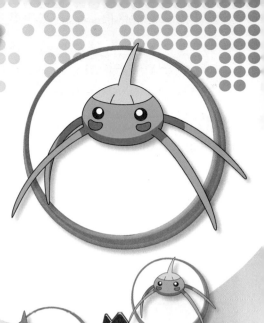

MASQUERAIN

SURSKIT

SWABLU

ALTARIA

# SWABLU
## COTTON BIRD POKÉMON

With wings that resemble cotton, Swablu can sit atop someone's head and look like a cotton hat.

**Pronounced:** SWAH-blue

**Possible Moves:** Peck, Growl, Astonish, Sing, Fury Attack, Safeguard, Mist, Take Down, Natural Gift, Mirror Move, Refresh, Dragon Pulse, Perish Song

**Type:** Normal-Flying

**Height:** 1'04"    **Weight:** 2.6 lbs.

**Region:** Hoenn

# SWALOT
## POISON BAG POKÉMON

For protection, Swalot exudes toxic fluid from its follicles, and can swallow anything whole.

| | |
|---|---|
| **Pronounced:** SWAH-lot | |
| **Possible Moves:** Pound, Yawn, Poison Gas, Sludge, Amnesia, Encore, Body Slam, Toxic, Stockpile, Spit Up, Swallow, Sludge Bomb, Gastro Acid, Wring Out, Gunk Shot | |
| **Type:** Poison | |
| **Height:** 5'07" | **Weight:** 176.4 lbs. |
| **Region:** Hoenn | |

GULPIN

SWALOT

# SWAMPERT
## MUD FISH POKÉMON

Swampert uses its thick arms to swat down foes, and can even fight while towing a large ship.

| | |
|---|---|
| **Pronounced:** SWAM-pert | |
| **Possible Moves:** Tackle, Growl, Mud-Slap, Water Gun, Bide, Mud Shot, Foresight, Mud Bomb, Take Down, Muddy Water, Protect, Earthquake, Endeavor, Hammer Arm | |
| **Type:** Water-Ground | |
| **Height:** 4'11" | **Weight:** 180.6 lbs. |
| **Region:** Hoenn | |

MUDKIP

MARSHTOMP

SWAMPERT

# SWELLOW
## SWALLOW POKÉMON

After circling the skies for hours, Swellow will dive directly at its prey.

Pronounced: SWELL-low

Possible Moves: Pluck, Peck, Growl, Focus Energy, Quick Attack, Wing Attack, Double Team, Endeavor, Aerial Ace, Agility, Air Slash

Type: Normal-Flying

Height: 2'04"   Weight: 43.7 lbs.

Region: Hoenn

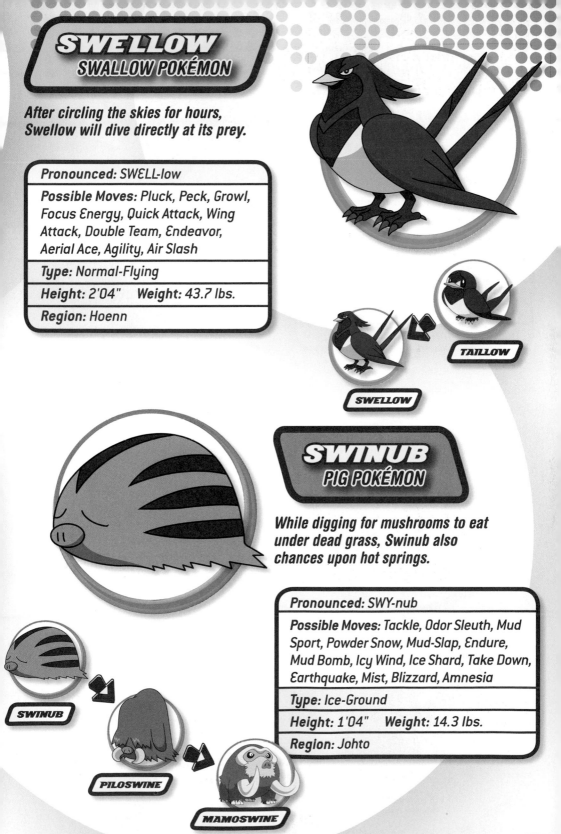

TAILLOW

SWELLOW

# SWINUB
## PIG POKÉMON

While digging for mushrooms to eat under dead grass, Swinub also chances upon hot springs.

Pronounced: SWY-nub

Possible Moves: Tackle, Odor Sleuth, Mud Sport, Powder Snow, Mud-Slap, Endure, Mud Bomb, Icy Wind, Ice Shard, Take Down, Earthquake, Mist, Blizzard, Amnesia

Type: Ice-Ground

Height: 1'04"   Weight: 14.3 lbs.

Region: Johto

SWINUB

PILOSWINE

MAMOSWINE

# TAILLOW
## TINY SWALLOW POKÉMON

Taillow will bravely take on the toughest foes, and will always look for warm climates in which to live.

**Pronounced:** TAY-low

**Possible Moves:** Peck, Growl, Focus Energy, Quick Attack, Wing Attack, Double Team, Endeavor, Aerial Ace, Agility, Air Slash

**Type:** Normal-Flying

**Height:** 1'00"　**Weight:** 5.1 lbs.

**Region:** Hoenn

TAILLOW

SWELLOW

# TANGELA
## VINE POKÉMON

No one has yet seen Tangela's face because it is covered in blue vines.

**Pronounced:** TANG-guh-luh

**Possible Moves:** Ingrain, Constrict, Sleep Powder, Absorb, Growth, PoisonPowder, Vine Whip, Bind, Mega Drain, Stun Spore, AncientPower, Knock Off, Natural Gift, Slam, Tickle, Wring Out, Power Whip

**Type:** Grass

**Height:** 3'03"　**Weight:** 77.2 lbs.

**Region:** Kanto

TANGELA

TANGROWTH

# TANGROWTH
## VINE POKÉMON

*Tangrowth doesn't care if predators take an arm or two, which are made of vines—they have enough to go around.*

**Pronounced:**
TANG-growth

**Possible Moves:** Ingrain, Constrict, Sleep Powder, Absorb, Growth, PoisonPowder, Vine Whip, Bind, Mega Drain, Stun Spore, AncientPower, Knock Off, Natural Gift, Slam, Tickle, Wring Out, Power Whip, Block

**Type:** Grass

**Height:** 6'07"

**Weight:** 283.5 lbs.

**Region:** Sinnoh

TANGELA

TANGROWTH

# TAUROS
## WILD BULL POKÉMON

Very violent by nature, Tauros will attack a foe by charging head-on.

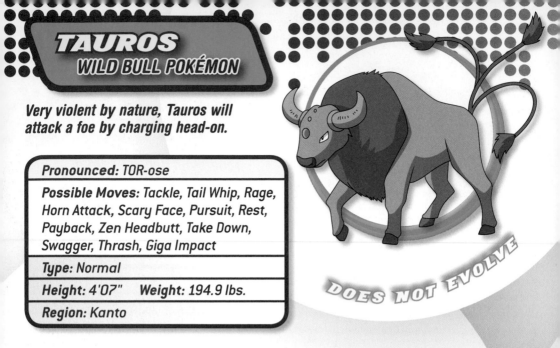

| | |
|---|---|
| **Pronounced:** TOR-ose | |
| **Possible Moves:** Tackle, Tail Whip, Rage, Horn Attack, Scary Face, Pursuit, Rest, Payback, Zen Headbutt, Take Down, Swagger, Thrash, Giga Impact | |
| **Type:** Normal | |
| **Height:** 4'07" | **Weight:** 194.9 lbs. |
| **Region:** Kanto | |

DOES NOT EVOLVE

# TEDDIURSA
## LITTLE BEAR POKÉMON

Teddiursa eats honey that soaks through its paws, and every paw has a different taste.

| | |
|---|---|
| **Pronounced:** TED-dy-UR-sa | |
| **Possible Moves:** Covet, Scratch, Leer, Lick, Fake Tears, Fury Swipes, Faint Attack, Sweet Scent, Slash, Charm, Rest, Snore, Thrash, Fling | |
| **Type:** Normal | |
| **Height:** 2'00" | **Weight:** 19.4 lbs. |
| **Region:** Johto | |

TEDDIURSA

URSARING

# TENTACOOL
## JELLYFISH POKÉMON

Made of mostly water, it uses beams from its eyes. Unfortunately, many fisherman have fallen prey to its poisonous barbs.

**Pronounced:** TƐNT-uh-cool

**Possible Moves:** Poison Sting, Supersonic, Constrict, Acid, Toxic Spikes, BubbleBeam, Wrap, Barrier, Water Pulse, Poison Jab, Screech, Hydro Pump, Wring Out

**Type:** Water-Poison

**Height:** 2'11"    **Weight:** 100.3 lbs.

**Region:** All Regions

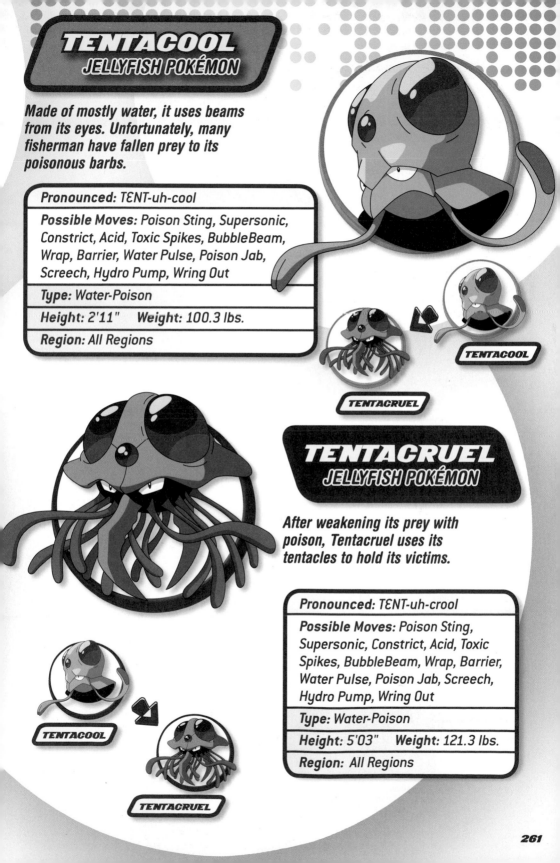

TENTACOOL

TENTACRUEL

# TENTACRUEL
## JELLYFISH POKÉMON

After weakening its prey with poison, Tentacruel uses its tentacles to hold its victims.

**Pronounced:** TƐNT-uh-crool

**Possible Moves:** Poison Sting, Supersonic, Constrict, Acid, Toxic Spikes, BubbleBeam, Wrap, Barrier, Water Pulse, Poison Jab, Screech, Hydro Pump, Wring Out

**Type:** Water-Poison

**Height:** 5'03"    **Weight:** 121.3 lbs.

**Region:** All Regions

TENTACOOL

TENTACRUEL

# TOGEKISS
## JUBILEE POKÉMON

This Pokémon does not like to appear where there is trouble, which would explain why it's rarely seen.

**Pronounced:**
TOE-geh-kiss

**Possible Moves:** Sky Attack, ExtremeSpeed, Aura Sphere, Air Slash

**Type:** Normal-Flying

**Height:** 4'11"

**Weight:** 83.8 lbs.

**Region:** Sinnoh

TOGEPI

TOGETIC

TOGEKISS

# TOGEPI
## SPIKE BALL POKÉMON

Where does Togepi's limitless joy come from? The secret is said to be contained in its hard shell.

**Pronounced:** TOE-geh-pee

**Possible Moves:** Growl, Charm, Metronome, Sweet Kiss, Yawn, Encore, Follow Me, Wish, AncientPower, Safeguard, Baton Pass, Double-Edge, Last Resort

**Type:** Normal

**Height:** 1'00"    **Weight:** 3.3 lbs.

**Region:** Johto

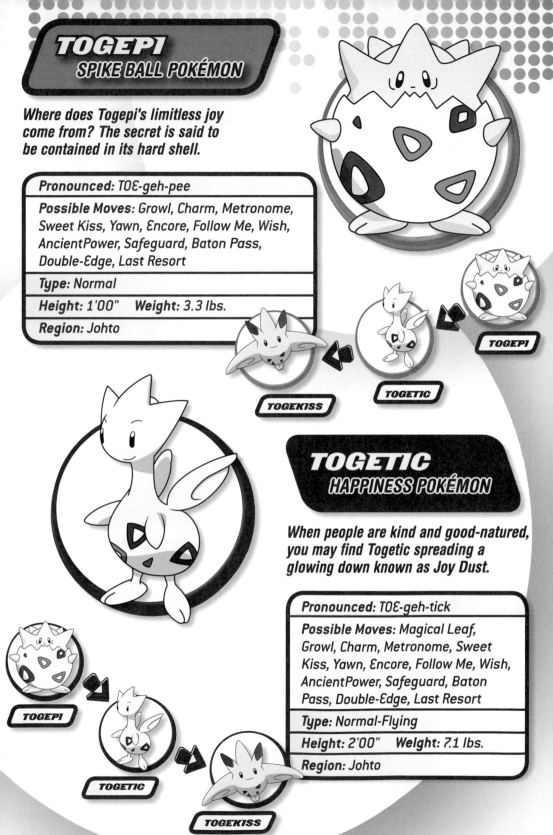

TOGEPI

TOGETIC

TOGEKISS

# TOGETIC
## HAPPINESS POKÉMON

When people are kind and good-natured, you may find Togetic spreading a glowing down known as Joy Dust.

**Pronounced:** TOE-geh-tick

**Possible Moves:** Magical Leaf, Growl, Charm, Metronome, Sweet Kiss, Yawn, Encore, Follow Me, Wish, AncientPower, Safeguard, Baton Pass, Double-Edge, Last Resort

**Type:** Normal-Flying

**Height:** 2'00"    **Weight:** 7.1 lbs.

**Region:** Johto

TOGEPI

TOGETIC

TOGEKISS

# TORCHIC
## CHICK POKÉMON

Torchic feels very warm to the touch thanks to the fire burning inside of it, and it can throw fireballs that are 1,800 degrees F.

**Pronounced:** TOR-chick

**Possible Moves:** Scratch, Growl, Focus Energy, Ember, Peck, Sand-Attack, Fire Spin, Quick Attack, Slash, Mirror Move, Flamethrower

**Type:** Fire

**Height:** 1'04"    **Weight:** 5.5 lbs.

**Region:** Hoenn

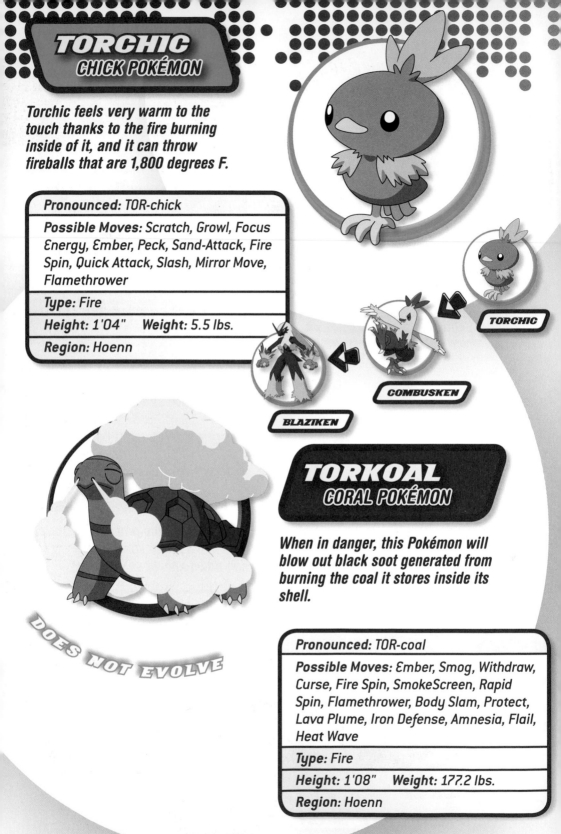

TORCHIC

COMBUSKEN

BLAZIKEN

DOES NOT EVOLVE

# TORKOAL
## CORAL POKÉMON

When in danger, this Pokémon will blow out black soot generated from burning the coal it stores inside its shell.

**Pronounced:** TOR-coal

**Possible Moves:** Ember, Smog, Withdraw, Curse, Fire Spin, SmokeScreen, Rapid Spin, Flamethrower, Body Slam, Protect, Lava Plume, Iron Defense, Amnesia, Flail, Heat Wave

**Type:** Fire

**Height:** 1'08"    **Weight:** 177.2 lbs.

**Region:** Hoenn

# TORTERRA
## CONTINENT POKÉMON

You can sometimes see smaller Pokémon living on the backs of Torterra and building nests. When in groups, Torterra have been mistaken for moving forests.

**TURTWIG**

**GROTLE**

**TORTERRA**

**Pronounced:**
tor-TERR-uh

**Possible Moves:** Wood Hammer, Tackle, Withdraw, Absorb, Razor Leaf, Curse, Bite, Mega Drain, Earthquake, Leech Seed, Synthesis, Crunch, Giga Drain, Leaf Storm

**Type:** Grass-Ground

**Height:** 7'03"

**Weight:** 683.4 lbs.

**Region:** Sinnoh

# TOTODILE
## BIG JAW POKÉMON

Prone to bite anything with its strong jaws, even Totodile's Trainer must be very careful when handling it.

| | |
|---|---|
| **Pronounced:** TOE-toe-dyle | |
| **Possible Moves:** Scratch, Leer, Water Gun, Rage, Bite, Scary Face, Ice Fang, Thrash, Crunch, Slash, Screech, Aqua Tail, SuperPower, Hydro Pump | |
| **Type:** Water | |
| **Height:** 2'00" | **Weight:** 20.9 lbs. |
| **Region:** Johto | |

FERALIGATR ← CROCONAW ← TOTODILE

# TOXICROAK
## TOXIC MOUTH POKÉMON

Toxicroak will build up poison in its fingers, and even one scratch can be fatal.

| | |
|---|---|
| **Pronounced:** TOCKS-eh-croak | |
| **Possible Moves:** Astonish, Mud-Slap, Poison Sting, Taunt, Pursuit, Faint Attack, Revenge, Swagger, Mud Bomb, Sucker Punch, Nasty Plot, Poison Jab, Sludge Bomb, Flatter | |
| **Type:** Poison-Fighting | |
| **Height:** 4'03" | **Weight:** 97.9 lbs. |
| **Region:** Sinnoh | |

CROAGUNK ← TOXICROAK

# TRAPINCH
## ANT PIT POKÉMON

Trapinch live in the desert and capture their prey by waiting at the bottom of sand pits they build as traps.

| | |
|---|---|
| **Pronounced:** TRAP-pinch | |
| **Possible Moves:** Bite, Sand-Attack, Faint Attack, Sand Tomb, Crunch, Dig, Sandstorm, Hyper Beam, Earth Power, Earthquake, Feint, Fissure | |
| **Type:** Ground | |
| **Height:** 2'04" | **Weight:** 33.1 lbs. |
| **Region:** Hoenn | |

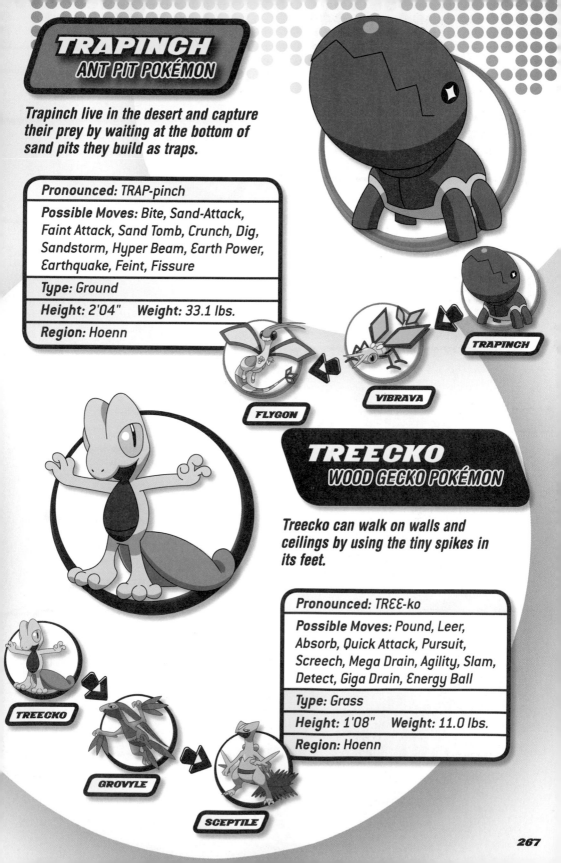

FLYGON

VIBRAVA

TRAPINCH

# TREECKO
## WOOD GECKO POKÉMON

Treecko can walk on walls and ceilings by using the tiny spikes in its feet.

| | |
|---|---|
| **Pronounced:** TREE-ko | |
| **Possible Moves:** Pound, Leer, Absorb, Quick Attack, Pursuit, Screech, Mega Drain, Agility, Slam, Detect, Giga Drain, Energy Ball | |
| **Type:** Grass | |
| **Height:** 1'08" | **Weight:** 11.0 lbs. |
| **Region:** Hoenn | |

TREECKO

GROVYLE

SCEPTILE

267

# TROPIUS
## FRUIT POKÉMON

Tropius packs away so much fruit, it actually has fruit growing from its neck.

**Pronounced:** TROH-pee-us

**Possible Moves:** Leer, Gust, Growth, Razor Leaf, Stomp, Sweet Scent, Whirlwind, Magical Leaf, Body Slam, Synthesis, Air Slash, SolarBeam, Natural Gift, Leaf Storm

**Type:** Grass-Flying

**Height:** 6'07"    **Weight:** 220.5 lbs.

**Region:** Hoenn

DOES NOT EVOLVE

# TURTWIG
## TINY LEAF POKÉMON

Turtwig tends to make its home near lakes. When it drinks water the shell on its back will harden.

**Pronounced:** TUR-twig

**Possible Moves:** Tackle, Withdraw, Absorb, Razor Leaf, Curse, Bite, Mega Drain, Leech Seed, Syntesis, Crunch, Giga Drain, Leaf Storm

**Type:** Grass

**Height:** 1'04"    **Weight:** 22.5 lbs.

**Region:** Sinnoh

TURTWIG

GROTLE

TORTERRA

# TYPHLOSION
## VOLCANO POKÉMON

Typhlosion creates walls of shimmering heat to hide behind, then blasts foes with intense fiery attacks.

**Pronounced:** tie-FLOW-zhun

**Possible Moves:** Gyro Ball, Tackle, Leer, SmokeScreen, Ember, Quick Attack, Flame Wheel, Defense Curl, Swift, Lava Plume, Flamethrower, Rollout, Double-Edge, Eruption

**Type:** Fire

**Height:** 5'07"     **Weight:** 175.3 lbs.

**Region:** Johto

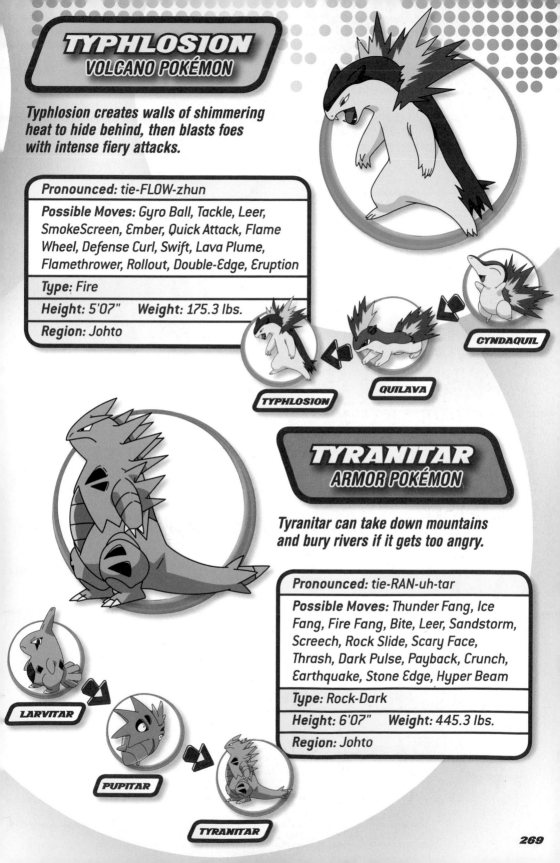

TYPHLOSION

QUILAVA

CYNDAQUIL

# TYRANITAR
## ARMOR POKÉMON

Tyranitar can take down mountains and bury rivers if it gets too angry.

**Pronounced:** tie-RAN-uh-tar

**Possible Moves:** Thunder Fang, Ice Fang, Fire Fang, Bite, Leer, Sandstorm, Screech, Rock Slide, Scary Face, Thrash, Dark Pulse, Payback, Crunch, Earthquake, Stone Edge, Hyper Beam

**Type:** Rock-Dark

**Height:** 6'07"     **Weight:** 445.3 lbs.

**Region:** Johto

LARVITAR

PUPITAR

TYRANITAR

# TYROGUE
## SCUFFLE POKÉMON

Tyrogue is a hothead with a very short temper. It thinks nothing of going against foes that are bigger and stronger.

**Pronounced:** tie-ROAG

**Possible Moves:** Tackle, Helping Hand, Fake Out

**Type:** Fighting

**Height:** 2'04"     **Weight:** 46.3 lbs.

**Region:** Johto

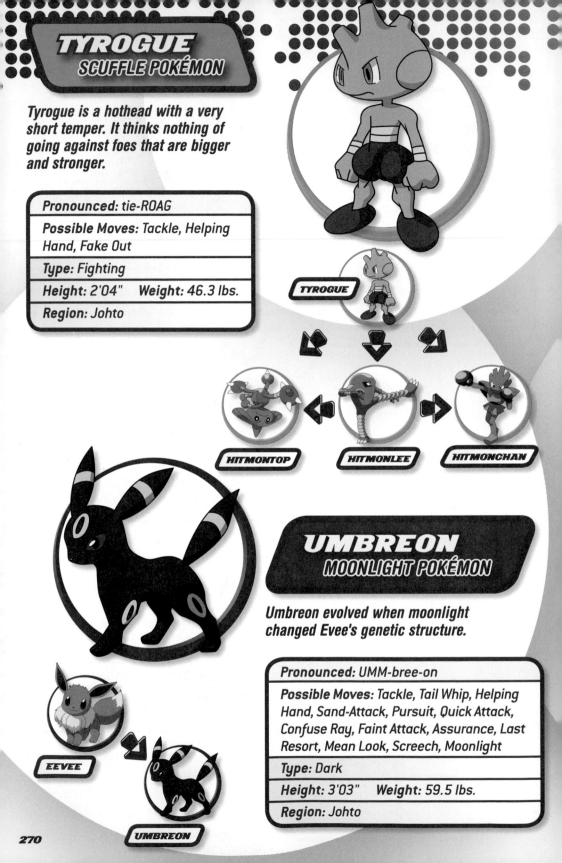

TYROGUE

HITMONTOP     HITMONLEE     HITMONCHAN

# UMBREON
## MOONLIGHT POKÉMON

Umbreon evolved when moonlight changed Evee's genetic structure.

**Pronounced:** UMM-bree-on

**Possible Moves:** Tackle, Tail Whip, Helping Hand, Sand-Attack, Pursuit, Quick Attack, Confuse Ray, Faint Attack, Assurance, Last Resort, Mean Look, Screech, Moonlight

**Type:** Dark

**Height:** 3'03"     **Weight:** 59.5 lbs.

**Region:** Johto

EEVEE

UMBREON

# UNOWN
## SYMBOL POKÉMON

Using telepathy to communicate, these alphabet-shaped Pokémon can be found stuck on walls. It is unknown which came first—these Pokémon, or human language.

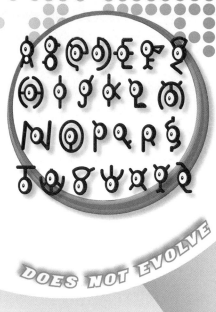

**Pronounced:** un-KNOWN

**Possible Moves:** Hidden Power

**Type:** Psychic

**Height:** 1'08"     **Weight:** 11.0 lbs.

**Region:** Johto and Sinnoh

*DOES NOT EVOLVE*

# URSARING
## HIBERNATOR POKÉMON

Ursaring is very territorial, and will often mark trees that have tasty berries or fruits.

**Pronounced:** UR-sa-ring

**Possible Moves:** Covet, Scratch, Leer, Lick, Fake Tears, Fury Swipes, Faint Attack, Sweet Scent, Slash, Scary Face, Rest, Snore, Thrash, Hammer Arm

**Type:** Normal

**Height:** 5'11"     **Weight:** 277.3 lbs.

**Region:** Johto

TEDDIURSA

URSARING

Also known as The Being of Knowledge, Uxie is rumored to have given humans the intelligence they needed to improve the quality of their lives.

**Pronounced:** YUKE-see

**Possible Moves:** Rest, Imprison, Endure, Confusion, Yawn, Future Sight, Amnesia, Extrasensory, Flail, Natural Gift, Memento

**Type:** Psychic

**Height:** 1'00"

**Weight:** 0.7 lbs.

**Region:** Sinnoh

## DOES NOT EVOLVE

# VAPOREON
## BUBBLE JET POKÉMON

Vaporeon has adapted so well to living an aquatic life that it can't be seen while in water.

| |
|---|
| **Pronounced:** vay-POR-ee-on |
| **Possible Moves:** Tackle, Tail Whip, Helping Hand, Sand-Attack, Water Sport, Quick Attack, Bite, Aurora Beam, Aqua Ring, Last Resort, Haze, Acid Armor, Hydro Pump |
| **Type:** Water |
| **Height:** 3'03"  **Weight:** 63.9 lbs. |
| **Region:** Kanto |

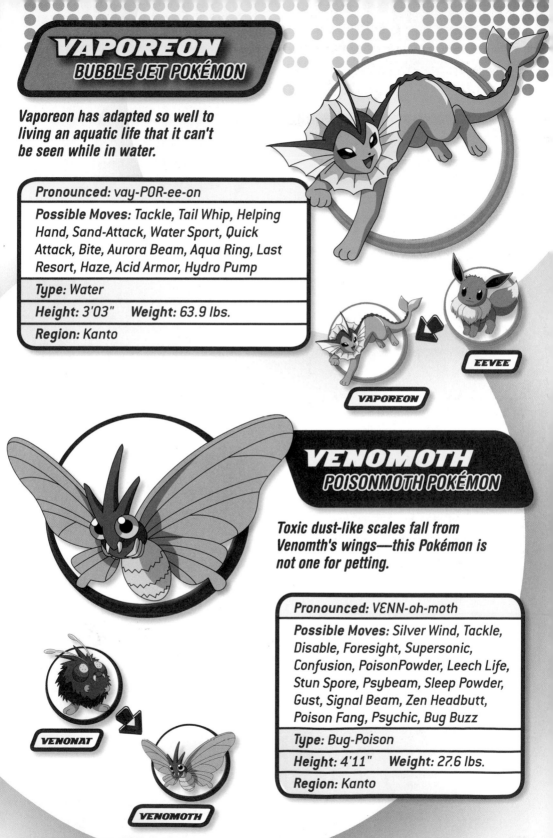

EEVEE

VAPOREON

# VENOMOTH
## POISONMOTH POKÉMON

Toxic dust-like scales fall from Venomth's wings—this Pokémon is not one for petting.

| |
|---|
| **Pronounced:** VENN-oh-moth |
| **Possible Moves:** Silver Wind, Tackle, Disable, Foresight, Supersonic, Confusion, PoisonPowder, Leech Life, Stun Spore, Psybeam, Sleep Powder, Gust, Signal Beam, Zen Headbutt, Poison Fang, Psychic, Bug Buzz |
| **Type:** Bug-Poison |
| **Height:** 4'11"  **Weight:** 27.6 lbs. |
| **Region:** Kanto |

VENONAT

VENOMOTH

# VENONAT
## INSECT POKÉMON

Venonat's big eyes are made up of tiny little eyes, and at nighttime it is drawn to light.

**Pronounced:** VENN-oh-nat

**Possible Moves:** Tackle, Disable, Foresight, Supersonic, Confusion, PoisonPowder, Leech Life, Stun Spore, Psybeam, Sleep Powder, Signal Beam, Zen Headbutt, Poison Fang, Psychic

**Type:** Bug-Poison

**Height:** 3'03"    **Weight:** 66.1 lbs.

**Region:** Kanto

VENONAT

VENOMOTH

# VENUSAUR
## SEED POKÉMON

The flower on this Pokémon's back gains a stronger smell after rainy days.

**Pronounced:** VEE-nuh-sore

**Possible Moves:** Tackle, Growl, Leech Seed, Vine Whip, PoisonPowder, Sleep Powder, Take Down, Razor Leaf, Sweet Scent, Growth, Double-Edge, Petal Dance, Worry Seed, Synthesis, SolarBeam

**Type:** Grass-Poison

**Height:** 6'07"    **Weight:** 220.5 lbs.

**Region:** Kanto

BULBASAUR

IVYSAUR

VENUSAUR

# VESPIQUEN
## BEEHIVE POKÉMON

There is only one Vespiquen in a colony and its stomach acts like a honeycomb for grubs. The grubs will strike at any foe that appears.

**Pronounced:**
VES-pa-kwen

**Possible Moves:** Sweet Scent, Gust, Poison Sting, Confuse Ray, Fury Cutter, Defense Order, Pursuit, Fury Swipes, Power Gem, Heal Order, Toxic, Slash, Captivate, Attack Order, Swagger, Destiny Bond

**Type:** Bug-Flying

**Height:** 3'11"

**Weight:** 84.9 lbs.

**Region:** Sinnoh

COMBEE

VESPIQUEN

# VIBRAVA
## VIBRATION POKÉMON

By using ultrasonic waves and flapping its wings rapidly, Vibrava can cause headaches in some people.

**Pronounced:**
VY-brah-va

**Possible Moves:** SonicBoom Sand-Attack, Faint Attack, Sand Tomb, Supersonic, DragonBreath, Screech, Sandstorm, Hyper Beam

**Type:** Ground-Dragon

**Height:** 3'07"

**Weight:** 33.7 lbs.

**Region:** Hoenn

TRAPINCH

VIBRAVA

FLYGON

# VICTREEBEL
## FLYCATCHER POKÉMON

*The fluid in Victreebel's mouth smells like honey, but is really a toxic acid.*

**Pronounced:** VICK-tree-bell

**Possible Moves:** Stockpile, Swallow, Spit Up, Vine Whip, Sleep Powder, Sweet Scent, Razor Leaf, Leaf Storm

**Type:** Grass-Poison

**Height:** 5'07"    **Weight:** 34.2 lbs.

**Region:** Kanto

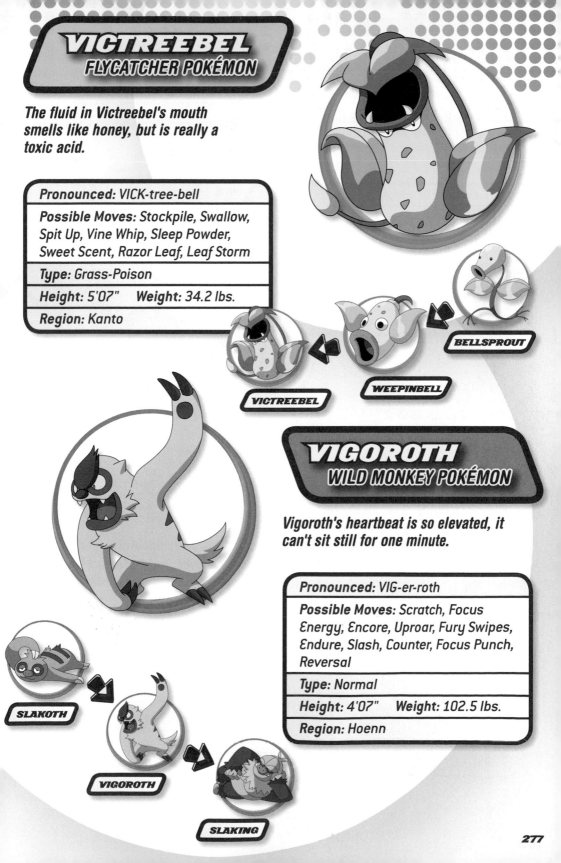

BELLSPROUT

WEEPINBELL

VICTREEBEL

# VIGOROTH
## WILD MONKEY POKÉMON

*Vigoroth's heartbeat is so elevated, it can't sit still for one minute.*

**Pronounced:** VIG-er-roth

**Possible Moves:** Scratch, Focus Energy, Encore, Uproar, Fury Swipes, Endure, Slash, Counter, Focus Punch, Reversal

**Type:** Normal

**Height:** 4'07"    **Weight:** 102.5 lbs.

**Region:** Hoenn

SLAKOTH

VIGOROTH

SLAKING

# VILEPLUME
## FLOWER POKÉMON

Vileplume's petals are so large that it spreads allergenic pollen over a wide area as it walks.

Pronounced: VILE-ploom

Possible Moves: Mega Drain, Aromatherapy, Stun Spore, PoisonPowder, Petal Dance, SolarBeam

Type: Grass-Poison

Height: 3'11"    Weight: 41.0 lbs.

Region: Kanto

ODDISH

GLOOM

VILEPLUME

DOES NOT EVOLVE

# VOLBEAT
## FIREFLY POKÉMON

Volbeat loves the sweet aroma that Illumise generates. It communicates with others by lighting up its rear at night.

Pronounced: VOLL-beat

Possible Moves: Flash, Tackle, Double Team, Confuse Ray, Moonlight, Quick Attack, Tail Glow, Signal Beam, Protect, Helping Hand, Zen Headbutt, Bug Buzz, Double-Edge

Type: Bug

Height: 2'04"    Weight: 39.0 lbs.

Region: Hoenn

# VOLTORB
## BALL POKÉMON

Although it looks as harmless as a standard Poke Ball, these Pokémon can explode or electrocute on contact.

**Pronounced:** VOL-torb

**Possible Moves:** Charge, Tackle, SonicBoom Spark, Rollout, Screech, Light Screen, Charge Beam, Selfdestruct, Swift, Magnet Rise, Gyro Ball, Explosion, Mirror Coat

**Type:** Electric

**Height:** 1'08"     **Weight:** 22.9 lbs.

**Region:** Kanto

ELECTRODE

VOLTORB

# VULPIX
## FOX POKÉMON

Its tail will split to make more tails and can control balls of fire.

**Pronounced:** VULL-picks

**Possible Moves:** Ember, Tail Whip, Roar, Quick Attack, Will-O-Wisp, Confuse Ray, Imprison, Flamethrower, Safeguard, Payback, Fire Spin, Captivate, Grudge, Extrasensory, Fire Blast

**Type:** Fire

**Height:** 2'00"     **Weight:** 21.8 lbs.

**Region:** Kanto

VULPIX

NINETALES

# WAILMER
## BALL WHALE POKÉMON

Wailmer likes to beach itself so that it can bounce like a ball and play. It also spouts water from its nose.

**Pronounced:** WAIL-murr

**Possible Moves:** Splash, Growl, Water Gun, Rollout, Whirlpool, Astonish, Water Pulse, Mist, Rest, Brine, Water Spout, Amnesia, Dive, Bounce, Hydro Pump

**Type:** Water

**Height:** 6'07"    **Weight:** 286.6 lbs.

**Region:** Hoenn

WAILMER

WAILORD

# WAILORD
## FLOAT WHALE POKÉMON

This massive Pokémon, the biggest of them all, can dive to depths of up to ten thousand feet.

**Pronounced:** WAIL-lord

**Possible Moves:** Splash, Growl, Water Gun, Rollout, Whirlpool, Astonish, Water Pulse, Mist, Rest, Brine, Water Spout, Amnesia, Dive, Bounce, Hydro Pump

**Type:** Water

**Height:** 47'07"   **Weight:** 877.4 lbs.

**Region:** Hoenn

WAILMER

WAILORD

# WALREIN
## ICE BREAK POKÉMON

The thick blubber on Walrein's body provides protection. It can easily crack icy surfaces with its big strong tusks.

**Pronounced:** WAL-rain

**Possible Moves:** Crunch, Powder Snow, Growl, Water Gun, Encore, Ice Ball, Body Slam, Aurora Beam, Hail, Swagger, Rest, Snore, Ice Fang, Blizzard, Sheer Cold

**Type:** Ice-Water

**Height:** 4'07"     **Weight:** 332.0 lbs.

**Region:** Hoenn

SPHEAL

SEALEO

WALREIN

# WARTORTLE
## TURTLE POKÉMON

It can live for almost ten thousand years, and a symbol of its longevity would be the furry tail it sports.

**Pronounced:** WAR-tor-tuhl

**Possible Moves:** Tackle, Tail Whip, Bubble, Withdraw, Water Gun, Bite, Rapid Spin, Protect, Water Pulse, Aqua Tail, Skull Bash, Rain Dance, Hydro Pump

**Type:** Water

**Height:** 3'03"     **Weight:** 49.6 lbs.

**Region:** Kanto

SQUIRTLE

WARTORTLE

BLASTOISE

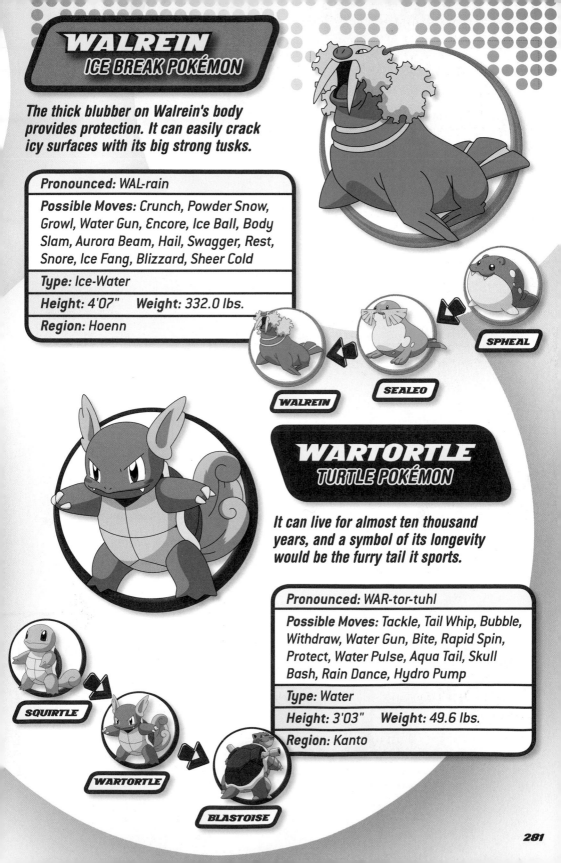

# WEAVILE
## SHARP CLAW POKÉMON

Weavile send signals to each other by carving them in frost-covered trees and ice.

| | |
|---|---|
| **Pronounced:** WEE-vile | |
| **Possible Moves:** Embargo, Revenge, Assurance, Scratch, Leer, Taunt, Quick Attack, Screech, Faint Attack, Fury Swipes, Nasty Plot, Icy Wind, Night Slash, Fling, Metal Claw, Dark Pulse | |
| **Type:** Dark-Ice | |
| **Height:** 3'07" | **Weight:** 75.0 lbs. |
| **Region:** Sinnoh | |

SNEASEL

WEAVILE

# WEEDLE
## HAIRY BUG POKÉMON

Weedle is voracious, eating its weight in leaves every day. Its only defense mechanism is the large needle on its head.

| | |
|---|---|
| **Pronounced:** WEE-dull | |
| **Possible Moves:** Poison Sting, String Shot | |
| **Type:** Bug-Poison | |
| **Height:** 1'00" | **Weight:** 7.1 lbs. |
| **Region:** Kanto | |

WEEDLE

KAKUNA

BEEDRILL

# WEEPINBELL
## FLYCATCHER POKÉMON

This Pokémon looks like a plant, but be careful! It emits a toxic powder to capture prey.

| |
|---|
| **Pronounced:** WEEP-in-bell |
| **Possible Moves:** Vine Whip, Growth, Wrap, Sleep Powder, PoisonPowder, Stun Spore, Acid, Knock Off, Sweet Scent, Gastro Acid, Razor Leaf, Slam, Wring Out |
| **Type:** Grass-Poison |
| **Height:** 3'03"    **Weight:** 14.1 lbs. |
| **Region:** Kanto |

VICTREEBEL

WEEPINBELL

BELLSPROUT

# WEEZING
## POISON GAS POKÉMON

This Pokémon grows by feeding on the gases emitted by garbage. Finding a triplet Weezing is very rare.

| |
|---|
| **Pronounced:** WEEZE-ing |
| **Possible Moves:** Poison Gas, Tackle, Smog, SmokeScreen, Assurance, Selfdestruct, Sludge, Haze, Double Hit, Explosion, Sludge Bomb, Destiny Bond, Memento |
| **Type:** Poison |
| **Height:** 3'11"    **Weight:** 20.9 lbs. |
| **Region:** Kanto |

KOFFING

WEEZING

# WHISCASH
## WHISKERS POKÉMON

Because Whiscash can create tremors in the ocean by whipping about, it has developed the ability to predict real earthquakes.

**Pronounced:** WISS-cash

**Possible Moves:** Zen Headbutt, Tickle, Mud-Slap, Mud Sport, Water Sport, Water Gun, Mud Bomb, Amnesia, Water Pulse, Magnitude, Rest, Snore, Aqua Tail, Earthquake, Future Sight, Fissure

**Type:** Water-Ground

**Height:** 2'11"    **Weight:** 52.0 lbs.

**Region:** Hoenn and Sinnoh

BARBOACH

WHISCASH

# WHISMUR
## WHISPER POKÉMON

Whismur shrieks as loud as a jet plane when it is scared, although when it cries, humans can barely hear it.

**Pronounced:** WHIS-mur

**Possible Moves:** Pound, Uproar, Astonish, Howl, Supersonic, Stomp, Screech, Roar, Rest, Sleep Talk, Hyper Voice

**Type:** Normal

**Height:** 2'00"    **Weight:** 35.9 lbs.

**Region:** Hoenn

WHISMUR

LOUDRED

EXPLOUD

# WIGGLYTUFF
## BALLOON POKÉMON

*By inhaling air, Wigglytuff can expand its body, and its fur feels soothing to the touch.*

| |
|---|
| **Pronounced:** wig-lee-TUFF |
| **Possible Moves:** Sing, Disable, Defense Curl, DoubleSlap |
| **Type:** Normal |
| **Height:** 3'03"    **Weight:** 26.5 lbs. |
| **Region:** Kanto and Hoenn |

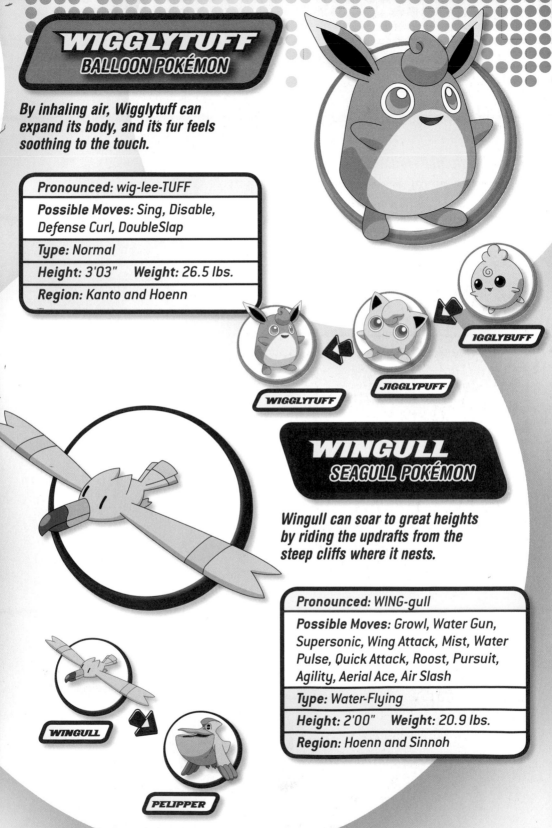

WIGGLYTUFF

JIGGLYPUFF

IGGLYBUFF

# WINGULL
## SEAGULL POKÉMON

*Wingull can soar to great heights by riding the updrafts from the steep cliffs where it nests.*

| |
|---|
| **Pronounced:** WING-gull |
| **Possible Moves:** Growl, Water Gun, Supersonic, Wing Attack, Mist, Water Pulse, Quick Attack, Roost, Pursuit, Agility, Aerial Ace, Air Slash |
| **Type:** Water-Flying |
| **Height:** 2'00"    **Weight:** 20.9 lbs. |
| **Region:** Hoenn and Sinnoh |

WINGULL

PELIPPER

# WOBBUFFET
## PATIENT POKÉMON

Some think that Wobbuffet's tail hides a secret, which is why it tries to keep it hidden.

| | |
|---|---|
| **Pronounced:** WAH-buf-fett | |
| **Possible Moves:** Counter, Mirror Coat, Safeguard, Destiny Bond | |
| **Type:** Psychic | |
| **Height:** 4'03" | |
| **Weight:** 62.8 lbs. | |
| **Region:** Johto | |

**WYNAUT**

**WOBUFFET**

# WOOPER
## WATER FISH POKÉMON

This shore-scavenger comes out when the temperature drops, and usually lives half-buried in the mud of riverbanks.

**Pronounced:** WOOP-pur

**Possible Moves:** Water Gun, Tail Whip, Mud Sport, Mud Shot, Slam, Mud Bomb, Amnesia, Yawn, Earthquake, Rain Dance, Mist, Haze, Muddy Water

**Type:** Water-Ground

**Height:** 1'04"

**Weight:** 18.7 lbs.

**Region:** Johto and Sinnoh

WOOPER

QUAGSIRE

# WORMADAM
## PLANT CLOAK BAGWORM POKÉMON

Depending on where Wormadam evolved, its appearance can be different. When it evolved from Burmy, its cloak became a part of its body.

**Pronounced:** WURR-mah-dam

**Possible Moves:** Tackle, Protect, Hidden Power, Confusion, Razor Leaf, Growth, Psybeam, Captivate, Flail, Attract, Psychic, Leaf Storm

**Type:** Bug-Grass

**Height:** 1'08"    **Weight:** 14.3 lbs.

**Region:** Sinnoh

BURMY ♀

WORMADAM

# WORMADAM
## SANDY CLOAK BAGWORM POKÉMON

If you want a Bug-and-Ground-type Wormadam, make sure your Burmy has a Sandy Cloak! Once Burmy evolves, there's no going back.

**Pronounced:** WURR-mah-dam

**Possible Moves:** Tackle, Protect, Hidden Power, Confusion, Rock Blast, Harden, Psybeam, Captivate, Flail, Psychic, Attract, Fissure

**Type:** Bug-Ground

**Height:** 1'08"    **Weight:** 14.3 lbs.

**Region:** Sinnoh

BURMY ♀

WORMADAM

# WORMADAM
### TRASH CLOAK
## BAGWORM POKÉMON

Looking for a Wormadam with awesome Steel-type abilities? You'll need to evolve a Burmy with a Trash Cloak.

| | |
|---|---|
| **Pronounced:** WURR-mah-dam | |
| **Possible Moves:** Tackle, Protect, Hidden Power, Confusion, Mirror Shot, Metal Sound, Psybeam, Captivate, Flail, Psychic, Attract, Iron Head | |
| **Type:** Bug-Steel | |
| **Height:** 1'08" | **Weight:** 14.3 lbs. |
| **Region:** Sinnoh | |

BURMY ♀

WORMADAM

# WURMPLE
## WORM POKÉMON

Wurmple uses its spiked back to protect itself, mainly from its chief predator, Starly.

WURMPLE

| | |
|---|---|
| **Pronounced:** WERM-pull | |
| **Possible Moves:** Tackle, String Shot, Poison Sting | |
| **Type:** Bug | |
| **Height:** 1'00" | **Weight:** 7.9 lbs. |
| **Region:** Hoenn | |

SILCOON

CASCOON

BEAUTIFLY

DUSTOX

# WYNAUT
## BRIGHT POKÉMON

Wynaut loves to chomp on sweet fruit, and grows in strength by pushing up against others in swarms.

**Pronounced:**
WHY-not

**Possible Moves:** Splash, Charm, Encore, Counter, Mirror Coat, Safeguard, Destiny Bond

**Type:** Psychic

**Height:** 2'00"

**Weight:** 30.9 lbs.

**Region:** Hoenn

WYNAUT

WOBBUFFET

# XATU
## MYSTIC POKÉMON

Although Xatu seems to do nothing but watch the sun all day, it does have the ability to predict the future and see into the past.

| | |
|---|---|
| **Pronounced:** ZAH-too | |
| **Possible Moves:** Peck, Leer, Night Shade, Teleport, Lucky Chant, Miracle Eye, Me First, Confuse Ray, Tailwind, Wish, Psycho Shift, Future Sight, Ominous Wind, Power Swap, Guard Swap, Psychic | |
| **Type:** Psychic-Flying | |
| **Height:** 4'11" | **Weight:** 33.1 lbs. |
| **Region:** Johto | |

XATU

NATU

# YANMA
## CLEAR WING POKÉMON

Prey will have a hard time hiding from this Pokémon, since its eyes can see 360 degrees without moving its head.

| | |
|---|---|
| **Pronounced:** YAN-ma | |
| **Possible Moves:** Tackle, Foresight, Quick Attack, Double Team, SonicBoom, Detect, Supersonic, Uproar, Pursuit, AncientPower, Hypnosis, Wing Attack, Screech, U-Turn, Air Slash, Bug Buzz | |
| **Type:** Bug-Flying | |
| **Height:** 3'11" | **Weight:** 83.8 lbs. |
| **Region:** Johto | |

YANMA

YANMEGA

# YANMEGA
## OGRE DARNER POKÉMON

Yanmega causes serious and critical injuries to its foes by creating shock waves with its wings.

**Pronounced:** YAN-meh-gah

**Possible Moves:** Night Slash, Bug Bite, Tackle, Foresight, Quick Attack, Double Team, SonicBoom, Detect, Supersonic, Uproar, Pursuit, AncientPower, Slash, Screech, U-Turn, Air Slash, Bug Buzz

**Type:** Bug-Flying

**Height:** 6'03"    **Weight:** 113.5 lbs.

**Region:** Sinnoh

YANMA

YANMEGA

DOES NOT EVOLVE

# ZANGOOSE
## CAR FERRET POKÉMON

This Pokémon uses its sharp claws to defeat its prey. Zangoose's greatest rival is Seviper.

**Pronounced:** ZANG-goose

**Possible Moves:** Scratch, Leer, Quick Attack, Swords Dance, Fury Cutter, Slash, Pursuit, Embargo, Crush Claw, Taunt, Detect, False Swipe, X-Scissor, Close Combat

**Type:** Normal

**Height:** 4'03"    **Weight:** 88.8 lbs.

**Region:** Hoenn

## ZAPDOS
### ELECTRIC POKÉMON
**Legendary Pokémon**

Zapdos, a Legendary Pokémon, can control lightning bolts, which would explain why it likes to nest in thunderclouds.

**Pronounced:**
ZAP-dose

**Possible Moves:** Peck, ThunderShock, Thunder Wave, Detect, Pluck, AncientPower, Charge, Agility, Discharge, Roost, Light Screen, Drill Peck, Thunder, Rain Dance

**Type:** Electric-Flying

**Height:** 5'03"

**Weight:** 116.1 lbs.

**Region:** Kanto

**DOES NOT EVOLVE**

# ZIGZAGOON
## TYNYRACOON POKÉMON

Why do they call this Pokémon Zigzagoon? Because it walks in a zigzag fashion. It's also great at finding items in the grass, or even in the ground.

| | |
|---|---|
| **Pronounced:** ZIG-zag-GOON | |
| **Possible Moves:** Tackle, Growl, Tail Whip, Headbutt, Sand-Attack, Odor Sleuth, Mud Sport, Pin Missile, Covet, Flail, Rest, Belly Drum, Fling | |
| **Type:** Normal | |
| **Height:** 1'04" | **Weight:** 38.6 lbs. |
| **Region:** Hoenn | |

ZIGZAGOON

LINOONE

# ZUBAT
## BAT POKÉMON

Using sonic waves that come from its mouth, Zubat can sense obstacles in its way.

| | |
|---|---|
| **Pronounced:** ZOO-bat | |
| **Possible Moves:** Leech Life, Supersonic, Astonish, Bite, Wing Attack, Confuse Ray, Air Cutter, Mean Look, Poison Fang, Haze, Air Slash | |
| **Type:** Poison-Flying | |
| **Height:** 2'07" | **Weight:** 16.5 lbs. |
| **Region:** All Regions | |

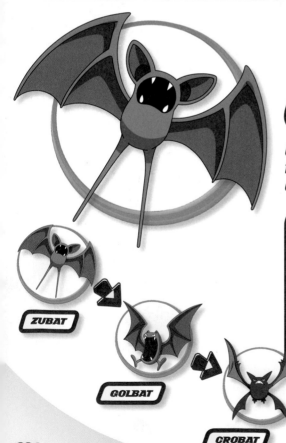

ZUBAT

GOLBAT

CROBAT

DARKRAI

# DARKRAI
## PITCH-BLACK POKÉMON

Although it is most active on nights with a full moon, folklore says that Darkrai actually lures people to sleep and gives them horrible nightmares on moonless nights.

**Pronounced:**
DARK-rye

**Possible Moves:** (known)
Night Shade, Disable, Quick Attack, Hypnosis, Pursuit, Nightmare, Double Team, Haze, Dark Void, Embargo, Dream Eater, Dark Pulse

**Type:** Dark

**Height:** 4'11"

**Weight:** 111.3 lbs

**Region:** Sinnoh

DOES NOT EVOLVE

# Darkrai

is a mysterious Pokémon who haunts Alamos Town in the movie Pokémon: The Rise of Darkrai. After being besieged by a flurry of bad dreams, the people of Alamos Town are looking for the source — and the arrogant but charming Baron Alberto is quick to blame this elusive Pokémon for the nightmares. But in the end, Darkrai's sacrifice proves that it only means to protect those it loves from harm.

# LEGENDARY LINEUP

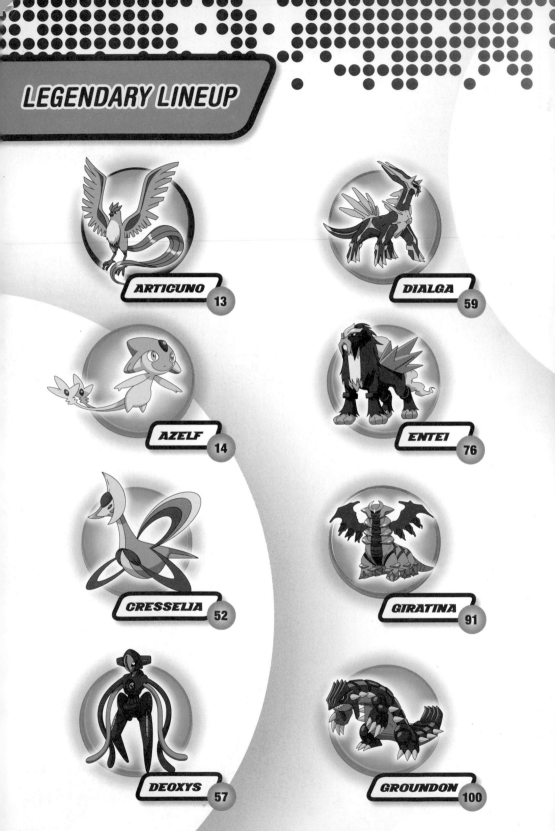

ARTICUNO 13

DIALGA 59

AZELF 14

ENTEI 76

CRESSELIA 52

GIRATINA 91

DEOXYS 57

GROUNDON 100

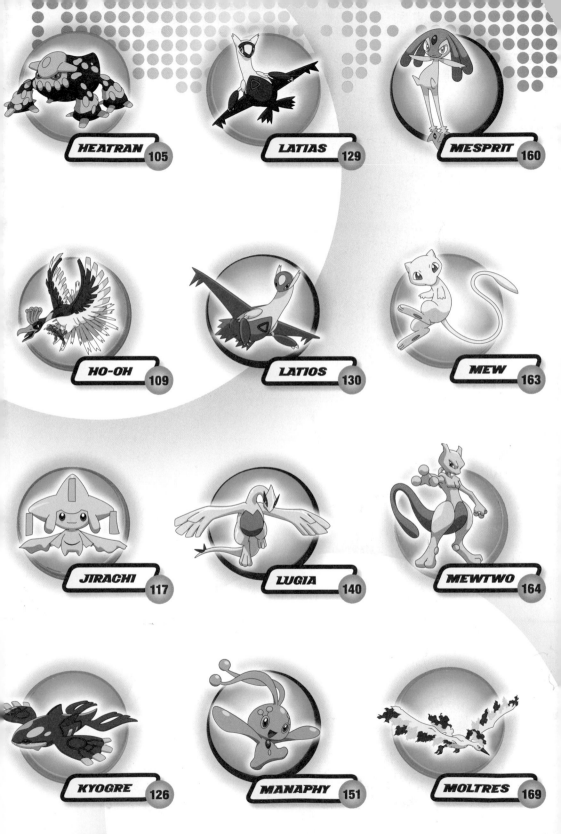

HEATRAN 105

LATIAS 129

MESPRIT 160

HO-OH 109

LATIOS 130

MEW 163

JIRACHI 117

LUGIA 140

MEWTWO 164

KYOGRE 126

MANAPHY 151

MOLTRES 169

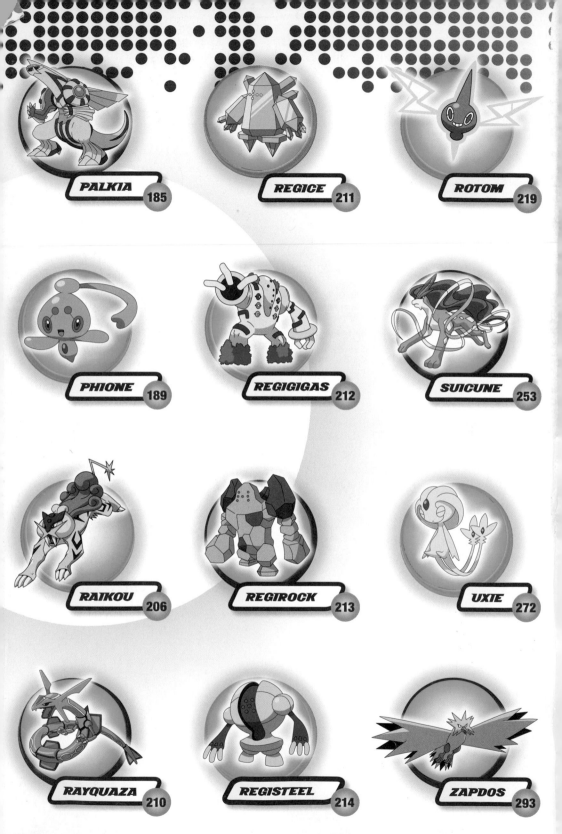

**PALKIA** 185

**REGICE** 211

**ROTOM** 219

**PHIONE** 189

**REGIGIGAS** 212

**SUICUNE** 253

**RAIKOU** 206

**REGIROCK** 213

**UXIE** 272

**RAYQUAZA** 210

**REGISTEEL** 214

**ZAPDOS** 293